A NOVEL

indigo
NIGHTS

LOUISE BAY
USA TODAY BESTSELLING AUTHOR

ISBN - 978-1-910747-25-4

the nights
SERIES

Parisian Nights
Promised Nights
Indigo Nights

Each book in the series is stand alone,
following a different couple.

chapter ONE

Beth

"Glass of champagne, miss?" a blonde flight attendant asked.

Champagne.

Once, it had been my drug of choice. There was nothing I didn't like about it. Everything from the cold, heavy bottle, to the gold foil wrapping at the top that made it seem like a present, to that beautiful sound of the air escaping when the cork was released. A maiden's sigh, it was called. I hated the sound of a pop; it was brash and hard and didn't do champagne justice. It wasn't seductive or subtle enough. No, I longed for that gentle hiss that promised inevitable pleasure.

But not anymore.

"No thank you," I replied. Two years ago, it would have been hard to say no. Three, almost impossible. But I was used to turning down alcohol now, and every time I did a buzz of pride flitted about under my skin. But that didn't stop me from remembering how good it felt from the moment it came out of the refrigerator until the end of my first glass. If I could have stopped there, that would have been great. Problem was, as soon as I had my first taste, I was greedy for the bottle, desperate to open a second. I had no control. Champagne was like a bad boyfriend (and I'd had plenty to enable me to testify). It reeled me in, promised the world and then left me vulnerable, alone, covered in regret and pain, and with a hangover the size of Africa.

In the words of Taylor Swift, champagne and I were never, *ever* getting back together.

"Has he definitely checked in?" the blonde flight attendant said to a shorter, brown-haired girl pouring chips into small bowls lined up on the bar.

"Yes, he's in 8A." They both glanced in my direction. I was in 9A. It sounded like they were expecting a celebrity.

The seats in first class on this carrier were arranged differently from most airlines. Instead of arranged in pairs, there were four long rows of seats all next to each other but at a diagonal, going end to end in the cabin. Each seat had high sides to form private space. That was why I liked flying with this carrier, especially when on my own. I wouldn't have to make polite conversation with the complete stranger next to me. I liked to disappear into my own world of recipes and baking when I travelled. I pulled out my notebook and clipped my seatbelt shut.

A male flight attendant I recognized—I flew the route from Chicago to London regularly—joined the pair and started to put ice into a tumbler. "Is he here yet?"

"No," the brunette said. "He's usually one of the last to

board. Can one of you take these chips? If he arrives and I'm walking, I'm likely to fall over."

"He's the kind of man that would spank you to teach you a lesson," the male flight attendant said.

I didn't catch the rest as they giggled conspiratorially. What did such a man look like?

Whoever Mr. 8A was, he was important if he managed to get the crew in such a fluster. They were used to flying with the rich and famous—airport lounges and airplanes were fertile ground for celebrity spotting. I'd seen Eva Longoria the last time I flew to New York. So tiny, but so pretty.

The blonde took the tray of snacks and began what would be one of many trips up and down the first-class rows.

I started to read through the last things I'd written in my notebook, trying to drown out the clatter of the bar. I'd been working on a ginger and cranberry cake. I liked the spicy, sweet and sour mixed together, but there was something missing.

Baking had become my salvation during my battle for sobriety. It had given me something to do, some structure to my day and a focus that had turned into a passion.

I'd started with brownies because my brother loved them and it was a small way to tell him how much I appreciated his never-failing support. I used to slip them into his lunch for work. I moved on to lemon bars and then worked my way through every type of pie ever invented and some that never should have been. Before long, I was baking every day.

As I got more confident, I started to vary the recipes I found, and even invented my own. I loved that even from the most basic of ingredients it was possible to create something that incited real pleasure in people. Through my baking, I got to make people happy, even for a few moments, and that fed my soul.

Champagne and I were over—I was now in a serious relationship with my stove.

Recently, I'd started to video myself baking and had created a channel on YouTube. I'd been surprised at how popular it had become in a short space of time—it had even attracted the attention of some TV executives in Chicago, which was the reason for my visit to my hometown. The idea that I might be able to give my baking meaning outside of my sobriety was exciting. It would mean that the last four years hadn't been just about keeping sober, that it had been building the foundations of a career as well. After spending the last four years in a protective bubble, concentrating on keeping sober, I was ready for a slice of real life.

"Good morning, Mr. James," the brunette said. The blonde and the male flight attendant snapped their heads around. It must be Mr. 8A.

I couldn't resist taking a peek at what all the fuss was about. The brunette's eyes were wide. I followed the direction of her gaze and found the back of a suit jacket. Whoever Mr. 8A was, he was tall, broad and wore expensive tailoring. I glanced up, awaiting a famous profile. His hair was almost black, just the ends shimmered brown, and was longer than most professional men tended to prefer. Perhaps he was a movie star that liked to dress in a suit. His profile and strong jaw came into view; he was clean shaven and wearing a serious look, as he pulled his eyebrows together sternly. I didn't recognize him, and his wasn't a face I'd forget.

I shivered as my nipples grazed the lace of my bra. I hadn't thought about sex for a long time—I'd shut down that side of myself while I focused on getting sober. That had been over three years ago.

The advice from my sponsor had been not to date for a year, not three. But after a long time of being miserable and out of control, I was happy and sober. Putting that at risk to date wasn't worth it. My last relationship had ended badly. In fact it had started badly, and continued disastrously, leaving me weak and hopeless. Memories of who I'd turned into meant staying single hadn't been a struggle, and anyway, it wasn't as if I was beating men off with a stick.

But something about Mr. 8A was deeply . . . sexual, almost to the point of disturbing, because it stirred something in me that was so unfamiliar.

I scanned his face as he pulled out papers from his carry-on.

"Let me know if I can help you put that in the overhead locker, sir." The male flight attendant bustled past, no doubt hoping for a spanking. 8A nodded once briskly. He looked like a man who did everything very deliberately, with no mistakes.

He slipped his jacket off, the expensive fabric yielding beneath his fingers. He handed it to the blonde, who just happened to be passing. He opened the overhead locker. I watched his muscles bunch beneath his tight shirt as he placed his bag inside. It was difficult to decide how old he was. His skin suggested early thirties, but his stern expression hinted he might be older.

As I deliberated over his age, his body, his mouth, Mr. 8A turned his head in my direction and caught me staring. I smiled, trying to cover the fact that I was thinking about him naked and between my thighs, not to mention wondering if every part of him was as solid as it seemed.

He offered no smile, no introduction. He just looked at me, or *into* me. I wasn't quite sure.

I laid my palm against my breastbone to calm the pulsing of my heart, but somehow I couldn't look away. Then, as if in understanding, like he'd got the measure of me, he offered me a brief nod and turned away.

I lost sight of him when he sat. I exhaled in relief, but at the same time, I wished the sides of my seat were slightly lower so I could watch him a little more.

I hadn't noticed a man in a long time. Not in a way where I wanted to touch him, and for him to touch me. Mr. 8A had prodded awake a part of me that had been asleep a long time. I'd been thinking about starting to date again for a few months now, but not because I missed being part of a couple. Not because I wanted to share my life with someone, but just because I thought I should. As much as anything, it was the next step in my recovery. I could see how it could become ten years between lovers if I didn't do something. Even my brother was regularly suggesting I get out and meet people. His wife, Haven, was even more vocal about it. She'd even tried to set me up a few times. As she said, I didn't have to fall in love but dinner and casual sex could be fun.

I wasn't sure if I could be casual about sex.

Was it possible to separate the physical from the emotional? Did I need to sleep with a stranger—to break the cycle of singledom I was in?

I wasn't convinced. A relationship was a risk, and if I was going to take a risk, shouldn't it be with a guy who might be my forever man? I was done with dating men who saw me as the girl they were with before they got serious, because drunk or not, I was always serious about them; I couldn't help myself. Nearly four years might be a long time, but if I found the man that was meant for me, I'd happily wait another three. At least, that was what I was telling myself.

A small, quiet voice from deep inside told me I was just frightened. Frightened of intimacy without the cloak of alcohol to protect me.

Alcohol gave me confidence.

Alcohol made me sexy.

When it came down to it, the pull of sober sex was easy to resist.

In the meantime, Mr. 8A was a mighty fine view, and I was happy to look but not touch.

I checked my phone for the time. Five minutes to takeoff and the cabin doors weren't even shut. We were late. I glanced behind me and out the window. Snow was falling thickly. I hoped we were still going to be able to take off.

The three cabin-crewmembers assigned to first class were gathered at the bar, chatting, waiting for the signal to start clearing people's glasses, and stealing furtive glances at Mr. 8A.

I understood their excitement.

There weren't many men who wore a suit like he did.

Or many men who were so handsome they elicited a short intake of breath on first glance.

Or many men who looked like if they touched a woman, they'd possess her forever.

I shifted in my seat. I had to try to distract myself. I leafed through the pages and tried to find where I'd left off.

"Sir. Miss," the blonde addressed me and Mr. 8A a few minutes later. "I'm afraid we're delayed due to the weather. We're asking people to make their way back to the lounge. We're hoping we can be back on track within a couple of hours. I'm very sorry for the inconvenience."

Used to travelling, it didn't take me longer than a minute to be off the aircraft and headed to the lounge. I wanted to find a free table in a quiet corner to work through my recipes, so I needed to get there quickly. It was for occasions such as these that I wore flats when I travelled.

After checking in to the lounge, I headed to my favorite place at the far right-hand side of the space, beyond the showers and the business center. There were only three tables of two in this section, and people who didn't fly regularly didn't realize they existed. It meant peace and quiet.

I pulled out my notebook, tucked my legs up under my skirt and started to scribble. Just a few seconds later, I sensed someone approach my section. Damn, I'd wanted this corner to myself. Head down, I watched the empty chair at my table as it was pulled out and someone put their bag on it. Wanting to know who was planning to sit with me when there were two other tables free, I snapped my head up and came face-to-face with Mr. 8A.

My heart started to thunder in the same way it had when I came across alcohol when I was first sober; it was warning me about temptation.

"Excuse me. Is this seat taken?" His voice was deep, gravelly. I'd not heard him speak on the plane.

I glanced across at the free tables. "No, please. Go ahead." I couldn't refuse, but why the hell did he want to share my table?

He pulled out his laptop and set it next to his phone along with a small black Moleskine.

I pretended to be engrossed in my notes, but all I could think about was him. All I could do was concentrate on not staring. I caught his scent: earthy and dark, expensive and sexual. Everything about him was magnetic. Hands unsteady, I gripped tighter onto my notebook.

A waitress approached, her eyes glued to my tablemate.

"Can I get you two anything?"

Did she think we were together, married? A grin started at the edges of my mouth. "I'll have a virgin mojito, and do you have any cake?"

Cake would stop my hands from shaking. Cake was now, as it had started then, a tonic for all that was wrong.

"We may have some. I'll have to check," the waitress replied.

"Thank you. Whatever you have." I smiled at her.

"And you, sir?" Mr. 8A's focus hadn't left his laptop. He glanced up, then back to his screen. "A soda water with a twist of freshly cut lime. Please." He didn't wait for a reaction before he recommenced typing.

"Yes, sir. Anything to eat?"

"No." His voice was firm. "Thank you," he said, almost as an afterthought. She scurried off with our order. Mr. 8A continued to divide his attention between his laptop, which got the majority of his time, and his phone and notebook.

Knowing he was doing anything but taking notice of me, I took the opportunity to do some more of the staring I'd started earlier. I guessed him to be six foot two or three—almost a foot taller than me. His hands were large, but moved quickly and precisely over the keyboard. His expression hadn't changed since the plane. He was definitely stern.

He took a deep breath and glanced up at me, catching me staring again. He held my gaze, and again I couldn't look away.

His phone vibrated on the table.

"Yes," he answered, but continued to return my stare.

His eyes were blue but an unusual shade.

Indigo.

I almost said it out loud.

Why couldn't I look away?

He held one finger up as if excusing himself and asking me to wait, then got up and wandered toward the showers to continue his call. Did he mean to ask me something when he returned? He'd gestured as if we'd been interrupted in the middle of something. He hadn't spoken to me since asking if the seat was taken, but perhaps he'd been about to? I realized I wanted him to ask me a question. I wanted to hear his deep, gravelly voice. I wanted to tell him something about me. A secret.

I craved intimacy with him.

But that's not who I was. I didn't give in to temptation anymore. I needed to shut him down. I needed to concentrate on my cake.

Dylan

She was delicious. Unusual. She looked like a fifties movie star: Vivian Leigh or a young Elizabeth Taylor. My cock had begun to twitch when she'd looked at me on the plane. And I could tell she'd been checking me out while I was working. I was used to it, and I quite enjoyed that she was taking her time, lingering over every detail of my physical form.

And when she hadn't looked away when I caught her? I loved that. She'd done it on the plane, too. It was intriguing, challenging. And I was up for it.

I needed a new fuck, and she'd do nicely.

Her tits were real, which was a plus. I was a connoisseur and could tell the real from the fake at a hundred paces. I'd choose real every time, but wouldn't rule a woman out for having a little help. And she'd ordered cake, which caught my attention. Most women I came across didn't eat. That was cute.

"That sounds fine, Raf. I'm in London for the week, so as long as I have it before I leave, it's fine."

I ended the call with my business partner and strode back. Luckily my meeting for the next day had been moved back, so if we didn't take off today it wouldn't be the end of the world.

In fact, given the company at my table, I'd say it might be just perfect.

I understood the dynamic between men and women. I got to sleep with hot women, and in exchange they got to fuck a rich guy in the hope that they'd become beneficiaries of my cash. I might be handsome, but I knew from bitter experience that if a richer guy came along, I'd be left in the taillights of the women I slept with. It just happened that now, there weren't many richer men, which gave me a certain satisfaction. I'd made peace with the transactional nature of relationships between men and women and had no expectations. At some point in my past I'd thought that love was possible. Not anymore. It was all about giving to get.

I checked out my table companion's hand. No ring. I couldn't remember meeting a hot woman in first class unless I'd bought the ticket.

Our drinks had arrived and we were still alone in this section of the lounge. I'd meant to sit near her when I'd arrived, as I'd been intrigued on the plane, but I'd not seen where she'd gone, so I'd headed back here. It was a place not many people knew about. Apparently, she did. Did she come to this lounge a lot? A wealthy heiress, perhaps? I was used to being with women who wanted my money, not women who had their own.

I finished off a few emails, then shut down my computer and put it back in my carry-on, leaving my notebook and phone in front of me on the table.

I leaned back into my chair, watching her slicing through her cake with her fork. "So, you like cake, virgin mojitos and red lipstick. I'd guess you also like fifties movies, kittens and the beach." I wanted to add *and I bet you fuck like a train*, but didn't.

It was true. I'd been with enough women to know the ones who were gorgeous but terrible lovers apart from the ones that were built for sex.

The woman in front of me was made for fucking. Those full, ripe breasts, that red, swollen mouth. I shifted in my seat at the thought of my fingers wrapped around her tiny waist and smoothing over hips that flared out into that incredible ass I'd caught as she'd left the plane. And I bet she was loud. We'd have to go somewhere private to allow her to let go and scream as hard as she was going to when I touched her.

She didn't respond to my assessment. Most women found it charming when I read them like that. More often than not I got it right. "Tell me what else."

She narrowed her eyes in suspicion. "I don't like kittens."

"But I was right about the movies and the beach."

She shrugged. "Who doesn't like fifties movies and the beach?"

It was a fair comment. "So tell me something unique about you."

She smiled, though it wasn't the flirty one I was used to. More of a polite smile, reserved for checkout girls and chumps like me who were crashing and burning. "I'm good. I'm busy."

Oh. A stab of disappointment hit me in the stomach. I wanted to have a little fun. Work was under control. I was ready to lighten up. I didn't normally have to work so hard to get a woman to play along, but I wasn't going to give up that easily—I liked a challenge. "What are you reading?"

She lowered her notebook. "You know, I'm sure any number of the flight attendants, male or female, would be happy to indulge you in"—she swirled her hand in my direction—"whatever it is you're doing."

I took a sip of my soda water, my eyes not leaving her. "I'm not interested in the cabin crew. I'm flirting with *you*, hoping you'll flirt back."

She set her book on the table and looked right at me. Her eyes were beautiful. Wide and deep brown and she had a beauty spot high on her right cheekbone. Stunning. "And what is the purpose of that? You seem pretty able to occupy yourself with your gadgetry. You can't be bored."

"I'm not bored. I want to get to know you." I grinned. I was happy to use all the weapons in my arsenal. She was worth it.

She cocked her head and frowned. "Stop looking at me like that."

"Like what? Like I want to make you come so hard you'll be seeing stars?" I held my breath for a second, wondering how she'd react. It could have been a step too far.

She shook her head but raised an eyebrow. I hadn't lost her.

"Oh really? You think that's ever going to happen?"

"I know it will. You're curious. You've been checking me out."

She blushed, but I wasn't trying to make her feel bad.

"I enjoyed it. Don't be embarrassed. I love attracting the attention of a beautiful woman." The cabin crew's attention was irritating, but being eye-fucked by a woman like her was invigorating.

She rolled her eyes. She thought it was a line. To be fair, it sounded like one, but I meant it. I'd noticed her, so I'd have been disappointed if she hadn't noticed me.

"Just because I saw something glittery and new in the shop window doesn't mean I'm going to hand over my credit card and take it home."

I chuckled. "Oh honey, I don't charge." She'd totally owned checking me out and given me a put down at the same time.

I needed a different tactic. "Shall we rewind slightly? My name's Dylan James." I held out my hand.

She took a breath as if she were trying to gather her patience, but eventually held out her hand. "Beth Harrison."

I pressed my palm against hers and savored the warm softness of her skin next to mine. So smooth. I'd happily lick every inch of her.

"So tell me about yourself. Are you going to London for business or pleasure?" I asked.

She sighed. "We're in an airport together for an hour, then we'll never see each other again. I'm not sure we need to get to know each other."

"If you never talked to strangers, you'd never meet anyone new. You're not interested in human connection?"

She narrowed her eyes, clearly considering my question. "I'm not interested in the kind of human connection you're suggesting."

The waitress appeared at our table. "Another virgin mojito, please, and I'll have another soda water with a twist." I didn't glance away from Beth. "Do you want more cake?"

She shook her head.

"Actually, sir, I wanted to tell you that your flight has been cancelled. The weather will get worse before it gets better. We're hoping it will be clear for the morning, and we've rescheduled for seven. We've secured a limited number of hotel rooms, and we're giving our frequent flyers priority. I can check you in remotely if you like, before everything gets booked up."

I glanced across at the waitress. She had an iPad in hand, ready to type in information, which presented an opportunity. I'd have the rest of my evening to persuade Beth to get naked, and the venue would be a comfortable hotel room rather than whatever place around here—probably the showers—I could find. "Sure. Check us in."

Beth began to say something, but changed her mind. Did she live in Chicago? Was she considering going home?

I watched as Beth concentrated on the waitress as she tapped the screen of the tablet.

Beth's lips formed a full pout as she focused on the iPad. Adorable. My eyes skated down her body.

"Mr. and Mrs. James, you're booked into room 302 at the Hilton. Your key will be waiting for you at reception."

I chuckled.

Beth flitted a look between the waitress and me, presumably waiting for me to correct the girl. *Yeah, that isn't going to happen.* "I'm sorry. I'm not Mrs. James." She waved her hand between us. "We're not married. Or together. I think he meant check us in separately." Beth's eyes were wide with panic.

I grabbed my phone and dialed my assistant.

The waitress gulped in a breath. "I'm so sorry. I assumed . . . Can I get your name?"

"Marie, could you book me into the Hilton for the night, please? My flight has been cancelled." Marie was resourceful; she'd find me a room if she had to come down to the front desk to organize it. And it wouldn't be the shitty standard rooms that the airline would book. "Call me back when it's done."

"Beth Harrison." Beth looked concerned. She probably thought I'd insist we bunk in together. It wasn't the worst idea in the world. Frankly, two rooms were a waste.

"My screen froze. I'll just be a minute." The waitress headed off to fix her IT problems.

Beth pulled out a tablet of her own and began to tap away.

"Hey," I said, smoothing my hand over hers. "Don't sweat it. My assistant will find me a room. You take room 302."

She moved her hand from under mine. "But it won't just be our flight that will be cancelled. Everyone is going to be looking for a hotel room. God knows how long it will take for the waitress to unfreeze her tablet. If I wait, we'll be left with just one room."

I looked at her. "Trust me. Take the room."

Her chest rose, then lowered as she took a breath and exhaled. "Okay." She paused. "Hey, is this a ruse to get me to relax, and then you'll give me some sob story about not having a room when your fake assistant calls you back?"

"Beth." My tone was serious. "I don't lie, and I don't force women to share my bed. Trust me." It'd been a while since I'd worked this hard. My money normally did the talking. To be fair, it had been a while since I'd thought anyone was worth working for.

My phone vibrated on the table in front of me. "Marie."

My assistant told me my room number at the Hilton—a suite on the executive floor—and I thanked her and hung up.

"What did I tell you?" I winked at Beth.

"You got a room?" she asked. It hurt my ego a little that she clearly didn't think I had the power to get a room at the Hilton. I could buy the fucking hotel if I needed to.

"So what's so bad about the idea of sharing a bed with me?" I asked. I was interested in what exactly might be holding her back. We had just met and she could be in a relationship for all I knew, though I was pretty sure she wasn't. I could spot an attached woman—ring or no ring—a mile off.

She laughed. "You mean other than the fact that we just met?"

I frowned. "Yeah. Give me three good reasons other than that."

"We should get going, or we'll miss the line for check-in at the hotel." She began to put her things back into her bag.

"That's what I thought. You can't think of any."

"I can think of plenty. First, you could be a serial killer—"

"I said other than the fact we just met."

She stood up, her weight on one foot, pushing one of her delicious hips out and emphasizing her curves. "Okay." She looked me straight in the eye. "One, I'm an alcoholic. Two, I've never had sober sex. And three, I'm scared shitless that when I finally do have sex again, I won't enjoy it in the way I used to."

Wow, that wasn't what I'd been expecting, at all. Women didn't try to discourage my flirtations through honesty; they didn't tell me their deepest secrets. Who was this girl?

She picked up her bag and spun round, heading quickly to the exit.

I stuffed my belongings back into my carry-on and tried to catch her up. This was a girl worth following. Incredible.

chapter TWO

Beth

I was used to telling people I was an alcoholic. Granted, not gorgeous strangers who made my skin buzz from a foot away, but still, it felt kind of euphoric to have told Mr. 8A. I hadn't stayed to watch his reaction. No doubt his jaw would have been on the floor. I laughed to myself and fell back onto the bed in my hotel room.

Dylan James' gruff exterior and curtness with the cabin crew had been a stark contrast to the way he'd spoken to me about wanting to make me come. I shivered. He'd wanted me and it had felt good, even if our exchange had been a little short-lived. Perhaps when I got back to London I *should* start dating again. It seemed that that part of me hadn't shriveled up and died as I'd suspected it might have.

I jumped as the hotel's phone buzzed. I reached across the bed for the receiver. "Hello?"

"What are you wearing?"

My stomach flip-flopped at Mr. 8A's voice. He was persistent, even after what I'd told him.

"Are you dirty dialing me?" I pretended to be haughty.

"If I thought you'd play along, I might." He laughed a deep, filthy chuckle and a desire to smooth my hands across his chest flickered through me. "But seriously. Why did you run off? Will you have dinner with me?"

I'd run off because I'd assumed my confession would put an end to his flirting and his change of heart wasn't something I wanted to stay and endure. Apparently, I hadn't scared him away. "Dinner?"

"Yes. Indulge me. It will help pass a few hours at least," he said.

Indulge him? I'd really like to kiss him. Have him kiss me. I took a deep breath.

"I don't dine with strangers," I replied. Should I let myself get to know him? Dinner in a whiteout was hardly a date, after all. More like a pre-date. And it would help me pass the time. He was also the best-looking man ever born, who had still called me after I'd confessed the things about me that should have made him run.

"So make an exception."

He said it as if it were simple. Like dinner with a man when I wasn't drinking wasn't a big deal.

"I don't date," I said.

"So make an exception."

"I'm not going to sleep with you."

He chuckled. "Maybe, maybe not, but I promise, you'll have no pressure from me on that score. We both have to eat, after all. We can fuck later if that's what you want to do."

I wanted to slam the phone down on him. He was so arrogant, but his complete confidence drew me in instead of pushing me away, as if it could shield me from hurt rather than expose me to it. If he was so sure of everything, maybe I didn't have to be. Like he said, it was just dinner. And dinner with someone I never had to see again. It could go really badly, and it wouldn't matter. I tried to stop the grin forming at the corners of my mouth. "Just dinner?"

"For now."

I took a deep breath. "Okay." What did I have to lose . . . other than my mind, my senses, and my confidence?

"Good. Come up to my suite. Room 2035." He hung up the phone.

I might have agreed to dinner, but I hadn't agreed to dinner in his hotel room.

How totally presumptuous of him. I'm sure it was obvious I found him attractive, but that didn't mean I was going to do anything about it. No, there was no way I was going up to his suite. A club sandwich and American Idol would do just fine.

I slid the receiver back on the stand, slumped onto the bed and picked up the remote.

I believed him when he said he wasn't going to pressure me into having sex with him—his ego wouldn't allow it. He was a man who didn't lose control or make mistakes. My going to his suite was convenient, I guess. Private. Better than having to endure the waitresses flirting with him.

I wasn't about to actually go up there.

But for the first time in years, I wanted to know more about a man. I could go up for a drink and stay ten minutes. Just dip my toe into the water and then leave, right?

I pulled out my makeup case from my carry-on, re-applied the red lipstick he'd noticed and made my way up to floor twenty.

My heart was thumping as I knocked on his door. Was I really about to do this?

Ten minutes.

That was it.

The door swung open and Dylan stood in front of me, his hair slightly more tousled than it had been back in the lounge. He no longer wore a tie or jacket, and the top few buttons on his shirt were undone. The gruff Mr. 8A had relaxed. He didn't say anything, and I ran through possible greetings to fill the silence before he reached out and brushed his thumb over my cheekbone. My skin burned where he'd touched me. He took a step closer so our bodies were nearly touching and the door swung shut behind him, leaving us both in the corridor. "Hey," he whispered as if he hadn't noticed that we were now locked out.

I took a step back. Having him so close had rendered me speechless. I'd expected him to make a move, but I expected a little something before—a drink, dinner, flirting and maybe even conversation. But his hand went to my lower back and he pressed me against him. I gasped and steadied myself by reaching for his forearms. I spread my fingers across the thick muscles under his shirt. His body was hard and tight as I molded against him.

"Look at me. I can see everything you are through those beautiful eyes, and I want to see everything I do to you tonight reflected back at me."

A pulse gained force between my thighs. "You didn't hear me earlier—" Had he forgotten that I'd told him I'd not had sober sex? Ever? I couldn't even remember a sober kiss since high school.

"I heard everything you said." He tilted my chin up, forcing me to look at him. He bent down and pressed his full lips against mine. "That lipstick is driving me insane," he growled and kissed me again, more forcefully this time. He pushed my lips open with his and my breath hitched at the sensation of his tongue skirting under my top lip. Jesus, each movement sent shock waves across my body and lit me up, as if I were Frankenstein's monster being plugged in for the first time.

He slid his hands up my back and my knees wobbled, made unstable by his touch. He caught me before I could fall, wrapping his arm around my waist. "Oh baby, if you like how my tongue does that, I can't wait to show you what else it's capable of."

The pulsing between my thighs grew stronger.

By agreeing to have dinner with him, had I effectively agreed to get naked and dirty? And if so, was there anything wrong with that? That toe in the water could be just a quick swim. My sister-in-law had called it a palate cleanser before I went on to find Mr. Right. I was never going to have to see Mr. 8A again after tonight. Maybe he was what I needed to find out what I liked these days, and get the embarrassing sober virginity out of the way before I started dating properly.

He kissed my forehead. "Come inside. I've arranged for

dinner to be set up, and don't worry, I won't fuck you until you need me to."

Need him to? I shook my head. He was pretty sure of himself, but I wasn't going to bet on him being wrong.

The door must have been ajar as he pushed it open and urged me inside.

His suite was huge—a seating area on one side with two large white sofas opposite each other and a dining area on the other side. The lighting was low and moody, and music played softly in the background.

"Let's eat." He took my hand and headed toward the table. There were a number of silver-domed platters spotted across the table for six. He pulled out a chair and sat, pulling me into his lap. "I ordered for us."

He lifted the lid on the plate nearest to him and revealed a huge slice of chocolate cake covered in fresh whipped cream.

"Cake?" I watched him as he took a forkful.

"You like it, right?"

Like it? I could eat dessert morning, noon and night. "I do."

"I thought we'd start as we mean to carry on. After all, tonight's all about pleasure." He held the fork up to my mouth. "Open wide for me." The pulsing between my thighs was back as I opened my lips.

The cake was delicious and obviously homemade.

"How is it?"

I opened my eyes. I had a tendency to want to block out all my other senses when tasting something great. For a second, I'd forgotten I was sitting on Dylan's lap. "It's good, really good."

He cupped my neck, pulling me toward him, and licked across my lips. "Hmmm, you do taste good. There was a little something on the corner of your mouth there. I thought I'd help you out."

I grinned and took the fork out of his hand, then reached for the cake. "You should have a bite for yourself. It really is good."

I held the fork up to his lips. His beautiful indigo eyes bored into me as he hungrily took the mouthful I offered him. He groaned, the sound an echo of the dam bursting inside of me.

I wanted him.

My desire sliced through any embarrassment I had at being so close to a man totally sober.

I dropped the fork and threaded my hands through his hair, watching him watching me. I dipped my head, sliding my tongue along his lips, in the same way he'd done to me. He growled again and pushed his tongue against mine—the chocolate, cream and him mixing together in perfect combination.

Dylan

My cock was used to beautiful women, but the one perched on my lap with swollen lips from what felt like hours of kissing was more beautiful than most. My cock agreed as I was uncomfortably hard. Her heavy breasts weren't helping—neither were the small movements she made against my thigh. Fuck, if I didn't get myself under control, I was going to come like a teenager as soon as I saw her naked. I growled and reached into her cleavage, pushing my fingers between her breasts, relishing the soft flesh. I wanted my dick to take the place of my hand, but it was too soon. She wasn't ready. I plunged my hand into her bra and fingered her already hard nipple. She tipped her head back and grabbed my knee.

"Dylan . . . I . . ."

She was nervous and it was adorable. The women I was used to had bigger balls than most men. "You don't have to worry about not enjoying sober sex." It was my favorite kind. I rarely drank, and never if I was planning to fuck. Drinking dulled my senses, and I didn't want to miss out on anything when my dick was busy. "You're going to come so hard, you'll forget what drunk feels like."

I yanked down her bra, exposing her breast. She gripped my head. I hesitated. If I got the slightest bit of reticence from her, we'd go no further. I'd have to excuse myself to the bathroom to relieve my aching cock, but I'd stop touching her.

But she wasn't trying to stop me. Her fingernails scraped my scalp as I took her nipple in my mouth and sucked. She tasted sweet and began to grind against my thigh as I alternated between flicking and biting, sucking and stroking her.

Her hands left my head, and for a moment I wondered if I'd gone too far. Her bra loosened—she'd been unfastening it, wanting more. Perfect. I dove back to her tit, reaching for the other. The loosened bra was still in the way, so I reached for her waist, pulling up her top. She held up her hands and I disrobed her from the waist up. I couldn't pull my eyes away from the glorious sight of her uncovered tits. They were full and tight and made for me. I cupped one in each hand, enjoying the weight of them, the way they were almost too big for my grip. A groan ripped through me. I moved her off my lap and stood. I wanted to get a better look at her.

"You are so fucking sexy." I kissed her briefly on her forehead as she watched me. Her arms went to her breasts, hiding them. "No. Don't cover these. They're mine."

She giggled. "I think, biologically speaking—"

"They're mine for tonight." I pulled her arms away and grazed my thumbs against her nipples. "Let's leave the cake for later. I want to taste *you* for a while." I trailed my fingers down her back and led her into the bedroom.

She lingered at the door. "I just . . ." She shook her head.

I removed my shoes and socks and sat on the bed. "Talk to me. What are you thinking?"

"Well, all that stuff I said earlier. It was true."

"Good. I wouldn't want you to have been lying to me." What she'd said had been intimate and somehow made her real. I'd hate for her to have been dishonest. I was sick of playing those same old tired games of cat and mouse with women.

She crossed her hands over her chest and looked at her feet. A memory of a feeling fluttered in my gut.

"Hey, we can stop and eat cake if you'd prefer." Perhaps fucking her wasn't the best idea I'd ever had. She seemed vulnerable, as if she'd been broken and the glue was still setting on her repairs.

"I'm just nervous. I know it's not like we're ever going to see each other again, I just—"

"Darlin', I told you I was going to make you see stars. The pressure is all on me. You just need to tell me what you're enjoying and what's not working for you. I promise, nerves are the last thing you're going to be feeling. But if you'd prefer to just talk, then that's fine. You can tell me what you were scribbling away in that notebook of yours."

She gave me a small smile, cocked her hip, released her hands from her chest and shimmied out of her skirt. Jesus, she was every inch the fifties movie star. The rounded ass, small waist and, of course, that beautiful red mouth. "You're a fucking goddess. Get over here." Hips swaying, she came toward me. I couldn't help but focus on the scrap of lace between her legs. I needed to feel her there.

I pulled her between my knees and sank my tongue in her cleavage, licking up and down the juncture. She cupped her tits, pushing them together, and I almost came.

I reached for her underwear, tracing my fingers across the top. They were flimsy and I was impatient. I gave them a sharp tug, and as expected, they came free as if they were willing me on. Ripping off a girl's panties never got old. Discarding them on the floor, I hesitated for just a second before touching her. I was a little nervous. It wasn't a feeling I had very often, and never when it came to fucking, but she was so goddamn sexy and vulnerable and she'd been so open with me. I didn't want to fuck this up. I wanted to make her first sober sexual experience special—somehow memorable.

She circled her hips, pulling me out of my own head, and my nerves disappeared. I ran my hand up her inner thigh;

my fingers coated in her lust for me as soon as I reached her pussy.

Perfect.

Wet and sweet and, I was sure, tight as a glove. I withdrew my hand and painted each of her nipples in her own moisture. She gasped and gathered up her tits again, pushing them toward me, urging me to take them in my mouth. "Tell me what you want," I whispered. I wanted to hear her need for me.

"I want you to suck it off," she said, her voice breathy and ragged.

"Oh, yes, I think we're going to be very well suited." I liked a girl who got so caught up in what we were doing that there was no room for inhibitions, no room for outside crap to seep in and interrupt our pleasure. I didn't know why she was nervous. She was perfect.

I bent forward and took her nipple in my mouth.

"Oh God, I'm loving that mouth of yours," she said as her head fell back.

My hand went to my dick as she spoke. I wasn't sure how long I was going to last if she was a talker.

I grazed my teeth over the puckered flesh and she bucked against me. She was so fucking responsive.

I pulled her onto the bed and slid to my knees. There was something about being fully clothed while getting a naked woman off. Maybe it was a power thing—yeah, it was definitely a power thing.

I pressed my palms against her inner thighs, parting

her legs for me. She squirmed, but I didn't think it was embarrassment. It was desire.

I blew against her pussy. "Tell me what you want."

She reached over her head as her back arched off the mattress. "I want your talented mouth on my pussy."

Oh yeah, she was ready. I groaned and went straight to her clit. Her hips flicked up and I had to hold her still. She tasted delicious. I didn't often go down on women, but I wanted Beth to relax, to understand she was going to enjoy tonight, that she needn't be shy or nervous. She just had to give her body to me.

I dipped my tongue at the edges of her entrance. She wouldn't have my fingers in her. I wanted her desperate to be filled up and rewarded for her begging with my cock, hard and fast. I didn't want her spoiled with my fingers.

I licked up and circled her clit as her hips continued to jerk and bounce. Later I'd have her sit on my face. I wanted to be totally surrounded by her smell, her taste. "You like that, darlin'?"

Her groans grew louder and her breath shorter. I wasn't ready for her to climax, not so quickly. When she came for the first time it was going to overwhelm her, and I was going to have my dick in her.

"God, I *love* your mouth." She sounded surprised.

I wasn't.

I pressed against her clit, rubbing the hard nub, and then released her, standing quickly.

"Hey, I was close. What happened?" She tucked one hand behind her head as she watched me with hazy eyes.

My gaze followed her other hand as it slid over her breasts, tweaking a nipple and then gliding down her stomach where her fingers found her clit. Fuck, she was spectacular. Creamy white skin and black-as-coal hair.

I stripped off my shirt. I had to be inside her. I found it difficult to understand why she'd thought she was going to be nervous. She seemed anything but.

"Take your hand away." My voice came out a jealous bark. I wanted every inch of her pleasure. It was my job to make her come, and I felt weirdly possessive about her orgasm. It was as if I had a burning *need* to give her orgasms. Her opening up to me about her alcoholism had created a need in me to get it right for her, to make it good.

"Make me." Her back arched as if she were turned on by the thought of what I might do.

Fumbling, my fingers unable to work quickly enough, I took a condom out of my wallet then stripped off my pants.

"Oh, Beth, your fingers are never going to be enough for you once I've fucked you."

Her gaze was on my dick, hard and flat against my stomach. She sat up, her eyes wide. "Jesus. Don't hurt me with that thing, will you?"

"It's all about pleasure, darlin'." I grinned at her as I slid a condom over my painfully hard dick.

Turning over, she crawled up onto all fours, her head twisted so she was still staring at my cock. Christ, she might very well turn out to be the fuck of my life. "That's it, Beth. You know how I want you."

I was going to be able to go again and again with her.

Her tits looked incredible from this angle as they swayed slightly with her impatience. Her ass was raised and waiting for me, and her hair tumbled across her back. I wanted this image committed to memory. I'd likely never see her again after tonight, but the sight of her, ready and waiting like this, was something I never wanted to forget.

I trailed the tip of my dick from her entrance down and around her clit and back up, coating myself in her juices. For a second I longed to feel her without the barrier of a condom. I shook it off. I never fucked without protection.

She pushed back, wanting me.

"Steady there, greedy girl." I grinned as I grabbed her hair.

I teased her a little longer, rubbing my tip over her entrance.

"Please, Jesus Christ. I want to feel—"

I didn't let her finish the sentence. I rammed into her up to the hilt.

chapter THREE

Beth

Jesus. Fucking. Christ. After teasing me for what seemed like days, the man I'd met only a few hours ago was buried so deep inside me I was close to being split in half.

Getting kissed by Dylan had somehow neutralized my nerves about being naked, sober, with a stranger. I wanted him. Wanted to be with him. Wanted a moment of madness. For the last three years, I'd been scared to enjoy life too much in case it descended into me chasing pleasure at the expense of my sobriety. I'd held onto everything so tightly, in such a controlled way for so long, that it felt good to let go, to breathe, and give in to something that made me feel good.

After bringing me to the brink two or three times, he'd refused to let me come. I'd always thought I'd never be able to let go enough without alcohol to get me to the point I'd have an orgasm, but Dylan knew exactly what he was doing. It was as if he'd made my body his life's work, and there was no way I was going to have a problem climaxing. Just staring at his monster cock was probably enough to send me over the edge at this point.

Finally, he was inside me, unmoving. It was only a fraction away from painful. If I'd had time to think after seeing him naked, I might have backed out. I hadn't been sure he'd fit.

Apparently he did. Just.

"You are *so* tight." His breath was heavy against my neck.

I tried to speak but just whimpered.

"You okay, Beth?" He sounded concerned. From my hazy memories of sex, my lovers had rarely been concerned with how I was feeling, with whether or not I came. Dylan's focus was on me and us, and not just him.

I nodded. "It's just so . . . big."

He grunted and pushed against my hips. He couldn't go any deeper. "I've never been so hard."

His hands stroked along my back as he straightened himself behind me. I shivered as he grabbed at my hair.

"You ready?"

Before I got a chance to answer him, he pulled back slowly, then crashed into me. My hand reached for my clit. I needed to get over the edge.

"No," he barked. "That's for me. Your clit, your pussy, your tits. They're all for me." He swiped my hand away, but replaced my fingers with his. I twisted my hips against his hand. He thrust once then twice, and in the distance I felt the beginnings of my orgasm begin to gather force. Again.

My head fell forward as I concentrated on the pleasure seeping into my limbs.

Holy. Crap. I couldn't stand any more, but I didn't want it to be over. "I'm so close—"

"So soon?" He picked up his pace, pushing harder and deeper as I spiraled into my first sober orgasm and the most intense feeling I'd ever had. I was floating and shivering, as if my body wasn't mine anymore. It was his.

Just before I collapsed, he pulled my limp body toward him so I was upright and kneeling on the bed as he pounded into me, as if he hadn't noticed I'd just had the orgasm to end all orgasms. One arm clasped around my waist, the other clamped at my shoulder, held me in place.

I gasped. The change in angle was like feeling him again for the first time. I reached back to bring his head to my neck, pushing my fingers through his velvety hair.

"You thought I couldn't make you come?" His voice was gritty. "I'm going to make you count your orgasms, because otherwise you're gonna lose track."

He wasn't going to have to wait much longer for the second. I watched as he pulled and twisted at my nipple, his fingers sending sparks down my legs and out of my toes.

"You're going to come again, do you hear me? My dick is going to explode this time when I feel those tight walls start to quiver."

I'd never had a guy talk to me like Dylan was talking to me. It was one of those things that only happened in porn, but it seemed like the most natural thing in Dylan and it made me pant.

I bent my knees slightly, meeting his thrust.

"Oh, yes. You know what you want, don't you? You want my dick as deep as it will go."

And there it was again, my orgasm barreling up my spine. My body juddered, supported in Dylan's arms, as my climax washed through me.

"Oh, yes, I feel you. So tight, Beth. So. Tight." He jerked sharply as his orgasm followed my own as he'd promised. As he'd said, he didn't lie.

He didn't let go as we collapsed, spent, onto the bed.

His chest heaved behind me and my stomach flickered with the remnants of my climax.

We lay in silence as our breathing returned to normal.

"You're astonishing," he said as I stroked his forearms. I was pretty sure I wasn't the only girl that had received that particular compliment.

He kissed my shoulder. It was such a sweet postcoital gesture, as if we were a long-standing couple. I sighed. I'd forgotten what this was like—what had he called it? Human connection—that was it. Or perhaps I'd never experienced it before.

It felt good to be held. It felt freeing to be fucked.

"You okay?" he asked, tightening his arms around me.

"Yeah. I'm good."

He kissed my shoulder again and then moved away, heading to the bathroom. *I should go back to my own room.* Perhaps I'd take one of those plates of cake with me. I sat up, wincing slightly at the way the muscles in my thighs pulled. I was going to be sore tomorrow. I slung my legs over the side of the bed, trying to find energy from somewhere.

"Hey." Dylan appeared from the bathroom. "A little unsteady?"

I grinned. "Ground-shaking sex will do that to a girl."

"Ground shaking, huh?"

My cheeks heated. He must know he fucked like a champion.

"I was going for world changing. It seems I've got a way to go." He headed back to the bed.

I smiled, still not able to take my eyes from his oh-so-perfect body. "Oh, I think you did just fine."

"Fine?" He frowned but nodded. "Hmmm. 'Fine' isn't a word I'm fond of. You'll have to give me a minute or two, and I'll see if I can notch up in your rankings."

I laughed. "You're a peach, but I should go."

"I fuck 'fine' and I'm a 'peach'? Are you trying to hurt my feelings?" He grinned at me. I think his ego was intact.

I crawled over and kissed him lightly on the lips. "You fuck like a machine. I had a blast. I gotta go." I twisted and hopped off the bed.

"You have a body made for fucking," he said, catching my fingers as I headed to collect my clothes. I turned to him.

I squeezed his hand and gazed at him. "Right back at you, Mr. 8A."

"Then stay for a little longer."

"Dylan, I'm going to hurt tomorrow as it is."

Casually, he cupped one of my breasts. Immediately my nipples pebbled. "But I promise it'll hurt so good."

"Do you want water?" Dylan called from the kitchen.

I reached for the clock on the nightstand. "That'd be great. Thanks."

It was 4:30AM and we were due to fly out at seven. I'd have to sleep on the plane; there hadn't been any chance of sleeping so close to Dylan. He was insatiable and I was more than happy going along for the . . . ride.

"What are we at?" He walked back into the bedroom and handed me a glass of water.

"It's four thirty. I need to get cleaned up."

"I mean, how many orgasms? I told you to keep count." He crawled across the bed, pulling the bed sheets down my body.

I slid away from him. "Four, but seriously. We need to get going. We have to check in again." I climbed out of bed and headed to the living room. I was pretty sure that my clothes had started to come off before we hit the bedroom. The silver domes were still scattered across the dining table. What a waste. I hadn't even seen what they were hiding. I picked up one to find a slice of strawberry gateau that looked incredible. I dipped my finger into the cream and tasted. Hmmm. I closed my eyes. Delicious.

"Your ass is the best I've ever laid eyes on." Dylan's hands were on my hips, smoothing down my ass. Every time he touched me, my skin tightened as if my body was preparing itself for another climax. But I really had to shower.

"Dylan. We have to check in."

He ignored me. "Lean over." He grabbed my waist with one hand, the other pushing me gently forward so I was gripping the edge of the table.

"And your pussy—it's so fucking sweet." Without warning, he slammed into me, forcing me farther onto the table. Vaguely, I heard a plate crash to the ground, but couldn't concentrate on anything but Dylan fucking me as though it was the first time.

He gripped my hips, pulling me back onto him.

"You want to get all checked in? You had enough of my dick?"

"No." I was trembling and weak from a night of monumental fucking, but I would never get enough of his dick.

I bucked away from him when he reached around and found my clit. He knew the exact pressure to use. I wasn't sure I'd survive another orgasm. I clasped my hand over his. "Please" was all I could manage.

"This clit is mine. I told you that. I'll do what I want with it."

I released his hand, steadying myself on the table. He was right; he owned my body when he touched me. There was something disturbing about the power he had over it.

Despite Dylan filling me like no other man ever had, I had the urge to have him deeper. I widened my legs, hoping to get more of him.

"Oh, yes, you can't get enough, can you?"

I shook my head. "Please." He slammed faster and faster into me, pulling me closer and closer to him. He groaned behind me as I twisted my hips in the hope that I could give him a fraction of the pleasure he was giving me.

The skin on my arms began to burn from the friction against the table, and I found I took pleasure from it. I wanted some kind of semi-permanent reminder of the fuck of my life. I'd never see him again after tonight. I'd like something to remember him by.

"Look at me, Beth. I know you're close and I want to see that beautiful face when you come."

I turned to him, pushing myself up with one hand. A thin sheen of sweat covered his muscle-bound body and the veins in his neck stood out with his effort. The sight of him was the last straw, and I gave him my orgasm, one final time.

Dylan

I set the temperature of my shower to cold. I'd been looking for a new fuck, but I hadn't expected to find the lay of the decade. We'd fucked all night and could have gone all day today if a flight to London weren't inconveniencing us. I'd never second-guessed myself in bed before, particularly when a woman had clearly climaxed, but I hoped it had been good for Beth; as good as it had been for me. I wanted it to have been memorable for her. There was something about her that brought out a protective side in me.

I was going to have to cool down—she'd be in the seat right next to mine and I didn't want to spend eight hours with a raging hard-on thirty thousand feet up. Just the thought of those perfect tits bouncing freely in front of me . . . *Argh*, I was done for. I shook my head, trying to get images of her out of my brain.

After I'd made her come five times, Beth had gone back to her room to prepare for check-in. She'd left in a rush, leaving me dazed, recovering from another explosion against her creamy skin. She'd seemed sated and I took satisfaction from that.

I showered quickly, hoping to catch up with her before we boarded. Grab her number, touch her. I'd really like to see her again, make it good for her again. If not today, then while I was in London.

Beth Harrison was everything a woman should be in bed: responsive, willing and a mesmerizing sight naked. She was also confident about her body and sassy enough to have called me a peach. She might have been a little shy at first, but any reticence had disappeared as my tongue touched her skin. I grinned and toweled off. I dressed quickly, eager to see her again.

I got to the lounge in record time and after scanning the main area and not seeing Beth, I passed the showers, heading to the table I'd found her at yesterday. I couldn't stop the grin on my face as I rounded the corner. Our table was empty. *Shit*. She wasn't here yet. I checked my watch. She was going to have to be quick; they'd start boarding first class any minute. Perhaps she'd got stuck on a call, but who would be calling her so early? Someone in London, maybe? A boyfriend? She didn't strike me as a cheater, and she'd told me she'd never had sober sex. She didn't seem like a liar.

I slumped in a chair and waited.

The same waitress who'd booked Beth's hotel room approached me. "Can I get you any refreshments, sir?"

I wanted to ask her if she'd seen Beth, but knew how desperate that sounded. "No. Thank you."

I tried to busy myself scrolling through the email on my phone, but before I knew it, we were being called for boarding. At least I'd see her on the plane. An exchange of numbers wouldn't be so private with the cabin crew gawking at us, but it would have to do.

I strode to the gate, on the way checking travelers, scanning faces. She'd probably just wanted to take her time to get ready. Not that she needed to. She'd looked pretty close to perfect when I'd last seen her—her silky hair mussed up, her lips well kissed, but I could understand if she hadn't wanted to travel with "I just got fucked" tattooed on her forehead. I grinned again.

I headed straight to the desk and down the ramp to the plane. I glanced down at my ticket. As I'd thought, 8A. They hadn't changed the seating. *Good.* I didn't want her far from me.

Jesus, Dylan, what are you thinking? She was a good lay. Calm down.

But I was anything but calm. I wanted to see her. I wanted to know more about her. Who might be calling her? Why was she going to London? Had she grown up in Chicago? All of a sudden, I had too many questions. Perhaps on the plane we could sit at the bar and just talk. I wanted to get to know her, which was unusual.

I turned left as I entered the plane.

"Good morning, Mr. James."

I didn't glance at whoever spoke. It was a man, which meant it wasn't Beth and therefore I wasn't interested.

There were passengers in front of me, so I craned my neck to see if she was already in her seat. The sides of each seat were too high to get a proper look. As I got closer to my seat, I saw hers. Empty. I spun to see if she was behind me.

"Champagne, sir?" A blonde flight attendant held out a glass.

I shook my head. "No. Are we all assigned to the same seats as yesterday?"

The flight attendant squinted at me. "Yes sir, you're still in 8A."

"And everyone else? They're all in the same seats?"

"Umm. Yes, I think so. There may have been some changes in economy, why—"

"Okay, thanks." I stripped off my jacket and she took it from me.

I kept one eye on the people trailing in. The cabin was pretty full already. The seat next to mine remained empty. I took out my laptop and notebook from my carry-on luggage and slid my case into the overhead compartment.

Damn. She still wasn't here. I checked my watch. I should have taken her number before she left my hotel room. I could get them to hold the plane if she was running a little late.

I took my seat. What would I say when I saw her? I'd just keep it casual.

The slamming of doors caught my attention and the crew began to round the cabin, collecting empty glasses. Where was she?

An announcement asked for all mobile phones to be switched off. She must have had her seat reassigned.

"Excuse me." I caught the blonde as she walked by.

She smiled. "How can I help you, sir?"

"You said the seat allocation had remained the same." Something gnawed in my gut. "But there was a young woman sitting next to me yesterday."

The flight attendant frowned. "Oh, yes. I think there was."

"So, where is she?" I was impatient and it was beginning to show.

"Let me check, sir." The blonde scurried away.

It would be inconvenient if she'd been assigned to a seat farther away. I couldn't recall whether there was a first class section upstairs on this flight. I would be really irritated if she was there when she could be next to me. I set my phone and my laptop to flight mode. When I glanced up, the blonde was heading my way.

She leaned toward me. "Sir, she didn't check in. She's not flying with us today."

What. The. Fuck?

I nodded curtly and fixed my stare on my laptop, trying to get a handle on myself.

Where was she? Had she fallen asleep? Was she embarrassed by the way I'd made her scream and decided that she couldn't face me?

Jesus, I was furious. With myself for not having made sure I had a way of contacting Beth, and with her for not checking the fuck in. What had happened? Beth fucking Harrison had got in my head; that was what had happened. And women didn't get in my head. Not since . . .

Well, not since a long time ago and it wasn't supposed to happen again.

chapter
FOUR

Beth

I couldn't stop grinning as I closed my hotel room door behind me, my thoughts fuzzy and my body deliciously sore. I needed to snap to attention and get my ass down to check-in. My shower would have to be a short one.

I grabbed my purse on my way to the bathroom, rifling through it to find my phone. I tried to unlock it single-handedly as I switched on the shower.

Seven missed calls? Shit. What had happened?

I stepped back from the shower and put my voice mail on speaker as I began to undress. I was going to have to multitask to make the flight.

The voice of my dad's second wife, Marissa, came through the speaker. She sounded muffled. The words heart attack caught my attention like a blade scratching over glass and I froze.

Heart attack? Another one? Quickly, I started to dress, grabbed my phone and headed back into the bedroom, glancing around to see what I needed to gather. The message ended and the next one was from my brother, Jake, asking where I was. Fuck. Luckily I hadn't unpacked. I grabbed my case and raced down to the lobby.

My father had had a heart attack last year but had recovered well. He'd been lucky. The third voice mail was from my dad's wife again. The message was clearer. They were at the hospital. My stomach began to churn as I spiraled into worst-case scenario. Was he still alive? Was I too late?

Guilt and fear ran through my veins.

Passing through the lobby of the hotel, I glanced around to see if I could spot Dylan. I wanted to tell him about my dad. To tell him that I wouldn't be on the plane. It was a stupid thought. He'd been a one-night stand. An epic one-night stand, but we weren't about to start sharing sob stories.

It was early so there wasn't a line for cabs. I looked up at the heavens, grateful for small mercies.

In the taxi, I called my brother. It went straight to voice mail, so I called Marissa back. Voice mail again. They were probably speaking to each other. Normally I'd be pleased. Their relationship wasn't a strong one, but the fact they were speaking this morning must mean things were very wrong.

The cab wasn't going fast enough.

"How long now?" I clicked my seatbelt, hoping that it might be a hint that I was ready to go a little faster.

"About thirty seconds less than the last time you asked." The cab driver pulled up at a light.

I was sure I smelled of sex, but I hadn't had time for a shower. I grabbed a hairbrush from my bag and started to work through some of the tangles Dylan had caused the night before. Guilt churned in my stomach. If I'd thought to take my phone with me, or if I hadn't been so stupid as to go up to Dylan's room, I would have known my father was being taken to the hospital sooner. There was a reason I didn't do one-night stands. And now I was being punished for it.

I needed to call my sponsor. My thoughts were spiraling out of control, and I knew that alcohol would calm me down, dampen the noise of the voices in my head—it would stop the guilt of not having my phone with me last night, the guilt of enjoying myself while my father was sick, and the shame that right then, I wanted to be on a plane, sitting next to Dylan, not in a cab racing to the hospital.

Nausea washed through me as I pressed dial. My sponsor was in London so would be wide-awake. It went straight to voice mail.

I'd been in Alcoholics Anonymous since I'd moved to London from Chicago. My brother had gone with me for the first few times, loitering outside, there to catch me when I fell apart. But I hadn't. AA gave me belief that things would be better, and with every meeting, I got stronger. I'd not had a drink since my first meeting. I'd learned that preventative action was the key to staying sober. I didn't get the urge to drink anymore, because I never let it get that far. I controlled my environment, so I wasn't exposed to any kind of pressure to tempt me to drink. Last night I'd given up that control and now I was paying for it. In some ways I was lucky I was in a cab on the way to a hospital. There was no temptation right in front of me. I wasn't quite sure whether I'd be able to resist if there had been.

We pulled up outside the hospital and I shoved some money at the cab driver and ran through the sliding doors. I should have listened to the rest of my messages. They would have told me where I should go. After several wrong turns, eventually I raced down the right corridor toward my stepmother.

"Oh God, Beth. I thought you'd be in London."

I scanned the corridor. There were several sets of double doors left and right. "Where is he? Is he okay? Can I see him?" My pulse was pushing through my skin.

"Yes, he's fine." She took my arm and we started through one of the double sets of doors. My stepmother and I hadn't had any kind of relationship until my father's first heart attack. His condition had brought us together, given us common ground.

"My flight was cancelled. Is he okay?"

"It wasn't a heart attack. They think it was just anxiety."

No wonder she was so calm. "Anxiety?" It was as if someone had opened a pressure valve, tension seeped away from my muscles, the voices in my head softened, and the fog began to clear. And it had happened without alcohol, without me having a drink.

She shrugged. "He's getting older. They said it's common to mistake it for a heart attack. I just have to sign some paperwork and he'll be out. You didn't have to come over. Didn't you get my message?"

My stomach twisted. I should have reacted more logically when I got the missed calls. Maybe not rushed right over here and missed my flight. Would Dylan be wondering where I was? Would he care? He was probably relieved he didn't have to have some awkward *goodbye, see you around* moment. I'd spared him that.

Why was I focusing on Dylan when I should be thinking about my family?

"Daddy, what have you been up to?" I forced a smile as I made my way into his room.

"I told her I didn't need to come to the hospital, but she wouldn't listen." His mood was normal at least. "When am I getting out of here, Marissa?"

Marissa glanced at me as if to say *See what I have to put up with*? But I knew she loved my dad and I was grateful for that. He deserved it. My mom had been killed in a revenge attack because my dad was a cop. I was sixteen and my brother was eighteen. If it were possible to die of guilt, my dad would have been taken from us a long time ago. Marissa had been good for him.

The day of my mother's funeral was the day I had my first drink, and I'd quickly learned that alcohol took the edges off reality. I wasn't sure I grieved my mother's death before I got sober. I just buried all my feelings at the bottom of an ocean of alcohol. The hurt wasn't as sharp when my head was dizzy with champagne, or wine, or vodka, or gin, or rum, or . . . I could slip into a different world where I didn't have to think about my mother's death. When I finally got sober, all the pain had still been there, perfectly preserved. I wasn't sure I'd ever get over it, but I was learning to live with it, sober.

I kissed my dad on the forehead and took his hand.

"I thought you were flying back to London, Beth?" Every now and then, I glimpsed my father and saw an old man instead of the invincible cop I'd grown up with. Now was one of those times as he lay in bed, machinery attached to his chest. I hated to see him vulnerable. It was as if our roles had been reversed, but I didn't have his strength.

"My flight got cancelled. I'm sorry I wasn't here." I squeezed his hand. Tears began to well but I didn't want him to see me cry. He was fine; my tears were of relief. That he was okay. That I was sober. Still.

It had been a lesson. I needed to keep control. There were enough curveballs to cope with in life without adding more to the mix. No more one-night stands.

"Marissa shouldn't have called you. I'm fine." My heart rate began to return to normal as I realized he really was going to be okay.

"Stop being a grouch. She did the right thing bringing you here, and you know it. So be nice." I turned to Marissa. "Does Jake know everything is okay?"

She nodded. "Yeah, I spoke to him."

"What time's your flight? The weather is better today. I don't want you here fussing over me. You have your own life to get back to." My dad looked stern.

Yeah, he was absolutely fine. I grinned and kissed him on the cheek.

"And then what?" my sister-in-law asked, looking between her best friend and me. Haven and Ash were perched on barstools in my kitchen, watching me bake while feeding and cooing at their babies. They'd become good girlfriends to me since my brother had started dating Haven, and my world, that had been just my brother for a long time, had opened up a little.

I was giving them the lowdown on Dylan. "And then we, you *know*." I felt like a teenager, confessing to her girlfriends about the night before. Apparently, this kind of sharing was par for the course with Haven and Ash.

"No we don't!" they screamed.

"We need details," Ash said, moving her daughter, Maggie, to her shoulder to burp her. "We're forced to live vicariously now. We don't get to have one-night stands. We need you to be *very* specific."

I laughed. "It was good. I mean, the best I've ever had." Since I'd been back in London, my mind had wandered to Dylan and our night together more often than it should have. He was a one-night stand, yet thoughts of him had stayed with me. Yesterday, I'd been shopping for cake tins and thought I'd seen him walk past the shop. My heart had started to thunder and my knees fizzed.

I kept waiting for thoughts of him to fade. I felt like a schoolgirl with a crush. No doubt I'd been long forgotten by him.

"Do you think it was because you're sober?"

"I have no idea, but I swear to God, if sex is that much better sober for everyone, then no one would ever drink." Dylan had warned me that it was going to be world changing. He'd been right. I wasn't sure I'd ever be the same again. It was as if he'd released something in me.

"Whatever it is, I think it's showing in your baking. This cake is orgasmic." Haven was making *ohhing* and *ahhing* noises.

I grinned. In a way, she was right. Dylan had inspired me, as if he'd been something of a muse to me. Apparently, great sex led to great cake.

"How did your meeting go with the TV people?" Ash asked.

I shifted my weight onto one hip. "Good, I think. They want me to do like a trial or screen-test for a slot on the Saturday morning show, *A Chicago Saturday*. I have to fly back next week and they'll set me up in the studio—"

"Are you serious?" Haven asked, her mouth still full.

I shrugged. "It might turn into nothing, but it's a bit of fun and perhaps I'll attract a few more viewers to my YouTube channel." Deep down I was excited. But I didn't want to let those feelings bubble to the surface in case things fell through, and I hadn't quite worked through the consequences of what a TV spot in Chicago meant. It was a long way away.

"That's amazing. Holy crap, you're going to be the Oprah of cooking." Ash's eyes were wide and sparkling. She truly was happy for me and that felt good. We were family, and I wasn't ready to move to Chicago and give that up, so as much as a TV spot sounded exciting, there was a serious downside.

Baking had started off as therapy, and I suppose it still was. Cakes were my favorite to create. Not occasion cakes—but cupcakes, carrot cake, chocolate cake, gateaux. And of course I loved a vanilla slice and fruit tarts, and I'd just mastered profiteroles—I liked to bake anything sweet or dessert-like.

"So, you're going to fly over to Chicago, bang a hot guy, record a TV show, then fly back to be vomited over by your nieces?" Haven had a way of getting to the heart of a situation; no doubt it was the journalist in her. "Before we know it, we'll have lost you permanently to the Windy City."

"Actually, it's something I'll need to discuss with WCIL. I'm not moving back to Chicago. I don't believe in going backward. I don't mind flying over regularly, but every week is crazy." I shook my head. "Anyway, I'm getting ahead of myself. They've not offered me anything yet."

"They will, though. They'd be crazy not to. Your breasts alone deserve to be on television," Ash said, as if she'd just told me she liked my haircut. I shook my head at her, smiling. "They should call your slot *The Baking Bombshell*."

"You're crazy." I threw a tea towel at her.

"She's right." Haven pushed Sophia in her bouncy chair, trying to get her to settle. "You are going to make guys come in their breakfast cereal. You'll be the thinking man's crush. Brains and beauty combined."

"Maybe Mr. International Lover will see you on television, swoop in and you'll live happily ever after," Ash said, waving her hands excitedly.

"Mr. International Lover?" I asked.

"Yeah, or Mr. I-Can-Go-All-Night." Ash looked at me as if I needed to keep up.

I giggled. Dylan. Would he see me on TV? And if he did, would he even remember me? My heart squeezed at the thought. I knew we'd had a no-strings-attached night together. Problem was, a few of my strings seemed to have become attached.

Ash sighed. "I can't believe you didn't get his number."

I shrugged, trying to act as if I didn't care, though it would have been nice if he'd asked. "That's the point of a one-night stand. You don't swap numbers."

"If you'd have made it on the flight, you could have joined the mile-high club," Ash said.

"Ewww. In some cramped bathroom that five hundred people have peed in? No thank you. Not even for his monster cock."

"Yeah, it wasn't particularly nice when Jake and I did it, and that was on a private plane." Haven looked off into the middle distance. There were things I didn't need to know about my brother. That he and his wife had sex at thirty-thousand feet was one of them.

"I bet he sees you on TV and gets in contact," Ash said. "I've got a feeling about this."

"I'll be long forgotten. He won't even remember my name." Dylan had been perfect one-night stand material, and I was thankful there'd been no awkward aftermath. I was pretty sure that if I'd seen him on the plane, he would have seen my desire to have more of him, and I'd not had to endure the pity in his eyes. I just had to distract myself and move on, perhaps get Haven to set me up. Now that I was over the hurdle of my first sober sexual experience, perhaps I could really date—find someone suitable, compatible, a forever man.

Men like Dylan weren't dating material.

Dylan

> *Beth Harrison.*
>
> *Beth Harrison.*
>
> *Beth Harrison.*

I couldn't get her out of my head.

Probably because I was in an airport lounge again, this time in London. My hankering for Beth was getting ridiculous. I'd asked my assistant to see if she could find the person sitting next to me on the plane on the pretense that I'd picked up the Mont Blanc pen she'd forgotten. Christ, I'd used a pen for an excuse. I was bordering on pathetic.

I kept telling myself that it was just about the sex, about her sweet, tight pussy and glorious tits. And yes, that was part of it, but there was something about Beth, about our night together, that meant I wanted to know more. I had an urge to find, protect and possess her. Perhaps it was because she'd disappeared into nowhere, denying me the opportunity to know more about her. I wasn't the one in control. She'd taken that from me. I didn't even know what she did for a living or what city she lived in.

All I knew was that she liked cake and had a body that would make any man weep. And that she was incapable of being anything but honest and open—qualities I'd valued in myself but in her they translated into something seductive and bewitching.

Why hadn't I used some of our hours together to glean the most basic of information from her?

I slammed my laptop closed. I needed to find someone else. My week in London had been non-stop meetings, business dinners and even a charity gala. A lack of sex was probably making my Beth Harrison obsession worse than it would have been if I hadn't had blue balls. Getting off in the shower just wasn't the same as sliding your hands up a woman's body, making her whimper before fucking her until she begged you for release. Masturbation might have given me release, but it didn't go deep enough to quench the thirst Beth had created. Worse, I wasn't sure another woman would help, but at least I could try.

I glanced around. The lounge was full of suits. I pulled out my cell. I'd line Mandy up—my regular, sure sex for a few years now—for when I landed. Low maintenance, she turned up at my apartment, we fucked and she left. We might swap a couple of pleasantries about the markets or the weather, but we both knew the score—it was all about the fucking for both of us. Every now and then I was tempted to ask whether or not she had a boyfriend, a girlfriend, a husband, and then I thought better of it, ripped off her panties and got on with it.

I stalked over to the self-service bar and poured myself a soda water as a shadow in the far corner captured my attention. It couldn't be. It would be too much of a coincidence. I'd be claiming to see water in the middle of the desert soon. I turned my head toward what had caught my eye.

I squinted. It really looked like her. I wandered closer, scanning the low tables, pretending to look for a newspaper.

It *was* her.

I wasn't imagining it. She looked as beautiful as I remembered.

Dressed in a tight red skirt and a black sheer blouse, she

looked every inch the fifties movie star. The disappearing woman, Beth Harrison.

I was part thrilled, part infuriated and entirely consumed with a desire to have her naked beneath me.

I watched her concentrate on her notebook, oblivious to everything going on around her. At least nothing had happened to her. Irritation prickled at the back of my neck as I wondered if she'd deliberately missed the flight to avoid me. Jesus, she should have been grateful that I'd fucked her, and begged me to do it again, not given me the brush-off.

Unable to take my eyes off her, I moved toward her table. I'd forgotten how full that dirty red mouth was. I'd not seen it around my dick, not yet. My cock jumped at the thought and I couldn't hold back any longer.

"So you *are* alive."

She snapped her head up, her mouth slightly open and her eyes wide. I bet she'd thought she'd never see me again. Well, I was determined to show her what she'd have missed.

At least she had the decency to blush. "D—"

"Stand up." My voice was tight and low as I tried to keep a grip over myself. I didn't want to draw any attention to us.

She frowned and dropped her notebook into her bag.

"Come with me," I said, my heartbeat thundering through my shirt.

I grabbed her elbow as she stood. I wasn't as familiar with this lounge as the one in Chicago, but I knew where the showers were. I pulled her in that direction. I needed to be alone with her.

"Are you okay? You seem upset," she asked.

I couldn't respond. I pushed through the doors to the showers. The lighting was low, and black slate lined the floors and wall. I tried the first door, but it was locked. The second one opened and I pulled her inside. Each large shower room was like a bathroom, with a dressing table, a couple of chairs and various lotions and toiletries.

Inside, I locked the door and backed her up against the wall. She looked confused.

"What are you doing?"

I wasn't sure, but I knew I wanted her overwhelmed by me, to melt under me.

"Did you forget what I do to you?" I asked. "How many times I made you come?" I pushed my hips against hers.

"No—I . . ." Her voice quivered and I got a small sense of satisfaction. Why was I so concerned about having an impact on this woman? Why did it matter?

I clasped her face in my hands and ran my thumb across the beauty spot on her left cheek. "Why did you run?" I stared at her, trying to uncover what she was thinking.

"I didn't run." Her voice was breathy, as if I had some effect on her. I knew I couldn't have been imagining it. "Not away from you. I . . . My father. I had to go to the hospital."

I bent forward to kiss her before registering what she was telling me.

"Shit." I pulled away, placing my hands on the wall on either side of her. "Your father was in the hospital?"

Her mouth parted as she gazed up at me. I was a fucking asshole for thinking her disappearance had been about us, about me. This woman had me upside down. "Is he okay?"

She skimmed her hands up my sides. "Yes. It was a false alarm."

Relief snaked through me. Not only because her father was okay but because it meant I didn't have to hold back.

She smiled and I couldn't resist her a moment longer. I buried my hands in her hair, tipped her head back and delved my tongue into her mouth. Her hands smoothed across my back; the feel had me yearning for more as I twisted my body to encourage her exploration. Her touch drove me wild.

"I've got to see them," I said as I fumbled with her blouse buttons.

"Careful. I have nothing to change into." She took over and I pulled out my wallet, trying to find a condom. When I looked back at her, she stood in her skirt and bra, her lips puffy, fiddling with the front clasp.

"Let me. Bras are my superpower."

"I bet they are." She grinned at me, but held her hands up in surrender. I released the front catch with a single touch. "Bet you have more than one, my friend."

Her breasts tumbled out, and immediately I reached for my cock. She brushed my hands away, making to open the fly as I fell under the spell of her incredible tits, pushing them up and together as she worked on my zipper. They were just how I'd imagined them over the last week—and I'd imagined them a lot.

I didn't know where to start with her. I wanted to bite, suck, kiss, lick and fuck all of her all at once. Possession was my aim.

Shit, I needed more time with her than a quick fuck in a

bathroom was going to give me. Could I ask for her number now?

"Champ, you're going to have to move this along. We board soon, and I'm going to be mighty upset if I don't spend takeoff in a post-orgasm haze," she said, snapping me out of the spell that her tits had cast on me.

I yanked up her skirt. "You think I can't make you come before we get called to the gate?" My heart was beating out of my chest.

"I'm counting on you."

I growled, and ripped off her panties. She was going to have to fly without underwear. I wasn't sure if that would be more tortuous for me, or her.

"Turn around." My trousers were around my ankles like some teenager, but I couldn't wait to be inside her.

She shifted sideways a little and turned, placing her palms against a full-length mirror affixed to the wall, sticking her ass out. My cock throbbed as she waited for me, her tits spilling out, her skirt around her waist. Perfection.

I grabbed her hips, pulling her back as she gasped at my touch.

Without ceremony, I slid inside her, watching her in the mirror as I pushed in as far as I could go. She made a choking sound, balled her hands into fists, and screwed her eyes shut. I stilled, taking her in. "You're going to have to try to be quiet." I cupped her breasts, pushing them together. She moaned. "I said quiet."

"I don't care if the whole fucking airport is listening." Her words came out strained and pleading as she pushed back against me.

I pulled out, then slammed into her. "Look at me while I make you come."

Her eyes opened, catching mine in the mirror. She was breathtaking. I couldn't hold back any longer, and placed my hands over hers and began to fuck her as if it were my job.

Her sounds grew louder and louder. Instinctively, I placed my palm over her mouth. Her eyes never left mine. They were desperate and needy and a reflection of everything I felt. In seconds, she began to spasm around me, her moans vibrating against my palm, sending spikes of pleasure directly to my cock. She really was the fuck of the century.

I wrapped my arms around her, rocking into her gently, not wanting to let go. Her hands barely held her away from the mirror.

"This feels too good to give up," I said, though I was really talking to myself. I knew I should walk away, satisfied with an easy, quick, incredible fuck, but something in me didn't want to. Something in me wanted to cancel our flights and spend the weekend locked in a hotel. I kissed her neck and pulled away.

"Shit, we're so late." She smoothed her skirt and started to fasten her bra. I couldn't take my eyes off her as I disposed of the condom. "Seriously, get out of here, I need to straighten up."

Was she blowing me off? "Give me your number, and I'll get out of your way." I spoke quickly, almost ashamed to ask.

I couldn't remember the last time I'd asked for a woman's number. Probably not since—well, a long time ago.

"I'll let you have it when we've boarded." She concentrated as she fiddled with the buttons on her blouse.

I fastened my trousers. "If you don't show up, I'm going to hunt you down."

She looked up and grinned at me, those plump lips begging to be bitten.

"Don't look at me like that," I said. I would have to have her again if she wasn't careful.

She raised her eyebrows. "Like what? Like I'm going to make you come until you see stars?"

I grinned and leaned toward her. "I can see every star in the universe right now." I dropped a kiss on her delicious mouth and unlocked the door.

chapter FIVE

Beth

The announcement that we would be landing shortly woke me up. I'd managed to sleep most of the way. I shifted in my seat and opened my eyes. Dylan stood in front of me, his face back to being stern.

I'd not seen him since he'd left the shower. I'd boarded the airplane, collapsed into my seat and fallen asleep, still relaxed from spontaneous sex and another Dylan-induced orgasm.

When I'd seen him in the lounge, any thought that I could resist him had dissolved. I wanted him, and even though it meant giving up control—to him, to my lust—he was worth it. The way he made my body come alive was nothing I'd ever felt sober or drunk. I knew now that with him, I could give up my control but still sustain my sobriety, and that made me want him even more.

And he seemed to want me, too, which gave me confidence, as if it made wanting him back okay. He could have very easily avoided me in the lounge but hadn't; he'd sought me out.

I smiled as my hand went to my head. Was I sporting bed head?

He held out his phone. "Number."

Jeez, he was moody. Did everyone just do exactly as he told them? Probably.

But did I want to be one of them? Should I give him my number? Giving up control for short, defined periods of time was one thing, but suggesting that we contact each other outside the confines of a trip was another.

"Number," he repeated.

I focused on him as if he was going to be able to answer my question before I asked it. He stared back at me before I said, "Is it a good idea? I mean—"

"I need to know what this is," he said. His expression didn't alter, and he kept his eyes on mine. I didn't know what he meant, but I took his phone. I'd spent the last week wondering about him, imagining him on street corners. I'd lived through a one-night stand with him, my father being rushed to hospital, and was still holding things together. The world hadn't fallen apart. Perhaps I was ready for a little ambiguity, a little less control, and a little more fun.

I took the phone and tapped in my number, adding my name in as *Airport Orgasm*.

I handed it back. He nodded once, his beautiful indigo eyes looked deep into me and then he stalked off.

I smiled. He struck me as a man who didn't ask for a number he didn't intend to use. Everything he did had intent. But if he didn't call, I'd survive. It was a powerful feeling— understanding how strong I'd become. Besides, I was pretty sure I could live off Dylan James memories until I started dating properly.

I gathered my things, ready for a quick exit. I had a lot to do tonight, including a little more research on the producer I'd be meeting tomorrow, and I'd have to call Haven and tell her about my unexpected encounter with Dylan. She'd be thrilled. Even more so when I told her I'd given him my number.

I'd only brought a carry-on with me on this trip, so I sped through the airport. I got through immigration in record time, and by some miracle, there was no line for a cab.

"The Langham Hotel, please," I said to the driver as I climbed into the taxi, carefully, as I was sans underwear.

The Langham made some of the best cake in Chicago. It was one of the reasons that they were my first choice of hotel when I was here.

I leaned back in my seat. I'd not expected to see Dylan again, but he'd been the perfect start to my trip. I'd arrived at the airport a little tense and nervous about filming my trial segment for *A Chicago Saturday* tomorrow. I'd boarded the plane floating and smiling. Dylan certainly knew how to make a woman come, that was for sure.

I could still feel his fingers pressed around my hips.

First class travel and great hotels were a particular indulgence of mine. My brother had been very generous to me when he sold his first company. It had taken a while, and a lot of nagging on his part, for me to accept his money and start spending it, but he'd set up a trust fund I'd actually started to enjoy.

Although my dad lived close by, it was easier on everyone, including his second wife and their kids, if I didn't stay with them. I'd spend much of my time on this trip at work anyway.

My phone vibrated. "Hey, Haven," I answered.

"So, I was thinking about making lemon meringue pie for Sunday dinner, but then I thought if you were going to be back, maybe you'd prefer to do it?"

Sunday dinners with my brother, Haven, Ash and Haven's brother—who was also Ash's husband—meant I got to test out my new recipes on a willing and enthusiastic audience who were brutally honest with me.

"Yes, I'll be home on Saturday so I can do the pie." I never turned down an opportunity to bake.

"Do you mind?"

"Nope. Not at all. In fact, I'm glad you called—I have an update on Dylan."

"I knew it. Fate. What's happened?"

I laughed. "Well, he was on the same flight. How weird is that? I mean, it's a huge coincidence."

"Oh, my God. I told you. Did you join the mile-high club?"

"I told you—yuck. But I may have joined the airport-lounge club, if there is such a thing. Does that make me a slut?" I whispered in the hope that the driver wouldn't overhear me.

Haven squealed. "Enjoying sex doesn't make you a slut. You're practically a virgin. It's about time you had a little fun."

I nodded, even though Haven couldn't see. When I saw Dylan, my desire overtook everything and I let him lead. It was liberating to not overthink things, to not let caution rule, if only in that contained space that existed between Dylan and I when he was around.

"And was he as good as you remembered?" Haven asked.

I sucked in a breath at the memory. "Better."

"It's fate."

"Don't be crazy. A good start to my trip is what it was." It had been more than good. I couldn't remember sex ever being so much fun, so intense, so uncomplicated. I couldn't wipe the grin from my face.

"Did you swap numbers? I mean, you don't have to marry the guy, but if the sex is that good, have a little fun."

"You don't think it'll mess with my head? I have a great life and now with the baking and the television thing just landing in my lap, I'm happy. I don't want to be greedy, or want something too badly. You know?"

"It's not greedy to take something on offer. Let Dylan be the cherry on the top of your cake. If he's offering, you may as well take a bite. It doesn't have to be anything serious."

I giggled at her mixed metaphor. "Maybe."

"I mean it. What he's offering is just what you need to get you back in the dating game. There are no emotions to knock you off kilter. If you don't care about him, he can't hurt you."

She was right. Expectations were my downfall. Expecting a man to return my feelings, or treat me kindly . . . Expecting someone wouldn't turn out to be a total shit. With Dylan, I had no expectations so I couldn't be disappointed.

"I gave him my number, so the decision is out of my hands." I didn't really believe that. Dylan had been gruff on the plane, but I got the impression he was fiercely private.

There was no way, with all the eyes of the cabin crew on him, that he was going to get my number, then not use it.

"He can be your Chicago lover when you're in town. This could be a perfect way of getting you back into men. No strings, a little stress relief, great sex. And you're not even living in the same town so there's no pressure."

Haven's words trickled through my brain, and the idea of more of Dylan James became more appealing with every moment.

Dylan

Goddamn it. I couldn't believe she'd run away from me—again. What was with this girl? She'd been willing and eager when I was fucking her, had given me her number without a fight, but she'd disappeared into thin air again as soon as the plane landed.

Standing in the queue for immigration, I typed "Beth" into my phone. Nothing came up. I tried "Harrison." Nothing. Jesus. I hoped she hadn't jerked me around. I cricked my neck, trying to relieve some of the cramped muscles. The girl was bad for my health. I scrolled through my contacts. Nothing under Beth, Bethany or Elisabeth. Fuck.

I put my phone into my breast pocket and gave border patrol my passport. I needed to work out a quicker way of getting through security. There were too many VIPs if it meant I had to wait in line.

As I made my way to baggage, I wondered why she hadn't given me her number. From the number of orgasms I'd given her, I was confident that she'd enjoyed the fucking, so why had she disappeared? Perhaps she was married and I'd misjudged her. My gut twisted. Misjudging women was not something I ever wanted to do again.

Jesus, I wanted to be home already. I was done with this week.

I took my phone out again and started scrolling. Perhaps I'd missed her entry. I scrolled right to the top of my contacts and saw it. *Airport Orgasm*. I grinned and my shoulders released. Funny as well as sexy. Ordinarily, I got the measure of women very quickly. I applied the same analytical skills in my sex life as I did in the workplace. My ex-fiancée, Alicia, had taught me that it was easy to misjudge a woman, and when she left me, I vowed never to do it again. So it was important to me to understand a woman really quickly. If they were after my money, it wouldn't stop me from fucking them, but I needed to know ahead of time. I wouldn't get caught out again.

Beth was the first woman since Alicia I couldn't pin down, or figure out. At first she was shy and nervous, but that had disappeared and the sexuality she cloaked when fully clothed caught back up with her and she seemed to enjoy fucking as much as I did—she hadn't faked anything. But she was full of contradictions. Where did her money come from for her to fly first class? It didn't fit—she didn't seem like the spoiled heiress type. And her obsession with cake was unusual. I wanted to know more. I wanted to understand all her apparent inconsistencies.

I'd become accustomed to being used for my money, but perhaps Beth was using me for my dick. I wasn't sure I'd mind—I just wanted to know.

Dylan: Airport Orgasm? Were you thinking it wouldn't stand out in my phone?

I grinned as I waited for her reply. And waited. And waited some more. My muscles bunched as I considered that she might never reply. Shit. Was it too much to call her?

I spotted my suitcase on the other side of the carousel, slipped my phone back into my pocket as I retrieved my luggage, and then I headed for the exit.

My driver, Don, always parked in the same place, so I made my way to where he would be waiting. Don was taciturn and although he'd worked with me for nearly two years, I knew almost nothing about him, which was why I liked him. Relationships that were uncomplicated and without emotion suited me. If I got to know him and he had a dying mother, or a sick kid, I'd feel an obligation to take some kind of responsibility and that wasn't what I was looking for.

I slid in to the back seat and pulled out my phone. I was like a fucking teenager, trying to get the pretty girl to notice me.

I didn't really know what it took to woo a woman successfully—I'd never had to try. Apart from my relationship with Alicia, there'd been no one serious. No one who had caught my interest. Mandy was a great, regular one-night stand, and I liked it that way. She didn't require work. None of the women I'd slept with since Alicia did, and that wasn't a coincidence.

Alicia. Hers wasn't a name I allowed to seep into my brain very often. And it wasn't that Beth reminded me of her. Physically, they were totally different. Alicia had been a fierce redhead. Beth was soft and sexy, and had the ability to pierce the armor I wore. No one had done that since Alicia. It was just a pinprick but I felt it all over. The effect of her was disturbing and compelling in equal measure.

Fuck it—I'd call.

I pressed dial, half wondering if I should have waited until I'd got home. Don didn't give a shit who I fucked, but I wanted our conversation to be private, and definitely didn't want to be blown off in front of my driver.

Straight to voice mail. I shook my head. I was being an idiot.

I needed to get my shit together.

My phone vibrated in my hand.

"Hey. Did you get that proposal?" Raf asked.

"I just got into the car. I haven't checked my emails yet. Any clear conclusions?" The business Raf and I had founded straight after college owned a bunch of companies. We'd started small, buying a failing tire company in Missouri the same year Alicia and I'd gotten engaged. We bought it for a dollar and took on a pile of debt, but after two years, we sold it for 3.5 million, debt free. The next business we bought for two million dollars and turned into a ten-million-dollar company in twenty months. Success was addictive—and we got used to it quickly.

As we got bigger, we had teams of people implementing turnaround plans across a portfolio of companies. Raf and I were in the middle of our annual strategic review, the time of year where we decided which companies we were going to keep, and which were ripe for a sale.

"I think things are pretty much where we expected. Except for Raine Media. WCIL TV in Chicago has lost a ton of viewers. I'm not sure media is our bag. They haven't hit their numbers again and I think management has lost focus."

"We might need to cut our losses. I'll take tires over television any day of the week." It had been Raf's idea to buy a media company. I'd gone along with it—he had a sharp eye—but I'd never really been convinced.

"Take a look at it. I think it's beyond hope."

I didn't need to take a look at it if Raf had already called time of death. "Okay. Anything else?"

"What, in the fifteen hours I haven't spoken to you?" His tone suggested that something had happened.

"Yeah. I know how you like to cause trouble while I'm away."

"Oh, that's right. I banged my assistant and she quit. I've got a temp."

"Jesus, Raf. Again? Can't you keep it in your pants? That's like the third one in a year. You're one step away from a lawsuit."

"Jesus nothing. Did you see the girl? She was totally smokin'. No way was I saying no. Especially when she asked me so nicely." His grin filtered through the phone.

"If she sues us, you're paying out of your own pocket."

"Calm down. She's not going to sue. You need to get laid."

I grinned. If he only knew. That was the difference between us. Raf and I were both believers in casual sex, I was just a little more discreet than he was.

I ended the call and scrolled back up to Beth's number. Against my better judgment, I pressed dial again.

"Hey," she answered.

I smiled. "Where are you?"

"At my hotel. Why?"

"You're like the disappearing woman."

"I like to get off planes quickly. The journey's done. There's nothing to be had from sitting around and enjoying the view."

I chuckled; it was true. "How come you're in a hotel?"

She sighed. "My dad's house is a little cramped. Where are you?"

I glanced out the window. "Just pulling up outside my house. You live with your dad?"

"Are you kidding me? You know I'm legal, right?" She laughed.

"So, you don't live in Chicago?"

"What's with all the questions?"

I was interrogating her as if she were a business proposition. "I'm sorry. I just . . ." I couldn't explain it to her without sounding like a sap. I wanted to know more about her. Maybe that way she wouldn't be quite so intriguing, so contradictory. "You can ask me a question. I think that's how conversation goes. You say something, then I say something."

"You're a lover and a comic."

I chuckled as I stepped out of the car and Don carried my suitcase up the steps to my brownstone. I nodded in thanks and he left me on the stoop.

She sighed as if exasperated. "Okay, if I get a question, what should I ask?"

My stomach fluttered as she deliberated.

"First I should really thank you for the orgasm."

My balls tightened at her words. She was most welcome. "The pleasure was all mine."

She laughed, a deep sexy laugh, and I imagined her red lips spread wide, ready for my cock. "You've thrown me off," she said. "I don't know what to ask you now. What do you suggest?"

I couldn't tell if she wasn't interested and she was trying to be nice, or if she was being genuine. "Ask me if I'm free for dinner."

I unlocked the door and pulled my case into the hallway, shrugged off my jacket and tie, catching the scent of her almond perfume as I did. Was I imagining things? It didn't matter; I wanted more of that scent.

Finally, she replied, "I can't have dinner with you tonight."

"Give me three good reasons." I snapped into business mode. Negotiation I could do.

"Well, I have to prepare for tomorrow. You're a stranger. The whole point of a one-night stand is that we don't have to make awkward conversation over dinner."

"I'm not a stranger, so that point disappears immediately. And you think our conversation is going to be awkward?" I asked, addressing her points one by one. "Why would you think that? We have so much in common." I slumped on the sofa and put my feet up on the small table.

She laughed and I couldn't help but grin in response, it was such a relaxed sound. "Like what?"

"We're both in Chicago. We like having sex with each other—Do I need to go on?"

"I'm not sure that's the basis of excellent dinner conversation."

"Look, I'm not proposing marriage. Just dinner." I loosened my tie.

"That's what Haven said."

Who the fuck was Haven? "Who?"

"My sister-in-law."

She had a brother. Interesting. Apart from her name, it was the first bit of personal information she'd given me. "She told you I wasn't proposing marriage?"

"She told me to have some fun, and that I didn't have to marry you."

"I like her; she gives excellent advice. Usually I save marriage for the second date. So dinner. Where are you staying?"

"The Langham. But no, reason one trumps them all. I have to prep." Her words were clipped, decided.

"Prep for what?" I asked.

"I have a thing tomorrow. A TV thing."

"Are you trying to be deliberately mysterious? Because, let me tell you, it's working." I couldn't remember the last time I had so much fun just talking. If she wouldn't have dinner with me, perhaps she would stay on the phone and just swap stories.

chapter SIX

Beth

I stood in front of the window watching the river and clutching the phone to my ear. Maybe I should agree to dinner with Dylan. As he said, he wasn't proposing marriage.

"I'm not trying to be mysterious. It's nothing, just something silly."

Truth was, I was a little embarrassed about the TV thing. I was almost certain nothing would come of it so I didn't want to make a big deal of it, then look like an idiot when I flew home with my tail between my legs. I didn't want to feel the disappointment or the shame because I knew the cure for both was booze. I'd avoided those feelings for a long time, so I wasn't sure how I'd cope with them sober. Problem was, I was already invested, so if it didn't work out, I was going to have to work through that. My baking was important to me. It didn't deserve the association that it had with my sobriety. It meant more to me than that.

"Tell me." Dylan wasn't giving up very easily—and I was quite enjoying his persistence.

"I'm just going to WCIL studios tomorrow to film a trial segment for their Saturday morning show. I'm sure it will be a disaster, but I just don't want to make it worse by not preparing. Does that make sense?"

Dylan took a deep breath. "Yeah, of course. You're going to try out for a presenting job?"

"Oh God no, nothing like that. As you know, I like cake."

"I had noticed that."

"I also really like to bake." It wasn't a secret but I hadn't mentioned the YouTube thing to anyone outside my London family. Dylan was so interested it seemed silly not to tell him. "I just put up a couple of videos of me baking on YouTube and WCIL called me about doing something similar on the Saturday breakfast show." I fell back onto the bed. "I just want to give it my best shot."

"I get that. So, you like to bake?"

"I love to bake—and eat what I bake, and I love other people eating my creations." I grinned up at the ceiling.

"Maybe, you'll bake for me one day. I should let you go. You have a busy day tomorrow."

As much as I wanted to prepare for tomorrow, I also wanted to continue talking to Dylan. But he wasn't looking for a friend; he was looking for a hookup.

"Okay. You must be tired from your flight."

"Have sweet, sweet dreams. And good luck, I hope it works out for you tomorrow."

He ended our call and I gazed up at the ceiling. I guess that was how this went—If I wasn't agreeing to meet up with him, then there was no point in just chatting. Problem was, I wanted to hook up with him again. I wanted a little orgasmic fun. He was a sure thing who could make me come. Perhaps I'd suggest a hookup tomorrow night, after going to the *A Chicago Saturday's* studio. I was going to stop by an AA meeting straight after—I wanted to make sure I was keeping my sobriety as my priority, however exciting or disappointing my day had been. The orgasm thing was becoming a little addictive. I jumped off the bed, feeling like a woman with a plan.

In the bathroom I examined the array of bath products, and chose a lavender oil that promised relaxation. I was pretty sure Mr. 8A would be more effective, but as I'd turned that down, a bath would have to do. I sprinkled the contents of the bottle into the bath and stepped in.

I grabbed a clip and put up my hair, and slid into the bath, feeling the oil-soft water against my skin. Delicious.

I ran through the recipe for tomorrow's show. I was going to do Muffin for Two that Haven and Ash always swore cured their hangovers. Feeling smug about not having hangovers when your girlfriends were suffering was one of the best things about being sober.

Someone knocked on my door and I sat up straight in the water. Shit. I'd not ordered room service. Who could it be?

I climbed out of the bath and pulled on a robe. There was another knock. "Coming," I replied.

I opened the door to a man with a trolley covered in plates. He clearly had the wrong room.

"Room service." He grinned at me.

I smiled back. "I didn't order room service."

Ignoring me, he pushed the trolley into my room, nearly knocking me over in the process. Perhaps he hadn't heard me.

He worked quickly, unloading six silver-dome-covered plates onto the small dining table in the corner of the room.

"Sir, I didn't order this."

"Yes, it was ordered," he replied. Jesus, I'd have to call room service to explain. I didn't seem to be getting through to him. He handed me a cream envelope, bowed and scurried away, pushing his trolley.

The envelope was addressed to *Miss (I hope) Beth Harrison (in case you'd forgotten your first name isn't Airport).* I grinned.

Inside was a card.

My Sweet Beth,

Good luck tomorrow. I hope this provides some inspiration. I hope to see you before you leave.

Dylan James

My heart tightened. I was pretty sure I wasn't leaving the US without my seventh orgasm courtesy of Dylan James.

I lifted the lid of one of the silver domes and found what I was expecting: the most spectacular cakes in Illinois.

I grabbed my phone.

Beth: Unexpectedly, I have a great deal of cake to eat. Care to help me finish it off tomorrow night?

I'd barely had time to take a breath before a response buzzed into my hand.

Dylan: If you're free, there's nothing I'd rather do.

There were a number of things I'd rather do than eat cake when Dylan was in the room. I tapped out a response.

Beth: Perhaps we could do cake AND orgasms? Just a thought.

Dylan: I take it back. That's what I'd rather do.

Butterflies flitted about in my stomach. He was cute. And so goddamned sexy.

Beth: I'd like to do you, too.

I couldn't stop the smile tugging at the corners of my mouth.

Dylan: Careful, or I might not be able to wait until tomorrow.

I could almost see the stern look on his face.

Beth: Until tomorrow.

Dylan: Sleep well, my sweet.

I fell back onto my bed, grinning. One-night stand sex with Dylan had been amazing. Being able to look forward to amazing sex with him added a whole new level of happiness that buzzed in my fingers and toes.

Who knew casual sex could be this fun?

I was looking forward to seeing him.

Cake and orgasms—life didn't get much better than that.

I sat in the busy lobby of the television studio, watching people rushing about. TV screens provided a backdrop to the reception desk and created a constant soundtrack to the live chatter and conversation all around me. Lots of women carrying iPads and talking on phones passed left and right, leaving me tired just watching them. I was used to calm, controlled environments. Even when Maggie and Sophia were screaming, it always felt safe. It might have been my second visit here but it didn't feel any more familiar.

A woman approached me. "Beth Harrison?"

This was it. I took a deep breath and stood. "Yes. Hi."

"Hey. I'm Amber, Bryan's assistant." Bryan was the executive producer of *A Chicago Saturday* and the guy I'd met previously. "I'll show you to your dressing room and Bryan will come see you in a few minutes. His last meeting is running a bit long."

"Sure, that would be great."

Between fantasizing over Mr. Dylan James—he really was quite the distraction—I'd rehearsed and rehearsed. Something I never did for my YouTube videos, but with those, I also had the opportunity to redo the bits that didn't go so well when no one was watching. I wasn't going to have the same luxury today.

As we headed down a long, white corridor, Amber leaned into me and handed me her card. "Call me anytime if you need anything. Think of me as your assistant when you're here."

"Thank you. But I'm only here for a test. There's nothing—"

"I've seen your YouTube channel. Believe me, if it's up to us, you'll be back."

I smiled. It was a nice thing for her to say, whether or not she meant it.

Amber wasn't wearing a scrap of makeup but looked beautiful with her shiny chestnut hair and wide mouth. "Listen, you didn't hear this from me." She stopped abruptly and herded us both into a room with a couple of chairs and a huge mirror in front of a built-in dressing table. "But Bryan can be a bit of an asshole. Don't take it personally. And don't let it put you off. The rest of us are great." She grinned at me as she headed toward the corner of the room, opening a refrigerator. "There's water and soft drinks in here, as well as fruit." She pointed to a basket on the low table in front of the chairs. "I can get you coffee, if you'd prefer."

"Thanks, I'm fine."

"Make yourself at home—"

The door opened and Bryan appeared, holding his hands out wide, his head cocked to the side. "She's here. Our sexy cake maker. You look stunning."

I glanced at Amber, who raised her eyebrows.

"Thanks so much for inviting me. I'm excited to get started."

"Great. Well, after you've spoken to hair and makeup, Amber can show you the set and make sure you have anything you need. Then we can start to talk about cameras and all that good stuff. I think I said on the phone that I want to make this very intimate, so it looks like your internet stuff with just a touch of gloss."

I nodded. I wasn't sure how a TV studio could be intimate, but that bit wasn't up to me. I needed to let go a little and allow the people around me to do the worrying. Even though I'd been discussing things for weeks, it all seemed so incredible that people were talking about *me* baking, on *television*. "Sounds great. You just tell me what you need."

"Honey, just be your sexy self." Bryan's cell chimed, and he waved. "I'll see you in a bit."

"Okay." I turned to Amber. "Hair and makeup."

She shook her head. "Just tweaks, they'll be in a second. I'll pop in when they're done in an hour or so."

Apparently *tweaking* took an hour. Wow. Way to make a girl feel special.

My phone buzzed in my increasingly sweaty hand.

Dylan: Good luck today, my sweet. Remember you thought sober sex was a hurdle—things are never as tough as you think they're going to be.

I grinned and my shoulders fell as my muscles relaxed. How had he known the right thing to say at just the right time?

Dylan

The natural light in my office was beginning to dim as I sat with Raf going through what had happened in London with a new potential acquisition we were looking at. I was distracted by thoughts of Beth, and I kept expecting Raf to call me out on my lack of focus.

I didn't understand why I was unable to put Beth to one side, why she brought out a side of me that made me want to protect and possess her. I'd fucked a lot of good-looking women, so I knew it wasn't just that. Perhaps it was her openness, the fact that she had opened herself up to me in a way most women didn't. She made it more than sex because every touch was full of vulnerability. And she didn't seem to want anything from me other than for me to be careful with her. My wealth or power didn't pique her interest, which puzzled me, but allowed me to imagine her as something more than just a lover.

"I've been looking at the strategic reports," I said. Raine Media had become more interesting to me knowing Beth was potentially going to be working there.

"Oh, right. We'll go through them in detail tomorrow. We have some time in the morning."

"Yeah, that's fine. I'm not so sure we should write off Raine Media. Perhaps we just haven't devoted enough attention to it." I held my breath, expecting Raf to see straight through my conflict of interest. I liked the link that Raine Media created between Beth and me. If we sold it, who knew what would happen to Beth's deal. I wanted a few days with her, some time to work out what the fuck I was doing, to organize my thoughts. But I knew I should come clean. Raf and I had a strict policy against mixing business with pleasure. When we first started out we nearly went under because I pushed to acquire a company that my ex-fiancée's brother was involved in, and Raf had reluctantly agreed. It had gone badly wrong and almost ruined us. It nearly meant the end of our business and our friendship. We survived partly because my ex-fiancée dumped me and because we vowed never to mix our personal lives with our business lives again.

Raf shrugged and stood up. "Not sure about that. Like you said, media isn't our sweet spot."

"But neither were tires, and look where that ended up." I should just be honest with him, but what would I say? I banged a girl who might work at the TV station? I wasn't sure there was anything to tell, yet. "We can talk about it tomorrow, but I thought maybe I'd go visit next week. Talk to some people on the ground to see if it can be salvaged. I think it deserves another three months." Not being honest with Raf felt like I'd just stepped off a ledge into a black hole. I hated lying. My palms started to sweat.

Raf looked at me with a furrowed brow. Could he smell bullshit? I was usually the more ruthless of the two of us. I didn't often fight to hold on to a business that hadn't made material progress within six months of us purchasing it. I was usually the one chomping at the bit, wanting to get rid of the dead wood. Raf was the optimistic one, the partner who got me to be patient and give things more time.

"If you think that's the best decision then I'm happy to support you. What did you see in the numbers that I missed?"

I'd not seen anything worth saving in the numbers.

"It's just a feeling," I mumbled, trying to be nonchalant.

"A feeling? You had a feeling? Wow, I'll get Marie to draft a press release." He swept his hand across the cityscape behind me as if reading a headline. "*Hard as Nails Billionaire Dylan James Has a Feeling*. This is going to go viral."

What had I been thinking, handing Raf ammunition like that? "I was thinking of the publicity we'd get if we sell it so quickly. You remember what the press was like when we bought it; they told us we knew nothing about media and would bleed all the creativity out of it. I don't think we can just drop it. We need to think, be smart about it."

"And of course, you have a feeling," Raf said.

I shook my head, trying to suppress a smile. "Get the fuck out of my office before I get *the feeling* to rip your balls off."

Raf chuckled. "That's more like it, my friend."

"I mean it. Fuck off. I need to wrap things up and leave."

"You're leaving work?" Raf looked at his watch. "It's six. Are you going part time? Do I need to reassess your salary?"

"You're a regular comic genius this afternoon. I have a meeting." I didn't want to open up to Raf about Beth. Not yet. I was continually busting his balls about his revolving door of women, so he wouldn't miss an opportunity to bust mine. Besides, since Alicia, there hadn't been much to share.

"Oh, right. I'll catch you tomorrow."

I pulled out my phone to see if I'd received a message. Beth hadn't mentioned a time to meet. The easiest thing would be just to send her a message or call, but something was stopping me. I guess I wanted the ball in her court—I wanted her to want to see me.

As I began to log off, a new message came in. I didn't recognize the sender's address.

Long time, no see, stranger. How are things going? Want to grab a coffee sometime?

Love,

Alicia

I closed the email, and then opened it again, clicking on the sender field to see the full email address.

My ex-fiancée was emailing me as if we were old college friends. As if she hadn't dumped me for a richer guy, and we'd not seen each other in a decade. Why was she getting in contact after all these years?

I hovered over the delete button, and clicked. I wanted to forget about it and get lost in thoughts of Beth.

Beth's hotel was just a few blocks from the office, so I

grabbed my coat and stepped into the cold. I couldn't stop grinning as I imagined having Beth to myself again.

In just a few minutes, I was entering the lobby bar. I found myself a seat on one of the stools, turning it kitty corner so I could watch the door. I ordered myself a soda water with a twist of freshly cut lime, took out my phone and began to work through the emails that had gone unanswered earlier in the day.

I sensed her before I saw her.

As I glanced up, she was grinning from ear to ear at nothing in particular, entering the lobby in high heels, a figure-hugging top and a full skirt that showed off her tiny waist. Men and women turned their heads as she clipped over the marble floor, heading in my direction.

An uncomfortable and unfamiliar swelling in my chest threatened to wind me. I felt a sense of pride looking at her. It didn't make much sense. I wasn't sure what I was proud of. Perhaps that she was turning heads, or just that she was so goddamned sexy. It was uncomfortable because she wasn't mine to feel proud of. But for the next few hours, I was going to do my best to make her mine.

Just for one evening.

She stopped in her tracks. Had she seen me? I sat forward in my seat but she spun around. She hadn't spotted me. Then she clamped her phone to her ear. Who was she calling?

My phone began to vibrate in my hand.

I grinned as I saw *Airport Orgasm* flash on my phone.

"You're very beautiful," I spoke quietly into the handset.

I watched as her palm flattened under throat. "Hey," she replied. "I was wondering whether you wanted to come over."

"Wondering or hoping?"

Her cheeks flushed and she cocked her hip out. "Maybe both."

Her whispered words sent electric currents straight to my cock and I shifted in my seat. "That's good to know. Keep walking in the direction you're facing."

She looked up and directly into my eyes. "Hey," she said again. "You're here."

I nodded and ended the call.

I glanced across at the barman, who seemed to be watching her approach, as mesmerized as I was. I wanted to punch him. I should be the only one allowed to look at her that way.

She slowed as she approached and I reached out for her waist, pulling her between my legs and kissing her firmly on the lips. "Really, very beautiful."

"You been here long?"

I held her in place. "Just a few minutes. I thought we should order some cake. I believe that was part of your plan for the evening?" I nodded in the direction of the afternoon tea menu in front of me. "Choose what you'd like."

I watched her as her gaze danced across the menu and I couldn't help but smile.

We were going to have a very enjoyable evening.

The waiter leaned toward her to get her order and raised his eyebrows. It was flirtatious, and I went from wanting to punch him to wanting to bury him.

I pressed my lips against her cheekbone and slid my hand up her back. It was a possessive, intimate move between a couple rather than two relative strangers about to have sex. She shot me a wide-eyed look but I smiled and lifted my chin toward the menu, indicating she should order.

"What would you recommend?" she asked the barman.

"Order quickly. I'm getting impatient," I said, loud enough for the bartender to hear, and kissed her cheekbone again.

"I think, maybe just one of everything. But a double portion of the chocolate mousse." Her voice was uneven and breathy. She sounded impatient, too.

I removed my hand and slipped off the stool. I pulled out my wallet and dropped some cash on the counter to cover our order.

Beth slid her hand over mine. "I'll just put it on my tab. You don't need to—"

A woman trying to stop me from paying for something? That was a first.

"I want to, Beth." For the first time in a long time, I set down my money not because it was expected, but because I wanted to.

"The faster that order reaches our room, the bigger the tip. You hear me?" I said to the bartender.

I pulled Beth toward the elevators. Thankfully the doors opened quickly. I wanted her away from prying eyes.

As soon as we got in, I pinned her to the wall with my hips and bent to suck on her bottom lip. She tasted sweet, like cherries.

She placed her hands on my shoulders. "Are you okay? What was that at the bar?"

"I'm okay, I just didn't like the way he was looking at you. I'm the only guy who gets to have dirty thoughts about you." I ground my hard-on into her stomach.

"He wasn't having dirty thoughts about me."

"Believe me, my sweet, every man you meet is having dirty thoughts about you."

"You're crazy." Her hands slid around my neck, her fingers dipping into my hair. I had to suppress a groan. The slightest touch from her pulled me under her spell.

The doors pinged open. "I'm going to go crazy unless I get you naked, STAT." I needed to rip off her clothes and check she was still the same, still as sexy as last time I saw her and then I needed to consume her, capture her, dull this ache inside of me.

The door to her room hadn't even shut when I began to unbutton her skirt. Briefly, I scanned the room. Floor-to-ceiling windows made up two walls of the corner suite, and boasted views of the river snaking through the city. How did this beautiful young baker travel in such luxury? I wanted to ask, but got distracted by her glorious ass, flaring out in front of me as her skirt hit the floor.

I loosened my tie and shrugged off my jacket. My impatience grew as I circled her waist with my hands and pulled up her top. Her breasts were pushed up and out, the sight making me dizzy.

She swept her hands across her taut stomach and pressed

her fingers against her lace-covered pubic mound as if she were trying to reassure her body. I groaned.

"That sweet pussy is mine to touch. I've warned you about that." I batted her hand away, pushed my fingers into the lace and yanked her panties off.

"Dylan," she sighed. The sound of my name on her lips washed over me like music.

"I need to see you." I stared at her pussy and she shifted her weight from one foot to the other, then reached behind her back and unclasped her bra.

I closed my eyes as I took a deep breath. She was magnificent and so beautiful I couldn't look at her for too long. I opened my eyes and she was looking back at me. "You are perfect," I said.

A shiver of hurt crossed her face. "I'm anything but."

I wanted to erase that darkness in her, scoop it out and swallow it down so she didn't have to endure it. I cupped her chin and dropped my lips to hers. "To me. You're perfect, to me."

Something about her naked body calmed me and dampened down the urgency that had threatened to send me over the edge since I'd laid eyes on her in the lobby. Now she was here in front of me, locked in to a bubble where the outside world wouldn't interfere.

A knock sounded on the door. "Fuck."

Beth gasped. "It's room service."

"Don't move. I'll collect it, and he won't be able to see you."

She wrapped her arms around *my* breasts.

"You know I don't like it when you cover yourself." I pulled her hands away.

She tried to turn away from me. "Beth." My voice was even. "I want you to stand here, like this, ready for me. Trust me. I'm not going to let the room service guy in to see you."

We stood silently face-to-face for a couple of long seconds while she decided. I wanted her to know that I wasn't playing games, that she could trust me.

She dropped her hands, giving me what I needed. Her— naked and exposed.

I walked backward toward the door so I didn't miss a moment of her naked body.

"Go get my cake, you pervert, then I want my orgasm."

I chuckled. "You greedy girl." I turned into the corridor to answer the door.

I gave the waiter a generous tip and pulled the trolley of cake inside, assuring him that I didn't need any assistance. The delicious Beth Harrison, naked apart from her peep-toe shoes, was for my eyes only.

I swept my hands across the trolley. "Your cake."

She arched an eyebrow at me. "I want the mousse first."

Anything she wanted was hers.

chapter
SEVEN

Beth

Dylan demanded, no *commanded*, my trust. Although my instinct was to shut down and close myself off, he was able to pinpoint my anxiety, name it and erase it.

How did he do that? When even *I* wasn't sure what I was feeling, what my reticence was, he knew. And that was liberating.

I'd never felt that before. Never fully trusted the man I was with, which always left me edgy, needy, wanting to please, wanting to do something to make it right—it was a constant reminder I wasn't enough. Dylan left no room for me to doubt him, or myself.

He was straining against the fabric of his trousers, and I planned to have a little fun with him. He passed me a glass filled with chocolate mousse and grabbed my ass. I picked out the *tuile* and popped it in my mouth, then dipped my index finger into the dessert and offered it to him. He grabbed my wrist and greedily took my finger in his mouth and sucked.

He knew me, but he still wanted me. It was an intoxicating combination, one I was unable to resist.

I could trust him. And he wouldn't break my heart, because I wouldn't let him. This was all about my vagina; it had nothing to do with my heart.

This was going to be fun.

Twisting my wrist free, I plunged my finger into the glass and coated my lips with the fluffy chocolate. I poked my tongue out and began to lick my lips clean.

The heat in his eyes was impossible to ignore. The promise they held making my feet unsteady. He pulled me toward his hard body and licked me clean.

I liked this game.

I pushed him away before he deepened our kiss and I lost all control. "Stay there," I said. He went to grab my ass, but I twisted away and stepped back so my ass was against the dining table—I wanted him to have a clear view of what I was going to do next. "Be patient." I scooped a little of the mousse out of the glass and dabbed a spot under each ear, then drew a chocolate line along my collarbone.

Dylan moaned and pressed his palm against his erection. "You're killing me."

I brought my hand down my body, then gently circled my nipples. The cold mousse felt delicious, but not as good as I knew his tongue and teeth would feel.

Dylan's patience ran out. He grabbed the glass out of my hand and slid it along the table. "We'll need more of that later." His voice was deep and thick. I shivered, knowing what came next.

He cupped my breasts in his hands and blew across them. I moaned and went slick between my thighs.

Just his breath got me wet.

He bent forward and licked me in one strong stroke across my lips, then buried his head in my neck, sucking at the skin beneath my ear. I tipped my head back, and thrust my hands into his hair, urging him on. I wasn't sure I'd ever felt so desired by a man.

He licked along my collarbone, first one side then the other, before breaking off to look deep into my eyes.

I scrambled between us, reaching for his fly, his hard-on making it difficult to unzip his pants. My fingers fumbled, the desire to fuck him—and have him fuck me—disconnecting my brain from my body.

"Please." It was all I could manage.

"Please what?" he growled against my skin as he dipped his head down and took my nipple between his teeth, bringing me to the edge of pain before he tongued and suckled me.

"I want to feel your dick. Please." I wasn't sure if the words had come out, if I was even capable of saying them, but every syllable was true. I'd never felt physical desire like I felt for Dylan. My pulse was loud in my ears—I was desperate for him.

He brushed his thumb over my chocolate-free nipple, then grazed his teeth over the other. My knees bowed as he straightened and grinned at me.

He lifted my chin with his finger. "You want my cock, baby?"

My heart was thudding against my ribcage. I nodded. I'd happily *pay* for his cock at the moment.

He unfastened his pants and pushed them down with his boxers, his dick springing free.

I took a deep breath and reached across the table for the mousse.

Dylan raised his eyebrows and I lifted a shoulder in a half shrug.

I sank to my knees and he groaned before I'd even touched him. I scooped some chocolate mousse out of the glass. Licking my finger clean, I leaned toward Dylan's dick. Starting at the base of his cock, I licked, leaving a trail of chocolate mousse.

I sat back on my knees and took some more mousse from the glass and placed it on my tongue, then swirled it over the tip of his dick.

I might have created my best recipe yet.

I glanced up at Dylan. He narrowed his eyes, his face so serious. "You are the most incredible woman I've ever met."

My stomach flipped.

Stand down, butterflies. Men always say the sweetest things before they come.

That was what casual sex was about—giving what you needed to give to get what you wanted. He'd say anything to ensure that the next thing I did was take his dick in my mouth.

I took a deep breath and licked again from his base, around the crown, and then clasped my lips around his tip, slowly edging him farther and farther in.

His panting and groaning made me want to take him deeper, and little by little, I took more and more. I gagged when he reached the back of my throat.

His hands pushed into my hair.

"Fuck, Beth. Look at me."

I glanced up, my sight watery from the strain of taking him so deep. His indigo eyes bore into me, frantic with need and lust. With one rough hand in my hair, he stroked the other lightly across my face, brushing my cheekbone with his thumb.

"Incredible," he whispered.

With two hands, one above the other, I held the base of him and took him in my mouth. I dragged my lips back up and swirled my tongue around the crown.

"You taste great," I said, continuing to twist my hands around the bottom of his dick, then taking him in my mouth again, shallower but faster this time as I began a rhythm. My heart beat against my chest and arousal built between my legs.

Dylan's hips started to rock into me, and the hand in my hair tightened. "Baby, no. Fuck. *So* good." The strain of pleasure showed on his face. "You have a beautiful mouth."

I pulled away and licked across his dick as he stabbed his hips toward me, fighting to get back into my mouth. I gave him a small smile and sucked on his tip as I moved a hand from his base to run my fingernails across his balls.

"Fuck, no. Beth, I'm going to come." He tried to pull away but I grabbed his ass, pulling him toward me. I wanted this. I wanted him.

I sank deeper onto him and he pulsed in my mouth, hitting me in hot squirts at the back of my throat. One touch from him and it would send me hurtling over the edge. How could his dick in my mouth be so arousing that I was a second away from coming myself?

I loosened my grip around his base and he pulled away. I leaned forward and placed small kisses down his shaft.

He stared at me, sweeping his thumbs over my cheekbones again. "You're amazing. The best."

"Don't." He didn't need to say things like that.

"Don't what?" He looked confused as he helped me stand.

"Pretend this is more than it is. I'll only trust you if you don't lie to me."

"I say things like that because I mean them." He dropped a kiss on my forehead. "I don't pretend. I told you I don't lie. That was the best head I've ever had. Come on. Let's get you to bed." He smoothed his hand down my back and over my ass and I shivered.

"Can we take the cake?" I asked.

He laughed. "Of course we can take the cake."

I picked up a plate with a slice of lemon drizzle. "I'm not sharing, so bring your own." I spun and headed toward the bedroom.

"Oh, I think I could persuade you to share if I wanted to, but that's okay, I won't make you." He picked up his own plate and followed me into the bedroom.

My bed was huge and we sat cross-legged and naked opposite each other.

"You are so fucking sexy. Look at you."

As I looked up, he snapped a photo on his phone.

"Hey." My stomach churned.

"My sweet, I need a reminder of this exact moment. That beautiful pussy, wet from giving me a blow job, those inflamed lips and your relentlessly phenomenal tits. And on top of that, you're eating cake. You can't expect me not to want to capture this. You're a vision."

"I don't like it. Delete it. I'm not adding to your collection." I didn't want to be one of a hundred naked women on his phone. I'd once flipped through my ex, Louis's, cell while he was asleep to find photo after photo of beautiful, naked women. It was as if they were his possessions. When I confronted him about them, he'd gone crazy that I'd checked his phone. He'd told me they were old photos, but if that was the case, why had he kept them? He never gave me an answer and he'd never deleted them. Every time I looked back at our relationship, I felt like an idiot. There were so many unacceptable situations that I'd just ignored.

"You're worried I have a gallery of naked women on my phone?" Dylan handed me his phone. "Delete it. But there's no one there but you. You can check."

I looked at the phone in my hand and then back at Dylan. "You're saying I can look at your phone."

He nodded. "I have nothing to hide."

I had to stop expecting him to disappoint me. I didn't want to go rooting through his photos. I didn't want to be that girl.

I shook my head. "If you show it to anyone, I'll kill you, and then my brother will hunt you down and kill you again."

He laughed and took another picture. "I don't want to share you."

My stomach flipped for the second time that evening.

"So tell me about your day. What happened?" he asked, as if we were on a date rather than enjoying a casual hookup.

I put my plate on the bedside table and stretched out on my side, propping my head up. "It was good, I think. We filmed two recipes. I thought it would be more like my YouTube stuff, but they filmed one with a moving camera and then the other with two static cameras. And of course, there were so many people watching." I was excited to see how the final version turned out.

"Did you enjoy doing it?"

"Once I relaxed and forgot about the people and the lights and just started baking, I was fine. I think they're going to look at it and then see if they want to use it. Who knows? I've lost nothing if they decide not to, and anyway I don't know how it would work. I mean, I can't travel from London every week."

"You live in London?"

I nodded. "I grew up here and moved after my mother died."

Dylan reached out and stroked my cheek with his knuckles. "You like London?"

"Of course. It's a beautiful city and it's home. It's where my family is—my brother and his wife and their daughter, and my sister-in-law's brother and his wife and their daughter. We've become a unit." As much as I'd grown up in Chicago, I'd never felt as *at home* anywhere as I did in London. Perhaps it was because that's where I'd found my sobriety.

"But your father is still in Chicago?"

"Yeah but . . . it's complicated." I didn't want to get into that with him. My father had remarried and had more children. It had happened quickly after my mother's death. My father's way of grieving was just to create a new future

112

and it hadn't really involved me and my brother, Jake. Things were better between us now but our relationship was forever changed.

He took a forkful of the cake he was eating. It looked like pineapple upside-down cake. "We have time."

I shrugged and he smiled, understanding that it wasn't something I wanted to discuss.

He discarded his plate and lay down opposite me, mirroring my position. "I looked for your YouTube stuff. I couldn't find anything."

"You did?" I grinned at him. "You need to search the Chicago Cake Maker."

"I'll do that. So, you had a long day. Were you just finished when you came back to the hotel?"

I had to think about it. "I went to a meeting after finishing at the studio, and then I saw you."

He ran his fingers down the side of my body. "A meet—oh, an AA meeting?"

I nodded. "I found a group I like when I'm in Chicago."

"You go every day?"

I turned over onto my stomach, lifting myself up on my elbows. "Not usually. In the beginning, yes. Now I go a couple of times a week, but usually in London."

Outside of my London family, I didn't usually discuss my alcoholism with anyone. Soon after getting sober, I'd made a decision to make sobriety rather than alcoholism my priority. Every alcoholic dealt with recovery differently, and I'd had to find my own path where I didn't feel that it overtook everything I did. "The way I see it, I'm an alcoholic like some people are diabetic—it's a chronic condition that I live with but it doesn't stop me living my life."

Dylan smiled at me. "And how long have you been a friend of Bill's?"

I looked up at him, trying to understand how he knew the term. I'd never heard it used outside of AA.

"I had a friend in college in AA," he explained, understanding my question before I asked it.

"Three years. Going on four." Saying that never got old.

"Wow. That's a long time without sex. I thought you must have still been in your first year."

I laughed. "It is a long time. But now you've broken the seal. You've ruined me. I'd forgotten how good it could be."

"My sweet, it was never this good, believe me."

"You should know." I smiled at him.

He raised an eyebrow at me in a question.

"I'm just saying." I shrugged. "You look like a guy who had a lot to compare it to."

"You're telling me I'm a man-whore?"

I looked up over his shoulder, considering my answer. "Not a man-whore. Just a man who's had a lot of women."

Dylan

I'd just been called a slut. I didn't normally give a shit what anyone thought of me, but for some reason I didn't want Beth to think badly of me.

"I suppose I've seen a few women naked." Since Alicia, sex had been about taking pleasure. It worked and I enjoyed it. But none had been as pleasurable as Beth. I'd forgotten how the physical could mix with the emotional to make it all the more powerful. Even from the first kiss, ours had been more than just a physical relationship. I couldn't imagine even looking at Beth without having some kind of emotional response. "Does it bother you?"

"If it bothered me I wouldn't have agreed to become one of them. I had a pretty good idea what I was getting myself into when I came to your room when our flight was cancelled." She smiled but my gut twisted. I wanted her to know that she was different, that I wanted to talk to her, not just fuck her. The more I found out about her, the more I wanted to know.

"Would it make you feel better if I told you that I rarely want to see a woman again after I've had sex with her?"

She laughed and sat up, swinging her legs off the bed. Was she leaving? The uncomfortable twist in my gut intensified. I was trying to distinguish her from the women I ordinarily slept with. "You just called yourself a man-whore. I'm going to get more cake. Want some?"

I followed Beth into the sitting room, taking a condom with me in case she wanted to get busy with that mousse again. Something outside the window had caught her eye. "Do you think they can see us?" I couldn't help but follow her.

I dragged my eyes away from her smooth curves and out of the window at the skyscrapers opposite us. "Maybe."

She placed her hands on the glass. "There are lights still on. People working late."

I stood behind her, gliding my hands down her sides then over her belly and around her waist. She leaned back against me, instantly grabbing my cock's attention.

"They're working hard." I pushed my hand down and reached for her clit. She sighed and swiveled her hips against my growing hard-on. I nudged her legs wider with my knee and she bent forward a fraction, the tiny movement snapping something in me.

She wanted to get fucked against the window—with an audience.

Jesus, this girl.

"Do you like the thought that people are watching you?" I whispered into her ear.

"Yes." Her voice cracked as I increased the pressure on her clit. "You do something to me. You make me wicked."

The thought of having an impact on her, over and above making her come, sent blood rushing to my dick.

I dragged my cock along her crack and she pushed back against me. I clenched my jaw, trying to stay under control.

"But you're mine to look at. Only mine." Possession crashed over me in a wave.

I rolled on the condom and lined up the tip of my dick at her entrance.

She gasped. I'd pay to hear the sound of her anticipation over and over.

"Dylan, people might see."

"I'm going to have you like this, and you're going to love it. If anyone sees anything, they can't possibly know how good it is. They can't feel what we feel. They can guess, but only we know."

"They can't have me. They can only watch while you do."

She got it. She understood how I needed to be special for her. I wanted to be different, wanted her to feel this energy between us—the familiarity, the passion, the trust.

I couldn't hold back a second longer and pushed into her, trying to go slow, to be patient; clamping my eyes shut because I knew if I caught a glimpse of that swollen mouth or the reflection of her tits in the glass I'd fuck her raw.

She groaned as my dick rammed into her. "So deep," she whispered and her head tilted back, and I buried my face into her neck, breathing in that almond scent she had.

"Do you think they know how deep I am?"

"Oh God, Dylan." I clasped my arm around her waist to support her.

"Answer me."

"They can't know. They can't understand how good it feels."

I pulled back, watching the sheen on my dick as it withdrew from her. She was always so wet whenever I went near her. Was she like that with all her lovers? Would she be that way with those who came after me?

Her whimpering broke my concentration. "You want more?"

"Please." She sounded desperate. I knew I was. I thrust into her, driving her forward so her breasts pressed up against the glass and her forearms lay flat. Jesus, as much as I was enjoying the view from this side, any lucky fucker watching her through the window must be getting images burned into his memory forever.

I thrust again. "I can't get close enough." I choked on the words as they crawled up my throat.

Her breathing became choppy and she spasmed around me; her forehead rested against the glass. Having the privilege of making her come made me the luckiest man on Earth.

But I didn't stop. I couldn't. I needed more. More from her, more for me. I folded my hands over her shoulders as she found the strength to hold her head up.

"Stay with me, Beth."

Her skin trembled beneath my fingers as I pounded into her again and again. I wanted this to last forever, but I was so close to the edge.

She removed one hand from the glass and pressed it between her legs.

"No," I barked. "You ask for my fingers. You don't use yours."

Her hand went back to the glass. "Please, Dylan. I need it. I need to come again."

I'd never get tired of hearing her beg for my touch. "You ask so sweetly, how can I say no to you?"

I dipped my hand between her thighs and gave her pussy one light stroke. She squirmed. "Dylan, please, God." Her voice, hoarse and desperate, got me harder than I ever thought I could be.

My fingers found her clit, swept down and quickly became coated in her moisture. How did she get so wet? I groaned and circled my hips, rubbing over her clit at the same time.

She leaned back, and with one arm reached over her head

and brought my face to her neck. "Tell me, is it good?" she whispered.

How could she doubt it? "The best. Your sweet, tight pussy surrounding my dick."

"Your"—she drew a deep breath—"huge dick."

"Yeah, you know it."

She bucked and she screamed my name at the shift in angle. The sound loosened my climax, it tearing through me from the ground up in sharp, delicious spikes. I exploded into her just as I felt her convulse against my fingers.

Jesus.

I'd never come like that before.

I didn't want to move but, post orgasm, the thought of anyone seeing her wasn't quite so appealing. I wanted to wrap her up and treat her like glass.

I pulled out, discarded the condom and turned her around, holding her front to my chest. I bent my lips to her head. "You really are incredible."

"You're not so bad yourself. With a little work we can get you above average." She giggled as I squeezed her ass.

"Let's move away from the window, shall we?" I walked her backward toward the bedroom.

"I can't believe we did that. Do you think anyone saw?"

I pushed her onto the bed. "If they did, they'll have seen the fuck of the century." I turned and headed back into the living room. "Stay there, I'll get sustenance." I grabbed some bottled water and placed it on the trolley, and pushed the whole thing into the bedroom.

"That is a fantasy come true," she said, grinning at me. "A hot, naked guy pushing a trolley full of cake? If I'm dreaming, I never want to wake up."

I chuckled. "I'm just interested in keeping your energy up. I'm not done with you."

"Are you going to stay? I mean . . ."

"Do you want me to? I can go." My gut twisted. Was she asking me to leave? I didn't want to; I wanted to stay surrounded by her.

"There's nothing I need to be doing. I just wondered if you needed to go home to your—I don't know."

I crawled on the bed toward her. "There's no one at home. I don't do that. I don't lie and I don't cheat." I sat against the headboard and pulled her into my arms.

"I know everything you *don't* do, but nothing you do. Tell me something."

I took a deep breath. "I buy sick companies and make them better." It was the simplest explanation of what I did.

"You're in private equity?"

Apparently I didn't need to dumb anything down for this girl. "In a broad sense, yes. I have a business partner and we use our own money and some of the bank's money." I stroked my fingers along her spine.

"Is there an ex-Mrs. James?"

I chuckled. "No one has been so unfortunate." She mumbled and I didn't catch what she said. "What?"

"Have you come close?" That wasn't what she'd said under her breath.

I took a beat, considering what I should tell her. "Yeah. A while ago. When I was first starting out, I got engaged to a girl." I hated to even think about Alicia, let alone talk about her. She represented a complete lack of judgment on my behalf.

"It didn't work out?"

"She dumped me for an older, richer man." I'd never said those words out loud before.

Beth pushed herself up on my chest and turned to look at me. I shrugged.

"You think she left you for the money?"

I nodded. "She admitted it. Said she wanted to enjoy her life and not have to struggle." I started to laugh. It was the first time I'd thought of Alicia and not hurt. I'd thought of us as partners, starting out on a journey together, with the same aims and aspirations—the same values. I'd been right in that we'd both been heading to success. It was just that I was planning to work for it, and Alicia wanted to marry it.

"Wow. True love, huh?"

"Is there any such thing?" Alicia had cured me of the idea.

Beth looked at me, her eyes sad. "You don't believe in love?"

I shrugged. "I believe in world-shifting sex with beautiful bakers from London."

She smiled and the sad look lifted—I was grateful. "Did she come crawling back when you made your money?"

I stretched my legs. I'd fantasized about Alicia trying to get me back since I made my first million. In my fantasy, I'd act as if I barely remembered her as I got head from a supermodel under my desk while Alicia begged me to take her back.

But she hadn't come back—I'd never seen her again, never heard from her until today. "She married the guy."

The wedding had taken place four months after we'd split. I'd gotten very drunk that day, and Raf had had to physically restrain me to stop me from crashing the ceremony. But not because I loved her by that point, but because I wanted to warn the groom.

I'd realized when she left me that she'd never been the woman I'd thought she was. I'd felt manipulated and lied to and I vowed it would never happen again.

Beth dropped a kiss on my stomach. "She's an idiot."

I cupped her face, stroking my thumb over the beauty spot on her cheekbone. When she said it, I could almost believe it.

"When do you go back to London?" Would we have some time together?

"Tomorrow."

My gut twisted. "Tomorrow?" I'd hoped we'd have longer. She was like a breath of fresh air sweeping through my tired routines. She was low maintenance, funny, beautiful—the sex was, well, the best I'd ever had. But more than that, she was real.

"When are you back?" I knew tonight wouldn't be enough. I wanted more of her.

"You wanna make this a three-night stand?"

I scanned her face as I tried to read her. Did she want to do this again? "Yeah I wanna make this a three-night stand. Do I have to convince you?" I flipped her to her back and held myself over her. I ran my teeth along her shoulder.

Her cheeks flushed. "I might consider it."

"Consider?" I reached for her pussy and ran my knuckle over her clit.

She pushed against my hand. "Well if you're going to play dirty, I guess I concede."

"My sweet, I'll play as dirty as you'll let me."

It was the easiest and most satisfying negotiation I'd ever had.

chapter EIGHT

Beth

I rang Jake and Haven's doorbell. The lemon meringue pie wasn't the best I'd ever made, not even close. But I'd promised I'd take one to our family dinner, so despite my jetlag and the memories of world-shifting sex, I'd put the ingredients together and come up with something that could vaguely pass for the pudding I'd promised.

"It's like a zoo in here," Haven said as she answered the door. "Enter at your own risk." She bent and kissed me on the cheek.

I stepped through the threshold to the sound of children screaming. "Jake's probably beating Sophia again."

I wasn't sure child abuse was something you should joke about, but as I was the only one without a kid, it wasn't up to me to set the standard.

Their huge Victorian villa was beautiful from the waist up. Below that, it had been hit by a baby hurricane. Underneath the buggies and blankets, the toys and bottles, I was sure the place was lovely. All I could see was chaos.

"Right, guys. You're in charge. We're going out to the garden." Haven pulled me through the kitchen as I managed to wave at my brother and Luke.

"The garden?" I asked. It was February—what the hell?

"We have patio heaters and blankets. It's the only place in the whole house that I can't hear the screaming," Haven said.

Ash followed, bringing a tray of drinks. "We can't be interrupted. We want to know *everything*."

My stomach clenched. It'd been years since I'd had anything to talk about.

"There's nothing to tell; I'm waiting to hear from the studio." Thoughts of my screen test had faded, replaced by an ache between my legs that Dylan had created and only he could cure. He and I hadn't had much sleep on Thursday, and he'd left for work early on Friday morning.

"Yes, yes. We'll get to the baking thing, but I want to hear about the sex first." Haven poured me a tall glass of something that had cucumber and strawberries in it while Ash opened a bottle of wine and filled two glasses.

I wrapped a blanket around my shoulders. "It was a nice coincidence running into him again." My cheeks heated. It wasn't that I was embarrassed about having sex, more that I didn't want to share it. Even though it was casual, it was beginning to feel like more than that.

"Was it as good as you remembered?"

I nodded and my heart began to thump. *Good* didn't come close. I'd collapsed on the plane and slept most of the way, waking to memories of Dylan's breath skirting over my skin, his fingertips over my hips.

"Are you going to see him again?" Ash asked.

I sighed. "He suggested next time I'm in town I should give him a call. Honestly, I'm not so sure it's such a good idea." I wasn't convinced I'd say no either. How could I pass up another night with Dylan? Still, that didn't mean it was the right thing to do.

"Why on earth not?" Haven raised her drink and we all clinked our glasses together.

I took a sip. "Because he's gorgeous, rich and powerful, *and* I think his penis might have magic powers." I felt as if I'd escaped, as if I'd woken up at precisely the right moment in the dream. Any more time with him was inviting danger and complications.

"Again with the *why on earth not*?" Haven said.

"I'm not sure I'm strong enough," I replied without thinking about my answer.

"Strong enough for what?"

"To hold him at arm's length. I mean, if I never see him again I'll have good memories. Why risk more? At the moment I'm not torturing myself wondering who he's sleeping with or questioning what he's saying. It's even between us. We both got what we wanted from each other. We should quit while we're ahead."

Haven stared at me. "You know, he's not Romano," she said finally.

Just hearing his name turned my insides black. My relationship with Louis Romano had begun just after my mother died—and had been the last relationship I'd had. My drinking had spiraled out of control when I'd gotten pregnant and he'd ended our relationship, stuffing some cash into my hands and telling me to get an abortion.

I'd had a miscarriage two days later.

The loss had threatened to engulf me. I'd held it at bay by alcohol. It'd worked—the booze dulled the pain and allowed me to sleep, to forget about my mother, my baby and the boyfriend who'd never loved me. It was so effective that I'd started to drink earlier and earlier in the day until every hour that I wasn't hazy with liquor seemed unnecessary.

"I don't want to talk about Romano." He was the symbol of a thousand bad decisions. I'd thought he was my salvation, and he'd ended being my destruction. It wasn't something I wanted to remember. He was the reason it had been easy to stay single for so long, the reason that dating was terrifying and seeing Dylan again felt dangerous.

A look passed between Haven and Ash. Questioning it would have meant talking about Romano, so I stayed quiet.

"I might call Dylan when I'm next in town," I said to bat the conversation away from bad boyfriends back to world-shaking sex.

"He might heal you." Ash looked concerned.

I just nodded. "He might."

"Your brother did that for me," Haven said, her tone serious. "Sometimes you just have to let them in, just a tiny bit."

"He's not suggesting we date. He's suggesting we fuck when I'm in town."

"So have fun. If you're not in the same city, he's not going to be able to hurt you. Assume he's dating other people and don't expect anything but his cock and an orgasm."

I laughed. It would never just be one orgasm. We were up to eleven. He made me count every one. "When you put it like that . . ." I wasn't convinced I could be so unemotional about it. I could feel myself being pulled toward him already. I wasn't the kind of girl who did just physical very easily.

"She shouldn't put her sobriety on the line, Haven," Ash said.

"I'm not saying she should, but having some fun doesn't mean she's going to start drinking again," Haven replied.

It wasn't so much my sobriety that I was worried about. It was more that I didn't trust myself, or my instincts, my judge of character. Dylan seemed like a good guy, but how would I know?

"I think she should do what she wants. You'll know if it's a good time to push yourself." Ash smiled at me.

"Sometimes you need to feel the fear and do it anyway," Haven said. "The things that are the most frightening tend to reap the biggest rewards."

They turned to me and I smiled. It was like seeing both sides of my brain battling it out in front of me. "So, the filming went well," I said in a not-so-subtle change of subject.

Ash topped up Haven's wine. "And when do you hear what's next?"

I dragged my seat slightly to the left; the heater was a little too hot. "This week, I think."

"Did you talk about whether or not you'd have to fly to Chicago every week?" Ash asked.

"A little. I said that I didn't want to do that, but I'd be happy to travel every few weeks."

Haven raised her eyebrows. "Dylan James is going to fall in love with you by the time you're done with him."

I rolled my eyes. "I can tell you that that is definitely not going to happen. The guy bangs supermodels and actresses."

"So did your brother," Haven said.

My phone vibrated on the table, so I avoided having to give a response as I checked the screen.

Dylan: Did you hear yet?

Beth: You are very kind to take an interest, but funnily enough, they haven't been in touch on a Sunday.

Dylan: It's my cock taking an interest. I want to fuck you against the shower wall. Right now.

I shivered.

Beth: I'm at dinner, surrounded by kids. You can't talk to me about your cock.

Dylan: I want to slide into you, filling you until you can barely breathe.

Jesus. I tried to keep my breath steady. I glanced up at Haven and Ash, but they were taking no notice of me. I peeled the blanket away; I was plenty warm enough.

Beth: Stop.

Dylan: You're going to be begging me not to when I twist my fingers around your clit.

Beth: I have to go.

I shut down my phone, knowing I couldn't ignore his messages if they were sitting there waiting to be read. I didn't need to be thinking about what Dylan's body could do to me while I was with my family.

"You okay?" Ash asked.

"Yeah. I thought it might be the studio. It wasn't."

"On a Sunday?" Haven asked.

"Yeah, I know. I don't know what I was thinking." I wrapped my blanket around myself, trying to hide my flushed skin and tight nipples.

Dylan James was relentless. But I liked it, was drawn to him.

He made it all so simple. So basic. He wanted to see me again because he wanted me naked. But when we were together, it seemed like more than that. And it was the *more* I was afraid of.

Haven took my hand. "If I hadn't taken a chance on Jake, I would never be where I am now. You were a girl when you met Romano. You needed someone. Now you're a woman. A strong, independent woman. You're not the same person. History isn't going to repeat itself. Take a chance."

Still gripping the phone in my hand, I relaxed back into my chair. She was right. I wasn't the same person. And Dylan wasn't Romano.

Just a taste more of him wouldn't hurt, would it?

Dylan

I looked out on the Chicago cityscape, then back to the president of Raine Media. "Tell me why we shouldn't sell you or shut you down. I don't see *any* plan to get your numbers back on track, let alone a viable one." I'd called Ted to my office to go through his numbers. When I'd taken a closer look at what was going on over there, I'd realized they'd only made small attempts to make any of the changes we'd asked them to. Changes that were essential if Raine Media was going to survive.

"I have to look at what's best for the company. The changes you asked for aren't good for my business."

The ego on this guy was incredible. "You get that this isn't your company, don't you? This is *my* business and if I ask you to make a twenty percent reduction in overall costs, then that's what you do. You don't nod at me, then ignore me and go back to business as usual."

"I stand by my decision." He leaned back in the chair. He must have read some shitty management book that told him going toe to toe with his boss was a good idea. He should ask for a refund from Amazon.

"I understand," I said. I stood and walked around my desk, toward the door.

Ted followed me, giving me a smug grin. I took his hand and shook it. "Thanks for coming in. You're fired." I opened the door to the outer office where my assistant sat. "Marie, Ted needs his exit paperwork. Can you arrange that please?" I'd warned Marie so she'd have everything prepared; she'd take his pass and notify everyone back at Raine Media.

I didn't glance at Ted's face. I wasn't interested. We were idiots for not spotting the problem sooner. I'd let the employees of Raine Media down by not realizing their boss was incompetent. Most of the time, I found, in business you just needed to hire good people and get out of their way. Somehow, we'd forgotten that. We needed to go back to basics.

I closed the door and went back to my desk. We'd almost written that business off. It felt good to have found the source of the problem, or one of them, at least. That familiar thrill of getting a decision right gripped me. I might have taken a second look at Raine Media because of Beth, but ultimately giving Raine Media another chance had been the right decision. Without knowing it, Beth had saved jobs, maybe even a company.

My cell vibrated against my desk. Beth and I had been texting for the last few days. She was fun and I found myself looking forward to hearing from her. She'd send me photographs of the desserts she'd made. I'd tell her all the different ways I wanted to make her come. I wanted to remind her what I could do to her, to convince her to see me again.

She'd sent me a picture of chocolate mousse in a martini glass, the caption reading *Where do you want it?* My dick jumped in my pants. It had recently become my favorite dessert. Fuck. That blow job should be recorded and distributed for women to use as instructions. The experience had been exceptional.

I typed out a response.

Dylan: Anywhere you care to put it.

Beth: You around on Thursday? I get in around lunchtime.

Part of me had thought that although she enjoyed our teasing over the phone, I'd never actually see her again. There was something about the way she'd said goodbye that'd made me think she'd gotten what she needed from me and wouldn't be back. Maybe I'd been wrong.

Dylan: You got the TV thing?

Beth: They're interested. I'm flying in to finalize details on Friday.

I grinned at my phone. I was looking forward to seeing her. I liked her smart mouth and perfect skin. I liked the way she talked to me, about anything I asked her, as if she hid nothing. It must have been why I'd ended up talking to her about Alicia. Her openness inspired the same in me.

I took a deep breath and jumped off a cliff as I typed.

Dylan: Do you want to stay at my place?

Having a woman share my space hadn't happened in forever. I fucked women at my place, but they didn't sleep, brush their teeth or unpack a bag. Ever. But it didn't make much sense for Beth to have a hotel room when I planned on keeping her in bed every moment she wasn't at WCIL TV. I wanted her to be comfortable with me. I wanted to show her I wasn't hiding anything from her. I wanted her in my home.

She didn't respond right away. I tried to distract myself, shrugging off my jacket and rolling up my sleeves, ready to deal with my inbox. Marie always flagged the emails I had to read, so if they weren't marked red they got ignored.

I kept checking my phone but nothing. No response.

"Marie," I called out.

She stuck her head into my office.

"Has he gone?" I asked.

"Yeah. A little shaken, but I got his pass and his phone and got Don to take him home."

Marie was great at cleaning up after me.

"Thanks. Well done. Can you arrange for me to have a tour of WCIL? Tomorrow if possible. I think it would be good to show our face and reconfirm our commitment to them. For the short term, in any event."

"No problem. Will Raf go?"

"You can ask him, but I doubt it." My cell vibrated on the desk. "I have to get this."

I waited until Marie shut the door before I tapped the code into my phone. I wanted to savor Beth's reply.

Beth: Thanks, but I'll stay at The Langham.

My stomach dropped. It wasn't the response I'd been hoping for.

I slung my phone on my desk and went back to my email.

Marie had arranged for me to meet with the WCIL TV people at 8AM the next morning. I'd need to replace Ted quickly, and I didn't know the team there as well as I should, so didn't know if there were any internal candidates for the role. Raf had agreed I should do a bit of digging. I often found people on the ground knew what was needed to fix the problems in the company. Tomorrow was about finding answers, getting to the root of the problem.

I toed off my shoes and headed toward the refrigerator. My housekeeper always left me dinner if she knew I was going to be home.

I pulled out a beer from the top shelf. Did Beth mind people who drank around her? I put the bottle back and pulled out a pot of something with a Post-it on it marked "dinner."

I took off the lid to find what looked like chicken. I wasn't really hungry.

Just restless.

I took off my jacket and put it over the back of one of my dining room chairs, then headed through the arch to the living room. I emptied my keys, wallet and phone onto the table, stuck my feet up and fired up my laptop.

I launched YouTube and typed in *The Chicago Cake Maker*. I tapped my finger against the mouse until I could skip the ads. The opening titles were Beth's greedy mouth in close-up taking a huge bite of cake. *Jesus*. I knew what else that mouth could do.

The titles cut to Beth standing in a kitchen, smiling into the camera. I grinned back at her. She was a beautiful girl. She was more than that; she was head-turningly stunning. On screen, her beauty was amplified; she was lit up, glowing. The camera loved her. My dick stirred.

I groaned. I should step away from the computer.

Nope, wasn't going to happen. I wasn't going to miss an opportunity to watch her, just stare at her, unashamedly, without her or anyone else knowing.

She started lifting up different ingredients, showing the camera what she was going to be using. I realized I didn't have the sound turned up. I tapped a few buttons, my eyes not leaving the screen. Her voice, huskier than I was used to, filled the room.

I could practically feel the blood rush to my dick. I placed my palm over my zipper in a half-hearted attempt to control my burgeoning hard-on, but it did anything but calm it. I groaned and pushed my hand down, growing harder with every movement.

Fuck me, two days before I saw her again, had her again, fucked her again, was beginning to feel like a lifetime.

She put some butter and sugar in a bowl and started to mix. The effort made her cleavage shake. I needed my dick between those tits. I took a deep breath.

The blood pounding against my ears made it difficult to focus on what she was saying, but I couldn't pull my eyes away from the screen for a second. I stroked harder and harder, up and down the front of my pants.

Guilt echoed through me. Somehow it felt wrong to be taking pleasure from her when I wasn't giving anything in return. I didn't want to be selfish with her. I wanted to give more than take.

I removed my hand and paused the video. I reached for my phone, clicking on the picture I'd taken of her, naked, cross-legged and eating cake. The zipper began to bite into my erection.

Without thinking about consequences, I scrolled through my contacts.

"Hey." She sounded breathy and sleepy, but I couldn't bring myself to feel bad about waking her.

"Were you asleep?" *I want to kiss you.*

"I'm in bed but not sleeping. Where are you?"

"I'm at home. I've just got in." *I want to touch you.*

"I was just thinking about you." She yawned partway through her sentence. I was a selfish bastard calling her this late, but I couldn't bring myself to end the call.

"What were you thinking?"

"I was wondering about Thursday."

My hand went back to my still-hard cock. "Tell me."

"I'm looking forward to seeing you. I . . ."

I grinned at her confession. "You, what?"

"No, sorry. I didn't mean . . . We'll have fun. If you can make it. It's no big deal if you have to cancel."

She thought I'd give up a chance to fuck her, see her, touch her? "I guarantee I can make it. Do you want me to come to the hotel again?"

"Yes." Her voice cracked.

My balls tightened at the memory of her pressed up against the glass. I ran my fingertips up my cock.

"What are you doing?" she asked.

Should I tell her? "I'm looking at you on YouTube." I seemed to lose my filter with her. I didn't want to hold back.

"You are? Do you like it?" I could hear her smile in her voice.

"I'm about three minutes in and hard as steel."

She inhaled. "Are you dressed? Are you . . .?"

She wanted to ask me whether I was masturbating and I wanted to tell her, but I understood her hesitation; it was an intimate question and it would be crossing a line. Hell, just calling her for no reason other than because I wanted to hear her voice was crossing a line.

"I'm dressed, but I wish you were here and we were naked."

"Tell me what you'd do to me if I was there."

I groaned and undid my pants. There was no way my dick

was going to tolerate being ignored for a moment longer. "I'd strip you naked—"

"And you'd keep all your clothes on," she finished my thought for me. "I like that."

We liked the same things.

I circled my cock with my fingers and pushed down to my base, my dick jutting out in front of me. I squeezed and exhaled as I released. "Yeah."

"I like your teeth, too." She spoke as if she was half asleep, though I heard the rustle of sheets. "When you put them against my skin."

I dragged my fist up the length of my cock, straining to speak. "I like your skin. It's so smooth and yielding. I like to watch my fingers press into it."

Her breaths came heavier. Was she . . .? I couldn't stop myself from groaning. "I like that you're always *so* wet. Tell me how that sweet pussy feels." I pumped my hand up and down my length.

She moaned. "It's so ready for you."

Dew beaded on the end of my dick. I wished she were here, astride me, hovering above me, ready to fuck me. I closed my eyes and let my mind take over.

"And I like how you fill me so deep that it blocks out all my thoughts. I have to . . . let go." Her words were jagged, verging on desperate.

My fist gathered pace. "I like your tits. They're so full and—" I couldn't finish my thought without coming and I didn't want to get there first.

"Are you close?" Her voice rose at the end of her question. "I'm so close. Just thinking about you makes me so . . ."

"If I can't feel you, let me hear you." I was seconds away from falling over the edge.

Her breaths turned into moans, which turned into her calling my name over and over. If I thought it was possible to take a flight to London tonight, I'd have raced to the airport right then. The sight of her coming was a precious thing, and I didn't want to be the chump that passed up any opportunity to revel in it.

She gasped, then fell silent. I was too far gone to hold back any more. "Beth, my sweet Beth," I called as my body went rigid, my orgasm claiming me.

My hand and shirt were covered in come, but I couldn't move. It was as if she'd stolen my energy. "Jesus, Beth."

She gave a small laugh at the other end of the phone. "Did we really just do that? We hardly know each other."

Even though I'd seen her less than a handful of times, we knew each other, better than the time we'd spent together would suggest. We had something—a connection.

I couldn't remember the last time I'd had phone sex. Probably with Alicia when I was travelling to Missouri. "I think we're getting to know each other pretty well."

"Maybe," she replied. "I'm so tired."

"Sleep, beautiful baker. I'll see you very soon."

We might not have shared many words, but it was as if something on a deeper level pulled us together and joined us.

I only hoped she felt it, too.

chapter
NINE

Dylan

My heart raced as I entered the lounge at Heathrow. Desperate to see Beth, I'd checked in a little early.

After phone sex on Tuesday, I'd arranged a last minute trip to London, flying out on Wednesday and back to Chicago on Thursday morning—on the same flight as Beth. The deal with Redux was dragging. Raf had been due to fly out next week, but I offered to go earlier. I kept telling myself it made good business sense.

I wanted to surprise her in the lounge. It would be like the first time we met. Maybe I'd have her in the showers again, like the second time we saw each other.

I scanned the lounge, looking for her unmistakable red lips but didn't see her. I found a seat toward the edge of the lounge, hidden behind a magazine stand that still gave me a view of the whole room so I could see when she arrived.

I went over to the wet bar, got myself a soda water and returned to my table, pulling out my phone and my laptop. I hadn't spoken to her since Tuesday night, but we'd had a few texts where she told me what she was baking and I told her that I wanted her naked. She would have said if she'd changed her plans, I was certain of it.

I started to scroll through my emails when I thought I heard her laugh. I glanced up, sporting a grin of my own. I saw the back of her head as she walked through the door, talking to someone on the way in. She looked beautiful, carefree and relaxed in the way that she was in the YouTube clips I'd seen. My eyes slid to her tiny waist, then back up, urging her to turn around and see me. She paused for a second, then threw her hands up in the air and laughed. My gaze followed hers and saw she was talking to a fellow traveler. They continued to chat animatedly as they approached the wet bar. Was he a colleague? A friend? My jaw clenched. I didn't like her spending time with men who weren't me.

My heart stopped as he slung his arm around her shoulder and she leaned into him.

The air around me froze. She was a cheat?

I shifted my chair farther toward the magazine rack. Jesus, I felt like a fucking asshole for following her to London just to have a few more hours with her.

I hadn't thought this through, and that wasn't like me. What was I doing flying three thousand miles for a few hours on a plane with a woman? Beth was great sex, but I didn't do relationships. After Alicia, I hadn't wanted anything more than sex. I'd certainly never gotten the urge to fly across an ocean for a woman. What the fuck was happening to me?

What an idiot. I didn't embarrass easily, but this was mortifying. I'd clearly thought there was something more between us than she did. I'd have to try to dodge her, and if she saw me, I'd pretend I'd forgotten this was her flight.

Yeah, right, that would be convincing.

I couldn't tear myself away from staring. The easy intimacy between them made me envious. I wanted to be the guy she linked arms with.

Fuck.

I ran through the possible explanations in my head. Perhaps she'd just met him, fallen crazy in love and planned to give me the brush off before we were due to meet? Perhaps they were just convivial exes? Nothing made sense. Why would she have agreed to meet me tonight if she was fucking someone else? I suppose it shouldn't matter. I never required monogamy from any of the women I fucked, but from her, it hurt.

Fuck, what was the matter with me? I was really good at things I set my mind to, and I'd been really good about sleeping with women without allowing it to ever be more than physical. How, in such a short space of time, had I allowed Beth to create this twisted sensation in my gut?

I logged off my laptop and packed up my carry-on. I needed to get the fuck out of the lounge. I checked the time. We were probably twenty minutes away from boarding.

Surreptitiously, I glanced over at the wet bar. Beth and her man weren't there. My gaze skirted the rest of the lounge and found them at a table, laughing, Beth eating cake. My gut churned. Part of me wanted to stay and watch as she took a forkful of whatever it was into her mouth, but I wasn't about to make a bigger fool of myself than I already had.

I slipped out of my seat and headed for the exit.

I made my way to the gate without noticing what was going on around me. I just wanted to be back in Chicago where I could pretend I'd never made this fucking trip.

I arrived at the gate, and after I flashed a smile, they allowed me to board early. My seat was 2A, right at the front of the plane. There was little chance Beth would wander past me. I might make it to the end of the flight without her knowing I was ever here, following her like some kind of pathetic stalker.

I unpacked what I needed from my carry-on, stowed my bag, and gave my jacket to the flight attendant.

I went to set my phone to flight mode when I saw an unopened text.

Beth: Just about to board. See you soon.

My body betrayed me as my heart expanded at her words. I had to remember she was texting me while she stood next to some other guy. Perhaps he'd gone to use the restroom and she'd used her time to juggle the rest of us. Perhaps I was one of several who'd just received a text. I shook my head and turned off my phone. I didn't want any fucking reminders of what an idiot I'd been.

I opened my laptop and did what I did best—work. I had the rest of the strategic reports to wade through, and they would be a good distraction. I wasn't going to let Beth-fucking-Harrison take up any more space in my head.

Two hours into the flight, I'd managed to avoid any run-ins with Beth, but going to the restroom was going to be risky. When I'd flown with Beth before she'd passed out cold for most of the flight. Hoping that was her MO, and not due to spending the night having world-shifting sex, I unclicked my seatbelt and moved to the restroom as quickly as I could.

Luckily, I didn't have to wait and I quickly locked the door behind me, my heart thumping through my chest. I just needed to get through the fucking flight without bumping into her and I could get on with my life as if I'd never met her.

When I unlocked the door, I took a deep breath and headed back to my chair. I made the mistake of briefly turning my head to my right, and there she was. Her seat was tilted back, and her eyes were closed, her black-as-coal hair framing her beautiful face. Even in her sleep, her beautiful red lips pouted.

I forced myself to look away, and I locked eyes with her man. I rarely got the urge to get violent, but I could have landed my fist to his face at that moment. He stared at me as if he wanted to return the favor. Thank God this agony would soon be over.

I went back to my seat and buried myself in my work.

By the time we landed, I'd decided that hanging back until the rest of the cabin had left the plane was my best chance of avoiding Beth. I didn't want to risk her man pointing me out as the guy who'd been ogling her earlier.

The cabin emptied as I made my way off the plane. I didn't dare look anywhere but straight ahead as I walked toward immigration.

I tried to ignore it, the first time I heard her call my name. I tried to convince myself I was imagining it. But of course I wasn't, and in seconds there was a tug on my arm.

"Dylan. It is you. What are you doing here?"

I didn't stop walking. Didn't look at her. "I had some unexpected business in London."

She was having to jog to keep up with me. "Did you know we were just on the same plane?"

I allowed myself a look. I longed to brush my thumb over that beauty spot on her cheek. My stomach tumbled. If only she wasn't so goddamn beautiful.

"Stop a second." She pulled me to the side of the throng of people making their way down the long corridor. I breathed in her sweet smell, unable to resist her. "Hey. It's good to see you." Her eyes narrowed as though she wanted to ask me a question. I knew how she felt.

I glanced around to see if the guy she was with was around, and found him emerging from the restroom. I looked back at her. "I have to go." I twisted my arm, setting me free, and I turned and continued up the corridor.

My heart thundered and even though I was in an airport surrounded by noise and activity, I couldn't see anything but her lips and her questioning eyes. How had I let her get under my skin? I'd told myself I'd never let that happen again. Beth wasn't Alicia, and I hadn't let my feelings for Beth get too far. It was a good reminder why I had the boundaries I did.

I didn't do feelings.

I didn't do vulnerable.

And I no longer did Beth Harrison.

Beth

I was grateful Jake had arranged for a car to pick us up from the airport; I wasn't sure I could stand in line without my legs collapsing from under me. I'd watched, baffled, as Dylan disappeared into the crowd. He'd seemed cold and angry. Had something happened at work? Had business in London gone badly?

The gnawing in my stomach after my encounter with Dylan was a reminder of why I hadn't dated. It felt like a mixture of guilt and shame with a hefty smattering of disappointment. I was used to him grinning at me, unable to keep his hands to himself. It was a shock to have him be so unfamiliar.

"You get in and I'll deal with the bags," Jake said. My brother was the last person I could talk to about Dylan's weird demeanor. I was pretty sure that although he wanted me to date, if any man ever put a foot wrong, best-case scenario Jake would tell me to move on. Worst-case, he'd kill the guy. How was I going to explain that we weren't even dating—we were just having casual sex? That was never going to go down well with my brother.

I hadn't expected to hear from Dylan before my trip back to Chicago, but we'd texted a lot—almost every day. He'd even called me, although I was pretty sure that was because he'd wanted me to get him off. I suppose it was kind of a compliment. I doubt he had problems finding willing volunteers for that particular job.

I'd found myself looking forward to hearing from him, to sharing parts of my day. He was meant to be an easy one-night stand, but things had begun to grow between us. But seeing him a few minutes ago—it had been as if we were strangers, as if he felt nothing. He must have known we'd be on the same flight, but he'd clearly made no effort to find me, and when I'd bumped into him, he'd acted as if he wanted to be anywhere but talking to me. I didn't get it.

"You okay?" Jake joined me in the back of the town car.

"Yeah. Men are such odd creatures."

Jake chuckled. "Any particular thing sparked this thinking?"

I shrugged. "I'm just tired, I guess." I held my phone in my hands, willing Dylan to text and everything to be as it had been.

Why should I have to wait for him? I shouldn't question and ruminate; I shouldn't assume *I* was the problem. I didn't want to feel wronged, like a victim. If he was mad then he'd have to tell me. I wasn't going to assume. I typed out a text.

Beth: It was good to see you earlier. Looking forward to tonight.

I'd been looking forward to seeing him but the butterflies in my stomach had been replaced with molasses. I wasn't ready for my one-night stand with Dylan to be over.

I walked out into the crisp Chicago air, my hair taking off in the wind as if gravity had deserted us. It was official. I had a TV show. Or a bit of one at least. Though, I probably shouldn't have signed the contract with WCIL TV without an agent. Or a lawyer, or both, but I had. It felt right to take the risk.

I'd gone straight from the studio to an AA meeting a few blocks from the hotel. Meetings always grounded me, and I'd needed it after signing on to do six Saturday morning slots on *A Chicago Saturday.* They'd agreed I could film them all in advance so I didn't have to fly over each week. I couldn't have been more delighted. The experience would be fun and, more than that, it felt as if I were cashing a paycheck for the nearly four years I'd spent baking my way to sobriety. Almost as if the universe were patting me on the back and rewarding me for a job well done.

I checked my phone. Still no response from Dylan. I turned right onto Wabash and a gust of wind almost toppled me over. I'd forgotten how unrelenting Chicago's weather could be.

As I entered the bright, high-ceilinged lobby of the hotel, I squinted to see if I could spot Dylan at the bar, waiting for me like he had been before, but there was no sign of him.

Perhaps I should just take the hint. My meeting had talked about how we couldn't control the behavior of others, only our reaction to it. It could have been a sign to accept that Dylan was done with me and I'd never know why. That we were only ever meant to be the casual thing it started off as. Perhaps I'd assumed a little too much, and missed the signs that he wasn't interested. But why had he kept in daily contact with me while I was in London if he didn't want anything to do with me? I could bring myself to believe that he'd not realized we were on the same flight, but his reaction to seeing me said there was more going on in his head than he'd let on.

The churning inside my entire body was the reason why people shouldn't date in their first year of sobriety. Alcohol would soothe the ambiguity and uncertainty. Alcohol was something I could count on. I knew exactly what it did to me—it blocked everything out and made the bad things better. Three years sober, I no longer had the constant urge to drink, but at the same time, I was thankful that I'd years of preparation for this moment. I had other ways to cope. Any earlier in my sobriety and I wouldn't have been so sure.

I checked in, and headed toward the elevators, except, I passed them and kept walking, toward the bar. I just wanted to *make sure* he wasn't here.

"Can I help you, miss?" The bartender smiled at me.

Half-heartedly, I smiled back. "No." Should I ask him if he'd seen a man on his own who seemed to be waiting for someone? No. I didn't want to come across as a total crazy person. "Actually, can I get some cake sent up to my room?" I wanted chocolate mousse, but couldn't bring myself to order it. "Perhaps a strawberry shortcake? Room 1204."

"Certainly."

"And maybe a selection of macaroons?"

He nodded and I turned back to the elevators.

As I rode up to the twelfth floor, I checked my phone again. Still nothing. I was pretty sure I'd been dumped.

As I entered my room, an image of being pushed against the glass the last time I'd been here flashed into my head. Jesus, that man knew how to fuck, or he knew how to fuck *me*. I'd never experienced anything like it.

My stomach flip-flopped at the knock on the door. Was he here? I raced to the door, and flung it open, a huge grin on my face.

It was the cake. I'd never been so disappointed at being given sugar.

I let the waiter in, and he set the tray on the table and I

signed his notepad and tipped him. I was being crazy. Why wasn't Dylan here?

I grabbed my phone.

Beth: I'm back at the hotel. I have cake. I'm hoping you'll join me?

I'd not even set my cell down when it buzzed.

Dylan: I'm sure you have others who can help you with the cake. You should have told me you were with someone. I don't like cheaters.

What the hell did that mean? Anxiety gripped at my throat. Who did he think I was?

Beth: Who have I cheated on?

I collapsed into a chair to read his reply.

Dylan: The poor chump on the plane. Get him to eat your cake.

I rolled my eyes as things started to click. He thought I was with my brother. He'd asked me to trust him on more than one occasion, but wasn't affording me the same courtesy.

Beth: First, ewwww. Second, if you'd stuck around I could have introduced you to my BROTHER, who is not a chump, btw. You, on the other hand, are an ass.

Silence.

Perhaps he didn't believe me. Perhaps he thought I was making it up.

Could he have really thought I was with Jake? Was that really the reason he was pissed off, or had it been a convenient get-out-of-jail-free clause?

Thank God I'd ordered cake. I reached behind me and

grabbed a couple of pink rosewater macaroons from the tray. Self-medicating with sugar was almost as good as drinking.

I sighed and closed my eyes. I'd really been looking forward to seeing Dylan, but now everything had become more complicated than it was supposed to be. Perhaps I should get out now while I was only a little disappointed.

My phone buzzed. I took a deep breath as I opened the message.

Dylan: You're right. I'm an ass. I'd really like to see you. Can I come over?

It would be better if I said no, easier. If I flew home without seeing him, life would be simpler. The hard shell surrounding my heart survived my disappointment today, but I wasn't sure if it would again. My phone buzzed again.

Dylan: I'm really sorry.

I stared at the screen. I couldn't and wouldn't say no to him. I was myself—the new reinvented Beth Harrison, with Dylan, and he allowed me to be her without it feeling fake or it being an effort. It was as if he was the final piece in rebuilding myself—he'd lodged in my soul and he'd be there forever.

I'd never be able to say no to Dylan, whatever he asked of me.

chapter TEN

Dylan

The sky was dark and very few people were on the street as I grabbed a cab in the cold. We were due a snowfall.

When I received Beth's text explaining the guy she was travelling with was her brother, I'd tried to dismiss it as bullshit. In a lot of ways it would have been easier if she were the cheater I'd suspected. Seeing her with him had made me realize she had the power to wound me, and I didn't like anything that had power over me.

It was too late.

I'd had a dull ache drifting through my muscles and joints since I'd first seen her in the airport lounge, and I wanted to be rid of it. I knew touching, kissing, sucking, and fucking Beth would chase it away.

But what she was saying wasn't bullshit. It made perfect sense and fit with everything she'd told me about him and about her and her life. As she'd pointed out, I'd been an ass.

I strode through the lobby and headed toward the bar. I

didn't see her, so I grabbed a stool and ordered a soda water and some chocolate mousse.

I waited twenty minutes before the elevator doors pinged open and Beth stepped out.

The ache inside me intensified as I took in her mouth, hips and beautiful eyes. I couldn't stop myself from grinning at her, but her lips were tight.

I slipped off my stool. "Hey." I leaned forward and kissed her cheek.

"Hey." She stared at my shoulder.

She took a seat next to me, her stool facing into the bar as mine pointed toward her.

"Can I get a virgin mojito?" I asked the waiter.

I grabbed her hand and ran my thumb over her knuckles. "I'm really sorry. I feel like a jerk."

She continued to look at my shoulder. "That's because you were a jerk."

"I should have trusted you. I'm not good with that—trusting people. Trusting women."

Finally, she glanced at me. "I struggle sometimes, too. But you can't ask me to trust you and then not do the same."

She was a setting out the first rule of our relationship. It was an acknowledgment that this was no longer a one-night stand. We had shifted into a different space. We'd been inching toward something with the phone calls and the texts, but my reaction to seeing her with her brother and her need for my trust—that took us to the next stage.

She mattered to me.

"I know. It won't happen again." For so long I hadn't concerned myself with trusting a woman, or having a woman trust me. I was rusty when it came to relationships, but I needed to remember quickly if I didn't want to lose Beth.

I linked my fingers through hers and squeezed her hand. I sighed in relief when she returned the gesture.

"How come you didn't tell me you were in London?"

It was a good question and I needed to be truthful with her, even if it was embarrassing. She'd asked me to trust her. She deserved that.

"I flew in overnight on Wednesday and was in meetings all day Thursday. Meetings I could have done by conference call in Chicago. I wanted to see you, and thought I'd surprise you at the airport." It felt good to be honest with her.

She spun her stool to face me and cocked her head. "Are you saying you flew to London just to surprise me at the airport?"

I nodded. "I told you I was a douche. I'm really sorry for jumping to conclusions."

She slid off her stool and stepped toward me. "You're a peach," she whispered as she leaned forward and kissed my cheek.

I chuckled. "I'll take that."

"We're going to need two chocolate mousse parfaits for room 1204, please," she called to the bartender.

"Make me a promise," she said as we headed toward the elevators, holding hands like long-term lovers.

"Anything." I meant it.

"Whatever this is and however long it lasts, let's agree that there will be no secrets or lies. I want to have fun with you. I don't want to spend time second-guessing you." She crinkled her brow, willing me to agree.

"My sweet, that's such an easy promise to make. No secrets or lies for however long this lasts." I kissed her on the forehead.

"I believe you and promise the same. I hope you believe me, too."

"I do. I really do." I shouldn't compare her to Alicia, or cast Beth with the same lack of compassion or morality. She was fresh and exciting, soft and authentic. She was nothing like Alicia.

The ache I'd had all day for her ebbed away and in its place a lightness settled.

I *wanted* to give more, wanted more in return. "But, I have a request." Her lips parted as she looked at me, waiting for me to say what was on my mind. "Whatever it is we're doing, I want to be only doing it with you exclusively."

Her pouty lips widened into a smile. "I can do that."

I bent forward and kissed the beauty spot on her cheekbone. "I'm glad."

We entered her room, walking straight through the living area to the bedroom.

"Talk to me about the TV thing." As soon as the words had left my mouth, I realized that I hadn't told her that I owned it. Was that technically a secret? A lie? Did she need to know? I just couldn't tell her before I told Raf; it felt disloyal.

She scooted onto the bed. "I signed."

"You signed?" I crawled over her, forcing her to her back.

"I did. Six shows."

I dropped my lips to her collarbone. She smelled like cinnamon. I placed small kisses across her throat.

"Does that mean you'll be back in Chicago for six weeks?" I pulled back to look at her.

She screwed up her lips. "No. They've agreed that they'll film them all so I just have to come over once."

"You don't like Chicago?" I moved her to her side, stroking my thumb between her tits and over her stomach.

She thought about it. "Yeah. It's where I grew up and where I remember my mom and still see my dad." She trailed her hands up my back. "Memories of her are one of the things that makes Chicago great, and one of the things that makes Chicago tough." I nodded, not wanting to interrupt her. I wanted to hear more, know more about her. "And there was other heartbreak here, too. In London, I feel like a new, adult Beth. She's really the only person I want to be now."

"She's a very special woman." London wasn't so far away, was it?

She cupped my face in her hand; I closed my eyes at her touch.

Facing the possibility of cutting her out of my life had made me realize what I could lose—and not just Beth, but something bigger. She represented a different possibility for me. A different kind of life, one where I shared it with someone.

The moment was interrupted by a knock at the door.

"Stay there. I'll get it."

She was sitting cross-legged on the bed when I returned carrying two martini glasses of chocolate mousse and two spoons.

I kicked my shoes off and joined her on the bed, sitting opposite her, copying her pose. Last time we'd done this we'd been virtual strangers. Now, sitting with her fully clothed and eating mousse was far more intimate than before. How was that possible?

I watched as she slipped the spoon into her mouth and closed her eyes. "You're so sexy." The words slipped from my mouth before I had a chance to stop them.

She opened her eyes. "Back at you. I meant to say so earlier, but this casual look you have going on suits you."

I glanced down at my jeans and shirt as she waved her hand toward me. I guess she'd never seen me out of a suit.

"I mean the suit thing is hot with a capital H, but you can rock a pair of jeans with that ass."

I chuckled. "Well, coming from the woman with the best ass in the universe, I'll take it as a compliment."

She leaned forward and kissed me on the lips. "You should. I'm picky about the asses I date." She blushed. "Not that we're dating, I just mean—"

My heart thudded as I lifted her chin with my finger. "I'd like it if we were dating. Exclusively, if you want to try that."

She smiled. "I'd like to."

I nodded. "Good."

Against my better judgment, I wanted more with this girl. More than I'd had with anyone since Alicia.

"I'm still hungry." Beth had finished her mousse and was looking at me with sad eyes.

"I can order some more."

"Not that kind of hungry." She cocked her shoulder and looked at me from under her lashes.

This was new: she was making the first move. I liked that her confidence had increased; it meant she trusted me.

I set my glass on the bedside table. "What kind of hungry are you?" I lifted up on my knees and crawled toward her, coaxing her to her back.

I dropped a kiss on the corner of her lip. "That kind of hungry?"

"Hmmm, maybe." She ran her hands up my chest and widened her legs as I held myself over her.

I dipped my head to her neck and swirled my tongue over her skin, then bit. "That kind of hungry?"

"Not quite, but almost." Her voice was breathy and labored and filled with the need for more.

I pulled her top out of her skirt and peeled it off, revealing her incredible tits. Amazing. But I couldn't stop to admire them. I needed her naked. I slid off her skirt and panties, followed by her bra. And there she was, laid out in front of me, naked and ready.

I smoothed my hands down her body, reminding myself of every curve. "Are you hungry for this?"

She grabbed my shirt and pulled me atop her, palming my cock through my jeans. "This."

I groaned. She wanted my dick. If I'd had any doubt she was perfect for me before, she'd just erased it.

"That, my sweet, I can help you with."

I pulled off my shirt, my eyes fixed on hers. She smiled and reached for her pussy. Fuck, she could make me hard so quickly. "No," I barked.

"No?" She began to circle her fingers. As much as I wanted her to stop, to let me give her pleasure, the sight of her, one leg bent, her hand between her thighs, was one of the most glorious things I'd ever seen.

I kicked off my jeans and boxers and crawled back to her, knocking her hand away and replacing it with my own. "This is what you want?" I asked, pressing her nub as she arched her back.

"More," she groaned. "I want you inside me."

I grabbed a condom out of my wallet. She watched as I slid it over my dick, then flipped to her stomach.

"Hey." I grabbed her hip and tried to pull her back. "Turn over. I want to see you."

I'd always fucked her from behind, but tonight I needed it to be more.

Her cheeks flushed and she moved to face me, reaching for my face. I crawled up between her thighs and slid my rock-hard cock over her entrance, up and across her clit. As usual, she was wet and ready, as if she had a constant need for me.

She writhed beneath me as I teased her. "More," she breathed. "Please."

I closed my eyes and took a deep breath, basking in her cries.

She grasped my shoulders as I positioned myself at her entrance and slid inside, inch by inch.

With each movement, she seemed to relax and melt against me.

If she were the only thing left in my world, I'd be a happy man.

Beth

I'd never felt so intimate with anyone. Dylan and I hardly knew each other, but it was as if he understood me, saw me, and wanted me, despite everything.

Our fight earlier had made me realize that although what we had was meant to be easy, losing him would have been anything but.

I cupped his face as he moved over me. We'd never had sex face-to-face, and watching him trying to hold back was the sexiest thing I'd ever seen.

I grabbed his ass, pulling him closer to me. He growled and dipped his lips to my shoulder.

"This is it," I whispered. "This is what I'm hungry for. You."

He thrust into me, winding me. "Jesus, Beth. If you say things like that, I can't . . ."

"You can't what?"

He groaned and pushed again. "I can't hold back. You feel too good—you're too beautiful."

I pushed my hips up to meet his, enjoying the sensation of him so very deep in me, of the physical connection matching the emotional one that had been created today. "Don't, Dylan. Don't hold back."

He began his rhythm in earnest, his strain written across his face. "Like this?" he choked out. I opened my mouth but only sounds came out. It was as if he were chasing away the unpleasantness of what had passed between us, leaving only the moment.

Sweat formed across his brow and his breath shortened. His thrusts were tighter and deeper.

I threw my hands above me, making sure I didn't hit the headboard, though I wasn't sure I would notice, even if I did.

"This is how you want it? Hard and deep?"

I shuddered beneath him as the beginnings of a storm gathered deep inside me. He knew exactly what I needed and how to give it to me.

I lost myself in the drag, each thrust heightening the sensitivity in every part of my body. The storm grew louder. I wasn't going to be able to stop my climax as it raced toward me.

I grasped at his shoulders and dug my fingernails into his skin.

"Oh God . . . so tight. Jesus." I didn't hear the rest of what he said as my climax crashed into me, leaving me breathless and desperate.

He buried his head in my neck, crying my name before collapsing on top of me.

I clutched him tight, wanting to freeze-frame this perfect moment.

We lay in silence as I trailed my fingers over his back.

Sated.

Exhausted.

Comfortable.

"It's never been like that before," I finally said. He pulled out, discarded the condom and lay on his back, pulling me toward him. "I mean we've never . . ."

"That wasn't fucking. That was something more."

My stomach flip-flopped at his words. He felt it too.

He kissed the top of my head. "How long are you here?"

"Just until Saturday. Tomorrow I have lunch with my producer and his assistant—I think they thought it would take longer to negotiate my contract."

"Did you get a lawyer to look at it?"

"No, I didn't bother."

"Beth, you should have said. I could have had a lawyer look at it."

"Haven's brother is a lawyer; he would have looked at it, but the way I see it I have nothing to lose. I'm getting what I need just by them asking. My main concern was ensuring I didn't have to fly over here every week."

"Nothing to incentivize you to do that, huh?"

I slapped him on the arm. "You know what I mean. I don't want to *have* to fly over. If I *choose* to, that's a different matter." He kissed me on my head. "I'll be over here to do the filming, then again when the first segment airs. I think they said they want to do a live interview."

"So you'll be back next when you film your segments?"

"Yeah, in about two weeks." I liked that he was interested—more than liked it.

"How long will it take?"

"A day, I think. They don't have much time and they're only five minute slots."

He grabbed his phone from the nightstand. "You're here on the twentieth?"

"Filming on the eighteenth." I pressed my lips against his six-pack.

"Well, could you stay a few days? I have a gala for the charity I'm a patron of. We could go together. What do you think?"

"A charity gala as our first date?" It was kinda public and very real. I knew I wanted to date Dylan, but going to a gala together just brought into focus that it was the first time since Louis that I would be someone's date.

But Dylan wasn't Louis. He'd given me no reason not to trust him.

"I might shout for dinner before then, but I'd love to have you as a distraction at the gala. It would make the evening much more interesting." He slid the phone back onto the table.

"Like in public when we've got clothes on and stuff? I don't know. I'm not sure it's my kind of thing." I laughed as I poked him in the abs.

He chuckled. "I promise we can do lots of things naked before and after."

"If you promise."

He rolled me to my back and claimed my mouth, pushing his tongue between my lips, making me want him again. Pulling back, he brushed my hair away from my face. "You could stay at mine when you come back. There's no need for you to get a hotel."

Only a few hours ago he'd been so mad he could barely look at me, and now here we were, dating, going to charity galas. He'd invited me to stay at his house.

"Can I think about it?"

He moved off me. "Sure."

"I want to. It's just, I'm so used to having my own space. I can be crotchety and mean sometimes, and I'm not sure I'm ready for you to see that side of me quite yet."

He chuckled. "I bet you couldn't be mean if you tried."

I stroked a hand down his chest.

"But I can be patient. You think about it."

"I like you. And I want to do this. I just may need a little time to adjust. I've been single a long time."

He smiled. "I know that feeling. And the alcohol stuff— is that something I need to be . . . I mean, do I need to do anything, or not do . . ."

I rested my chin on his chest and gazed at him. "I'm the alcoholic. You can't make me drink or stop me from drinking. That's all me. But what's between us is new, so I need to just make sure I'm working my program."

"Do you have a sponsor and stuff?"

I smiled at him. "Sure. I went for a meeting today after I left the studio. My sponsor's in London, and I check in with her. I'm not newly sober; I just need to make sure I don't get complacent."

He smoothed the hair from my face. "Do you mind talking about it?"

"With some people, maybe, but not you." Because I'd already told him the most intimate thing about me, the first time we met, it had laid a foundation that made it easy to talk to him, easy to be honest. "It's not like I go around with a placard saying I'm an alcoholic—my life is not my alcoholism. Not now." I wanted him to know that I wasn't weak and fragile. Overcoming alcoholism had given me strength.

"WCIL asking me to do this show means the last four years haven't just been about getting sober. Does that make sense?"

"I get that," he said, stroking the hair from my face. "Were you always an alcoholic? What caused it?"

I liked that he was asking questions, that he wasn't afraid of the intimacy it would create.

"I'm not sure it was the cause—I think the disease has always been in me—but I started to drink when my mother died, then I had an asshole boyfriend and I just tumbled into a cycle of feeling terrible and drinking to feel better, and then drinking so much I felt terrible, so I drank more to make that go away." My stomach twisted at the memory of those dark times. They felt like a lifetime ago.

"What made you get help?"

"Jake." I blinked to try to stem the flow of tears. "He brought me to London, told me he loved me and wanted to have his sister back." I smiled, trying to stop from descending into an ugly cry. I was just so grateful that my brother cared so much.

Dylan stroked his thumb across my cheekbone.

"He took me to a meeting the next day and waited outside. I think he thought I was going to skip town if he left me." I smiled. "But I didn't. I didn't want to escape. I wanted to be happy. And that's what keeps me sober. I want to be happy."

He trailed his knuckles between my breasts and over my stomach. "I think you're very brave."

"I think I'm very lucky. Lucky to have Jake and lucky that my life never got to the point of no return. Nothing happened that I couldn't fix. I see some people come in to meetings and they've lost everything—their families, their jobs, their homes. I was saved before I ever got that far."

"And the asshole that you dated, what happened to him?"

"Oh, I'm pretty sure he's still an asshole. Actually, Jake's wife dated him. They went out twice. It's a long story. But Jake ended up punching him in front of her." I laughed. "He'd been waiting for an opportunity to do that for a while."

"Double win." He smiled.

"Right."

"And he broke your heart?" he asked.

I thought about it. "Looking back, it's hard to tell. I would have said yes, definitely, if you'd asked me straight after it happened. But I'm not sure he did break my heart. After him, I stopped trusting people, stopped trusting myself to know what was best for me. He took my power away. I think I'm still getting that back."

He stroked my fingers splayed across his chest.

"I'm sorry. I wish I could make it better." His brow furrowed.

I trailed my fingers over his lips. "You're used to solving problems."

"I guess."

"I don't want you to fix me. Just be with me. Be real with me."

He nodded. "Should I put my boxing gloves on when I meet your brother?"

My stomach flipped in the most delicious way. I wasn't sure how Jake would react to meeting Dylan, but it sounded like Dylan wanted to find out. He was thinking about our future. Part of me shone with excitement, but there was still a part that wasn't quite ready to let Dylan into my life in London.

chapter
ELEVEN

Dylan

My days had become longer since Beth had left for London. I wanted to get as much done as possible so we could spend the time she had away from the studio together.

My phone vibrated on the desk in my office; the number wasn't familiar.

"James," I answered.

"Dylan, it's me." I froze. "Alicia."

I hadn't thought about the email she'd sent me since I'd deleted it, so I was shocked to hear from her. I hadn't heard her voice in years, not since I caught her cheating on me with her now husband.

"It's been so long since we spoke. How are you?"

I took a deep breath; was she attempting to make small talk with me? "What do you want, Alicia?"

"Hey, is that the way you greet an old friend?"

Was she serious?

I'd always found her so charming. However much she did things that would burn and sting, she was always able to talk her way out of it, convince me that I'd misunderstood her intentions.

"I wondered if I could buy you lunch? Or dinner?"

I winced. What was she plotting? With my cell tucked under my chin, I Googled her husband—a wealthy, not to mention elderly, Chicago entrepreneur. They had married shortly after I'd discovered their affair—good business, she'd called it. Perhaps he had died.

"How did you get this number?"

From time to time, I wondered if she'd kept track of my career. My wealth now far exceeded her husband's.

"Oh, Dylan, I have my ways. You must remember that I can be very persuasive if I set my mind to it."

I ended the call. I didn't need her bullshit.

She called back and I put my phone on silent, turning it face down so I wouldn't even have the distraction of the flashing screen.

What the hell was Alicia calling for? I glanced back at my search results and scrolled down. It looked like her husband was having some financial difficulties—maybe she was looking to trade up again. The recession had been brutal. Raf and I were cautious investors, careful to ensure that we never got pulled into bidding wars with investors, but the economy had taken a lot of casualties.

Raf crashed into the office. "We just got regulatory approval on the Redux transaction." He was panting.

"Fucking great." We'd never done anything in the sector before so we'd been told that approval was by no means a certainty. "I knew we'd get it."

Raf stalked over to my desk and held out his hand. "You were right, my friend."

"As usual." I winked at him.

"Okay, don't be an asshole about it." Raf slunk into one of the chairs opposite my desk.

I chuckled. "Guess who just called me," I said. "Alicia."

"Are you fucking serious, dude? Have you spoken to her since that shit went down when you split?"

I shook my head. "Nope, never even laid eyes on her. She emailed me a week or so back, but I just deleted it."

"What did she want?"

"No idea. I hung up on her."

"Wow. I mean, you were cut up about her. I'm not sure you've ever been the same. Would you go back there?"

Beth's beautiful smile came to mind. I still hadn't told Raf—or anyone else—about her. I liked that we were wrapped up in a bubble, just the two of us, but perhaps it was time. "Not if my dick depended on it. And anyway, I'm seeing someone."

"You mean you're fucking someone."

"Well, we're definitely doing that, but we're also dating. In fact, she's coming to the gala on Friday." The corners of my mouth twitched. I couldn't wait to have her on my arm.

"And why am I just hearing about this now?"

"Because, unlike you, I don't like to over share. Which unfortunate girl are you bringing to the gala?"

He rolled his eyes. "Christ, I hate the drama. Christie threw a vase at me last night. I didn't even know I owned a vase."

"Christie's the Art History major?"

Raf looked at me as if I was stupid. "No, that was Tasha, and weeks ago. Do you listen to anything I tell you?"

"I try not to."

Raf ignored me. "Christie's the one who looks like Gisele ten years ago." I shrugged. "Anyway, she's a maniac. I think I'm going stag on Friday. I'm getting too old for this shit."

I chuckled. "You were too old to be chasing girls five years ago. You need to try a woman. Someone who has her shit together."

"Are you really giving me relationship advice? You haven't gotten laid for a decade before this mystery chick came along."

"Her name's Beth—and if you call her a chick I'll miscalculate your quarterly dividend on purpose—and I was having plenty of fun before her, but I never chased. I never had to."

Raf pushed his hands onto the chair arms and stood. "You're an asshole. I hope you marry her, then she divorces you and takes all your money."

"Love you, bro."

"Yeah, whatever."

I picked up my phone. Four missed calls, all from the same number. I also had five texts. Hoping they were from Beth and not Alicia, I opened the first one.

Alicia: Seriously Dylan, I have a business proposition for you. I think we should talk.

Business? She'd probably suggest marriage. That was how she approached relationships.

Alicia: I'm just suggesting lunch. If you don't like what I have to say then you never have to see me again.

Alicia: I really miss what we had. It was so simple and you were so good to me.

Jesus, did she think I'd fall for this shit? What we'd had was anything but simple. Looking back, everything had seemed strategic where Alicia was concerned.

Alicia: I really need your help. Please. You're the only one I can turn to.

There were plenty of rich men in Chicago, others who would be taken in by her.

Alicia: I'll email you my proposal.

I took a deep breath, deleted her texts and dialed Beth.

"Hey," she answered. "How come you're calling me in the middle of the day?"

My MO was to call Beth before work, and then after if it wasn't too late. We spoke most days and I'd gotten to know her routine. We were four thousand miles apart, but somehow I felt closer to her than ever.

"I just needed to hear your voice." I wanted to neutralize Alicia's poison by talking to Beth. "Am I interrupting?"

"No. It's always good to hear from you, and I'm just baking."

"Of course you are."

She laughed. "Yes, I suppose I do it a lot. How's your day."

"Good and bad. Weird."

"That sounds intriguing." The scrape of utensils against metal clattered down the phone. "Tell me."

"Well, we got regulatory approval on Redux."

"Congratulations. That's the pharma company in England, right?"

"Yeah." I grinned. Our worlds had begun to mix together as I got to hear about her day and I shared mine. I'd forgotten how comforting it could be. "And then my ex called, which was the bad and the weird."

"Alicia? I didn't realize you were in touch."

"We're not. I haven't spoken to her since we split."

The clattering at the other end of the phone went silent. "What did she want?"

"She suggested lunch. I hung up."

"You hung up?"

"Yes, I don't want to speak to her. I have nothing to say, and I'm sure she's got nothing I want to hear."

"Perhaps she wanted to apologize, set things right? Maybe she was offering you both closure."

"I'm pretty sure whatever she was doing, it was entirely to benefit Alicia. Anyway, I don't want to talk about her. I want to talk about you. What are you making?" Images of Beth naked except for high heels and an apron sprung to mind.

"Hmmm, I'm not sure I should say."

"Hey, I thought we said no secrets."

"Chocolate mousse. It's a current favorite of mine," she confessed.

"Is that right? I'm quite fond of that dessert myself." I grinned. "What are you wearing?"

She laughed. "I always bake naked. Apart from my heels and a short, frilly apron, of course."

I groaned and palmed my twitching cock through my pants. "I wish I was there."

"I'm going to see you tomorrow; we can make up for some lost time. Unless you're busy?"

"I'll make time for you. Are you sure I can't convince you to stay at my place?"

"I'm not saying never, Dylan, just not this time. We'll see plenty of each other. I'm staying a week this time."

"I hope to see all of you."

She laughed. I was serious. If I thought she'd let me, I'd keep her naked for her entire trip.

"Perhaps I should cancel the gala," I said. I didn't want to share her.

"You can't do that. You're a patron. Unless . . ."

"Unless what?"

"Well, we've just started dating. Maybe it's too early to—"

"It's not too early to anything. I told Raf that you were coming with me."

"You did?" I didn't understand why she was surprised but she sounded happy, which made me happy.

"Sure, we're exclusively dating; why wouldn't I tell people?"

I ran my finger round the inside of my collar. "Okay, you're not saying anything. What are you thinking?"

"Ummm, I'm thinking I'm glad we're exclusively dating."

I grinned. "Well I'm pleased that you are."

She laughed. "Perhaps I should tell my brother."

"You've not told him?" This conversation was long overdue. We needed to be on the same page with stuff like this.

"I've talked to Haven and Ash."

Well, that was something. Her sister-in-law and her kinda sister-in-law seemed to be her closest girlfriends, so at least she'd told them.

"What's stopping you from telling Jake?" She wasn't dating anyone else and neither was I, but she hadn't told her brother despite the fact that they were close. Was she having doubts?

"Nothing. He's been telling me to date for a while now, so the general concept isn't a problem. I guess I don't want him to worry, and I think he'll want to meet you when I tell him and I don't know—"

"Okay, well, we can do that."

"You think? I mean, the family thing, can't we just skip it? If you ran into each other that would be one thing, but an introduction? It all seems a bit . . . over the top."

"I want to meet your brother, Beth. Everyone who's important to you. Don't let this be a big deal. I'm not going to ask him if I can propose." Though it was a big deal. I'd not met a girlfriend's family since I'd asked Alicia's father if I could marry her.

"Okay. I'll tell him, but I'm warning you, he'll want to meet you properly." I could hear her smile, even from four thousand miles away. I wished she were closer.

"Good. I have plans for our weekend, so bring some outdoor clothes."

"Outdoor clothes?"

"You know, stuff you can go outside in?"

"Yeah, thanks, genius. I understand what you're saying, but why?"

I laughed. "Because I want to show you something."

"But the things *I* want to see are indoors where clothes are optional."

I shook my head. She was the perfect balance between sweetness and joy, sexy and dirty. "I think we can do both."

I couldn't wait to prove it.

Beth

I woke from a dream about lemon curd, shortbread and poppy seeds. I reached for the switch on the side of my chair that tilted it back up to a sitting position and I grabbed my notebook from the pocket to my side. I scribbled down some notes, then peeked over my shoulder and out the window.

My stomach tumbled, and I grinned.

I'd never enjoyed landings, but now my excitement at being stateside was threatening to bubble over as I willed the plane to the ground as fast as possible. I'd never been so enthusiastic to go back to the place I grew up.

Since my last trip to Chicago I'd returned to London, barely dating someone, and yet, here I was, going back to Chicago to see my *boyfriend*.

I'd resisted his numerous attempts to get me to stay with him. Moving quickly was one thing, but I wanted a life jacket to cling on to as I got swept down the river.

With Louis I'd moved in with him after our third date, and I'd become completely dependent very quickly. I was a different person now, but I wanted to make sure I didn't fall into old patterns. Dylan and I could spend time together without me being a guest in his house.

Haven and I had gone shopping for a suitable dress for Friday's gala, and we'd picked something that I thought Dylan would like. I was pretty sure he'd be okay with anything I chose, but as he'd told me I had the best ass in the universe, I wanted to make sure I had a dress that showed it off.

As soon as we were landed, I scrambled off the plane, texting Dylan on the way to immigration.

Beth: I just landed. See you later.

Dylan: I have the live arrivals board for O'Hare open on my laptop. I'm sorry I'm not there to meet you.

Beth: Make it up to me later.

I'd rather he finished his work so we could have the whole evening together than stop to collect me, then have to go back to the office. Once I was with him, I knew I wouldn't want to let him go.

Dylan: It will be my pleasure.

An image of him licking my breast flashed into my mind.

Beth: I was hoping it would be mine.

Dylan: I'll make sure it is.

It was a promise I knew he could deliver on.

At check-in, I was greeted by name. Clearly, I was spending far too much time here.

"You're in 1204 again, Miss Harrison. Roger will take your bags up for you."

"Thank you. I'm fine to take my own." As much as I didn't want Roger missing out on a tip, I didn't want to have to wait on my suitcase.

I headed to the elevator and pressed the up button, glancing across at the bar where Dylan and I had sat when we were last here.

I squinted, and he came into view. He was here? He grinned, slid off his stool and walked toward me.

I breathed in the sight of his strong jaw and wide shoulders wrapped up in a beautiful navy suit that brought out his indigo eyes.

He circled his arms around my waist, pulling me toward him and kissing my forehead. "Are you eye-fucking me?" he asked.

I tilted my head as if considering my answer. "I really think I am."

He chuckled and kissed me again on the forehead before reaching for the elevator button.

"What are you doing here?"

"I'm sorry I didn't meet you at the airport. I had a call, but got here as soon as I could."

"I wasn't expecting you until much later. My other lover is about to arrive."

He shook his head as he pulled me into the elevator car. "Don't joke about shit like that. It makes me restless."

"Would it make a difference if I told you my other lover's a woman?"

He growled and pushed me against the glass wall of the elevator, slamming his tongue against mine, plowing deep and hard. My hands slid into his hair as I tried to stop from collapsing. Lust overtook me. I liked him, and I enjoyed our phone calls, but seeing him was different. Seeing him made my breath short and panties damp. I wanted to press my fingers against every part of his body in the hope that it would soothe my need for him.

"I'm so pleased you're here," I said as he kissed down my neck. "I told myself that I could wait until tonight, but I think I would have turned up at your office, naked beneath a coat."

He pulled back to look at me. "I should have waited."

The elevator doors pinged open and we scrambled out. "I need a shower. I'm airplane grubby."

He bent his head to my neck as I fiddled with the key card in the lock. "A shower sounds good."

I grabbed some additional pillows from the top shelf in the dressing room, pulled back the bedcovers and started to build a pillow wall down the middle of the bed.

Dylan wandered back into the bedroom, a towel around his waist, eating an apple. "I brought the menu. We should eat. What are you doing?"

"Yes, we should eat. Good idea."

I pushed a pillow down to the foot of the bed. The wall should probably be two pillows high.

"Seriously, what's with the pillows?" He grabbed the belt of my robe and pulled me toward him. We'd made it to the shower, then the sofa, then eventually back to the shower.

"I'm building a pillow wall. I need to sleep tonight, and won't if we're lying naked next to each other."

He sighed. "I can sleep at home. It's fine and you're right, as much as I'd like to keep you up all night, you've got to make whole sentences in front of a camera tomorrow. It's best if you get more than thirty minutes of rest."

I tried to peel his hands from around my waist, but he wasn't budging. "But before we make it into the bed, anything goes, right?"

I grabbed the discarded menu. "What shall we eat?"

He leaned into my ear. "How about I eat you?"

"You did that already." I smacked his hand. "Good job by the way." He chuckled. "I think I'll have the pasta. Shall I order you the steak?"

He cocked his head and smiled. "Yeah, that would be great."

I placed the order and Dylan pulled me into the living room and onto his lap, facing the view of the river.

"I have to be up at six tomorrow. The car is coming for me at seven."

"Friday has turned into a bit of a nightmare for me. I have meetings all day. I'm sorry."

I leaned into his chest, savoring the feel of his skin against my cheek. "I'd planned to go and see my dad, then I'll have to get ready for the gala. It's fine."

"We'll have all day Saturday and Sunday together."

I was concentrating on the vibrations in his chest as he spoke, so I didn't register what he'd said at first. "Oh no, not Saturday. Didn't I tell you? They've decided to show the first segment this Saturday, so I have to go into the studio for an interview, then meet with their publicity team. I think I'm going to be there most of the day."

He took a deep breath and I sat forward so I could see his face. "Are you mad?"

He smiled. "Of course not. I just want to spend time with you."

"Sunday, though. And I brought outdoor clothes."

The door buzzed and I scampered off his lap. The sounds of the television filled the space behind me.

"Beth," he called as I was answering the door.

"What?" I screamed when I saw my face on TV. "What's that?"

I looked up at Dylan but he was staring at the screen. "That's you."

I sank to the sofa before my knees gave way. "Christ on a bike. What the hell am I doing on television?"

"Bake with Beth" scrolled across the screen, and then I was gone.

"Excuse me, can I get a signature?" a voice from behind me asked.

I couldn't move. Dylan must have dealt with it as when I finally stood, the waiter had gone.

"Did you see that?" I asked.

Dylan nodded, his eyebrows raised. "Did you do publicity shots already?"

"I had some taken in London. I didn't think, didn't realize . . . I just didn't expect this." I couldn't believe they were advertising *my* show. Or my slot on someone else's show.

"You didn't expect to be on television, even though you have a baking segment on *television*."

"Well, when you say it like that it makes me feel stupid."

Dylan chuckled. "You're not stupid. But perhaps you're not quite prepared."

"I'm thinking you might be right. I've been concentrating on getting the recipes right, and making sure I've rehearsed. I guess I didn't think about broadcasting into peoples' homes."

The more time that passed, the more it felt like I was leading some kind of double life. In one, I lived in London, dreaming up recipes and having my nieces spit up on me. In the other, I was in Chicago, on television, and had a boyfriend who looked like a Greek god and ordered me dessert whenever I wanted it.

I was living the best of both worlds but needed to mesh them together if I was going to be able to hold on to both of them.

chapter
TWELVE

Dylan

I glanced at the clock, again. This meeting had been dragging on far too long, and we were due to be at the gala in an hour and a half.

"Ultimately, if you're not on board with this, then I'll find someone who is," I interrupted the guy telling me again why my integration plan wasn't going to work. "We're due to take ownership of Redux in less than two weeks so if you want out, let me know now."

"It's not that. I just want—"

"Let's reconvene next week. Email me over the weekend with your decision. I don't want to spend any more time debating this."

I stood and strode out of the meeting room, and didn't stop even for Marie. She'd expected me to catch up on my phone messages and emails, but that shit would have to wait. I'd not seen Beth properly all day, and I wanted to squeeze out every last drop of time together.

I took the elevator to my waiting town car and hit dial as I got in.

"I've just got into the car; I should be with you shortly," I said as soon as she answered.

"I told you I'd be happy to meet you there. I know how busy you are."

"Well, I need to change into my tux—"

"Which Marie could have had Don collect."

I'd brought my things to the hotel yesterday so I wouldn't have to go home. I still wasn't quite sure why Beth wouldn't stay with me, particularly when I was effectively staying with her. It wasn't as if we were getting any space from each other. We'd slipped into coupledom—working during the day, racing home to get naked in the evening. We'd not even made it out for dinner yet. But tonight was different.

"And anyway, I want to take you to this gala. This is our first date, and I'm not meeting you there. I just pulled up to the hotel. I'll see you in a few."

I raced up to the twelfth floor and used the key Beth had given me. As the door sprang open, my breath caught in my throat as I came face-to-face with the most beautiful woman I'd ever seen. She stood looking out of the window, her back bare and red velvet flaring out from her tiny waist. I'd never seen her hair up—it felt so good trailing against my skin that I couldn't ever have imagined wanting to see it up—but now, it gave me a better view of her perfect skin and that delicious neck. "You're a goddess."

She smiled at me over her shoulder. "And you have perfect timing. Can you help me with this necklace?"

I wasn't sure if, once I started, I'd be able to stop touching her.

I let the door slam closed as I strode toward her, my cock tightening with every step. Sliding my hands around her waist and dipping my head into her neck, I took a deep breath. "You smell like cinnamon."

She laughed. "That's your imagination."

I took her necklace and fastened the clasp, my hands smoothing down her neck to her waist, then pulled her back against me.

"We don't need to be there by six thirty. In fact, we don't need to go at all."

She tilted her head so it rested against my chest. "We do need to be there by six thirty, but we don't have stay too late. How about that?" She pushed her perfect ass against my now rock-hard cock and I groaned.

"Are you sure I can't convince you to ditch the whole thing?"

"I'm sure. I think a man as successful as you can control his penis for a couple of hours. I Googled you today. Apparently, you're quite the eligible bachelor about town."

I chuckled. "You Googled me? You didn't think about doing that before we had sex the first time?"

She slid her hands over mine. "Apparently I liked your tight ass too much to be bothered by what Google had to say."

"My tight ass likes you back." I kissed her neck. "Right, if you insist on going to this dumb gala, I'm going to grab a shower."

She swiveled around in my arms. "Do me a favor?"

"Anything." I traced the swell of her breasts with my thumb, desperate to taste her. I wasn't going to be able to keep my hands to myself this evening.

"Keep this," she said, scratching her nails over my five o'clock shadow. "I like it against my skin."

I groaned. "You're killing me."

"But it's such delicious torture." She grinned.

Less than an hour later, we were pulling up outside the Drake Hotel. I ignored the flashes of the cameras as I stepped out of the car and rounded the trunk to open the door for Beth.

She looked confused at the attention, but I held out a hand. "Why are there photographers here?"

"Publicity for the charity," I explained.

I put an arm around her waist and pulled her toward me.

"Mr. James, who's your date tonight?" one of the photographers yelled. Beth looked up at me and I grinned at her, leaning toward her and placing a small kiss on her pouting mouth. The flashes of the cameras intensified.

"This is Beth Harrison. Baking goddess and my girlfriend," I replied to the photographer.

"Can we get inside?" she whispered through her smile.

I chuckled.

"As in *Baking with Beth* on *A Chicago Saturday*?" another photographer asked. "The trailers have just started to air."

"Apparently, it should be me Googling you." I squeezed her again and led her inside.

"My show hasn't even gone out and frankly, given the disastrous day yesterday, it probably never will."

"My sweet, it wasn't disastrous. It was television." Now was a perfect moment to confess that Raf and I owned Raine Media and WCIL TV, but I didn't want to complicate anything. Our ownership didn't and wouldn't impact her in any way. We didn't get involved with commissioning the programming in any detail. We just approved policy and strategy decisions. I didn't have time or the inclination to explain that all to her. I'd do it before she left to go back to London.

As we entered the hotel, we were immediately offered champagne. Out of habit, I reached to accept a glass on Beth's behalf before realizing what I was doing, and I set the glass back down.

"You can drink, Dylan. It doesn't bother me."

"No, sorry, I never drink on occasions like this. I was getting a glass for you but then—"

"If you don't drink at events like this then there's something wrong with you. I imagine it would be much more fun." She scanned the lobby, her head tilted toward the candelabra. "I wonder if I could make a cake that pretty."

"I think you could do whatever you set your mind to." I dipped my head and kissed her on the cheek.

I spotted Raf coming toward us. He glanced to my left and his eyes widened. I saw the word *fuck* form on his lips. I grinned. Yeah, she had that effect on me, too.

"How did you get so lucky?" He shook my hand and slapped me on the back before taking a step back and raising Beth's hand to his lips.

He kissed her knuckles. "It's a complete pleasure to meet you," he said.

"Really?" I interrupted. "Are you kidding me? Do women fall for that—the kissing the hand stuff?" I looked at Beth and she just smiled. She wasn't falling for it.

"Well, given you're still a virgin, I'm guessing it works better than whatever it is that you do."

"I'm guessing you're Raf," Beth said before I could punch him.

"And you're the mystery woman I've heard nothing about until this week. How did you two kids meet?"

"We were sitting next to each other on the plane on the way to London a few weeks ago," Beth replied. "All the cabin crew were excited about him; I couldn't see what the fuss was about. He was so serious and moody." She looked up and grinned at me.

I shook my head. I was confident she'd been interested since we'd locked eyes that first time.

"He is desperately moody, that's for sure, though less so the last few weeks. We should put you on the payroll. I like him better since he met you. Do you live in Chicago?"

"I grew up here and my father's here but I live in London now. I might be spending a bit more time back here though."

"Do you know what table we're at?" I asked, interrupting the natural course of their exchange. Beth was a sentence away from saying she was here to film for WCIL TV and neither Raf nor Beth knew about the connection. I needed to be the one that filled them in.

Raf peeled his eyes away from Beth. "Table one, I hope. We're paying for this thing."

"Come on, let's go." I walked us in the direction of the entrance to the Gold Coast Room.

"Does he irritate you?" she asked.

"Of course." I opened the door and gestured for Beth to go in. "He's irritating."

We were the first ones into the room, as dinner was yet to be called.

"I like him. He knows how to handle you."

I laughed and stopped, pulling her toward me. "You think? I think *you* know how to handle me."

"How so?" She looked at me, sweeping her fingers across my jaw.

I shrugged. "I'm not sure. I'm more me when I'm with you." My heart tripped under my shirt. I felt so comfortable around her. There weren't many people in my life with whom I could just kick back and relax. Most new people I met liked my money or my connections a little too much. In her own words, Beth had been attracted to my tight ass. The fact that we'd started with the physical somehow meant we had started out equals in our relationship. She hadn't expected more from me, and that gave me room to relax and be myself.

"That's one of the nicest things anyone has ever said to me. I really like the *you* that you are when you're with me."

Could she feel the thud of my heart as I held her? It was as if my love for her were knocking, trying to get out.

I loved her.

I wanted her to know. No one had ever made me feel as good as she did.

"Beth . . ." I needed her to understand what she did to me, how different she was to any other woman I'd ever met.

"It's beautiful," she said, glancing up at the ceiling.

"You're beautiful."

She looked back at me and smiled. "This being out in public thing is overrated."

"Now you agree." I sighed.

"When's your speech?"

"After the entree. We can leave then, right?"

Before she got a chance to agree, someone tapped me on the shoulder. I was irritated at the interruption and would have ignored it had Beth not nodded in the direction of the intruder.

Without loosening my grip, I turned to see who was ruining this moment I was having with Beth, and came face-to-face with the last woman who'd had any kind of hold over me.

Alicia.

Beth

"What are you doing here?" Dylan snapped at the woman who had just approached us.

I was used to him being surly and gruff but never angry.

"Well, that's not the way to greet the love of your life," the redhead replied.

"God forbid." Dylan's arms pulled me closer. "What are you doing here?"

"I'm here to catch up with old friends," she said, turning to me. "And make new ones. I'm Alicia Munroe, and once upon a time I was engaged to the man you're clinging to." She smiled at me as if she'd complimented me.

"You poor girl, you must feel so silly to have let him go," I replied, my smile equally big. I turned back to Dylan. "I won't be making the same mistake." I should have taken the high road, but something about her trying to claim him created a red mist in me. Dylan was a good man who hadn't deserved to be traded in for a richer model.

His grin was wicked as his hands rounded my ass.

"I wanted to follow up on our lunch date," Alicia said, her focus on Dylan now. He didn't look at her. Instead he tried to kiss me but I leaned away. What the fuck was this about a lunch date? My stomach twisted.

"There is no lunch date. I hung up on you, if you remember. Can you leave us please? I've got a hard-on and you're ruining it."

She rolled her eyes at Dylan, and I wondered how they could have ever been together. They both seemed so different. "I'll call you." She headed out through a flurry of guests.

I slid my arms around his neck. "So that was Alicia, huh?"

He grinned. "You're quite the force to be reckoned with."

"Don't you forget it." I tapped his nose with my finger. "Talk to me about her inviting you to lunch. Does that happen a lot?"

He frowned. "Never. It was just that time I told you about. No, wait, she'd emailed me just a week or so before that. I'd forgotten about it until she called me. Before that I hadn't heard from her since she called off the wedding."

I pulled out of his arms and tried to steer us to our seats as the room filled with people and noise. But he grabbed me by the waist and pulled me into him, keeping our bodies tight against each other as we headed to our table. "Did you give any thought to what I said? Maybe she wants to apologize. Meeting her might give you closure."

"I don't know what closure is, but I'm sure I don't need anything from her."

Louis had always been in constant contact with various ex-girlfriends, which he'd used as a tool to make me jealous. When I turned up at his hotel to tell him I was pregnant, the girlfriend he'd had before me was just leaving. I tried to tell myself that they were just friends, but he'd clearly still been fucking her. Looking back, I didn't understand how I allowed myself not to see it. I suppose the thought of losing him completely after the death of my mother had been too much to bear.

But I was a different person now. Dylan had given me no reason to doubt him, and the fact was that he obviously still had so much resentment toward Alicia; maybe he should meet her so he could put the past in the past and move on—with me.

"Hey." He squeezed my knee under our table. "I'm not lying to you. We're not in contact, and I'm not interested in anything that she has to say. I got over her a long time ago."

"I think you should consider hearing her out. Maybe you're not as over her as you think you are." I didn't want our relationship to be in any way a reaction to what Alicia had done to him.

"Look at me," he growled and I turned to face him. "I'm with you. She had her chance."

"All I'm saying is think about it. Just promise to tell me if she gets in contact, or you decide to see her."

He needed to know that transparency was important to me. It was at the core of my sobriety. I demanded honesty from myself and I needed it from the people in my life.

"I'm not going to see her again, and I don't want to talk about this anymore."

"Okay, but I want to be clear about my expectations. I need openness from you. Don't hide stuff. If you decide you want to meet her, that's fine. Just tell me."

I watched his chest rise as he took in a breath. "Okay, but I don't want to meet her."

"Just think about it." I smiled tightly at him.

"Are we okay?" he asked. I clearly wasn't good at faking my smile.

"We're more than okay. I'm crazy about you, and I don't want either of us fucking this up."

He grinned. "I'm crazy about you, and I really want to make you happy."

He looked sincere, vulnerable and so damn sexy. I smoothed his hair away from his face.

I was falling for Mr. 8A.

Our table filled up and Dylan introduced me to various people. Raf and Dylan's business was quite the supporter of the charity at the center of the evening's gala. I hadn't realized that they would be such a focal point of the evening. When the speeches started, it became clear that the charity was a mental health organisation. It wasn't the most obvious cause and that Dylan had chosen to support them added a depth to my understanding of him.

"I just need to thank some people." Dylan dipped his head and kissed me on the cheek as he stood up and made his way to the stage.

He looked so handsome in his black tie, his hair swept back from his beautiful face. I couldn't quite believe he was mine.

I was so focused on the fit of his tux and the sparkle in his eye that I wasn't focused on what he was saying until I heard the words "my experience with depression."

"I couldn't remember a point in my childhood that wasn't marred by the debilitating disease that is depression. My mother's illness began when I was born. As a result, I remember her being only a peripheral character while I was growing up." Dylan stared out into the crowd as he spoke, his eyes searching for something. I wanted to rush up on stage just to hold his hand, to let him know that I was here for him. "It was my dad who took my brother and I to school, cooked us dinner, taught us how to ride a bike and checked our homework. I have no memories of my mother doing normal, motherly things. I don't remember her smile, her laugh. All I remember is her being in bed and being told she was sick. I spent nights worried that she would die, that my dad, my brother and I would catch whatever she had and get sick too."

Tears formed at the corners of my eyes. How had I not known just how incredible this person in front of me was? The idea that this man, who was so in control, so considerate and confident, was once a vulnerable boy who just wanted a normal life was almost too much to bear. It was easy to assume that Dylan's life had always been as charmed as it was now, but it clearly had been anything but. I wanted to take away his pain and make him happy. I had an urge to comfort and soothe him. How could I have not known this?

His voice was calm and steady, but I could tell by the way his hands fisted by his sides that what he was telling the room wasn't an easy confession.

"When I left home for college I found this incredible charity, which we are here tonight to support. They educated first me, and then my father, on my mother's condition, and they paid for my mother's medication and her therapy. Eventually I got the mother I should have had twenty years earlier, and my father got back the wife he married. Tonight, with your generous donations, we've made it possible to give countless people back their families. Thank you."

My forehead was tight with sorrow; as he returned to the table I tried to hold back my tears for him.

He'd never mentioned his parents before. My stomach dipped, and I felt as if I hadn't had enough time with him. I wanted to know everything about him. In some ways, it felt as if we'd known each other forever. I didn't think I'd experienced real intimacy before Dylan, and his speech was evidence that there was so much more to know.

As he sat down, I grabbed his hand under the table and ran my thumb across his wrist. "I think you're very special," I whispered into his ear.

He smiled tightly, keeping his eyes facing forward.

"I meant what I said to Alicia. I'm not going to let you go. I was actually thinking of extending my trip."

He turned toward me and raised his eyebrows. "Because of my speech?"

"For of a lot of reasons. You're probably busy, but while you're at work perhaps you'd lend me your kitchen for an afternoon?"

"Will you promise to greet me at the door in nothing but an apron and high heels?"

I laughed, pleased he could still make me happy as well as sad. "How long have you held that image in your head?"

His grin spread wide across his face. "A while."

"Well, you'll have to tell me every one of your fantasies and we'll see which ones we can make come true." I winked at him.

"You're all I need," he whispered. My heart expanded in my chest as I reached up to kiss his cheek. He had other ideas and explored my mouth urgently, as if we were at home without an entire ballroom watching us.

The next evening, I woke in Dylan's arms as he carried me up the steps to his brownstone. I'd agreed to spend Saturday night at his place, and Don had picked me up from the studio. I'd been up since four, and we hadn't slept much after the gala. With the run-in with Alicia and getting to know about Dylan's mother, I hadn't wanted to a miss a moment with him. I was clearly paying for it now.

"You can sleep, my sweet."

"I want to talk to you."

He kissed the top of my head, setting me down on a softer-than-air sofa.

"This is comfy."

He chuckled. "Can I get you a drink?"

"Some water would be good."

I combed my fingers through my hair and sat up, taking in my surroundings. The room had a bright, almost beachy feel. A dark wood table sat in front of the squishy sofa and another, higher table was placed over by one of the long, shuttered windows. A collection of photographs adorned the surface, and as much as I wanted to go and investigate, my legs didn't share my enthusiasm. The walls were decorated with black and white photographs of scenes of what looked like Cuba.

"I like your place," I said as Dylan came in carrying a tray.

"I'll show you around later," he said, setting down the tray. "Are you sure you don't want to go straight to sleep? You've had a long day."

I shook my head. "Oh my. You are the perfect man, aren't you?" Along with my drink, he'd brought in a slice of chocolate cake.

He pecked me on the lips, but before he could pull away, I grabbed his collar and pulled him over me. He groaned and kissed me properly, pushing his tongue against mine, as if he were looking for a deeper connection.

He pulled back, leaving me panting, and handed me a glass.

"Thank you. And cake? You're spoiling me."

Dylan grinned as he rearranged himself and pulled me

into him. "I watched your slot and your interview. You were amazing."

My face heated. "I wasn't amazing, but it was fun. I enjoyed myself."

"You were amazing. I imagine most of the male population of Illinois had their right hand down their pants while they were watching, so I'm not sure how many of your viewers you'll convert to baking."

I slapped him on the arm. "It was only a teeny segment."

"Yeah, but they were running trailers all morning, and they interviewed you live. You were the focus of the whole show. I recorded it; we can watch it if you like." He reached for the remote control but I grabbed his hand.

"No. Please. I'll die of embarrassment." I curled up against him.

"Later then."

"Maybe never," I mumbled.

He wrapped his arms around me and pulled me closer. "You can't pretend it didn't happen. It's exciting—like the stuff you do on YouTube, just bigger and with more people watching."

"I guess. But I don't want to think about any of that now. I just want to be here, with you."

My phone rang and Dylan went to collect my purse, though I didn't ask him to. It was such a small thing, but it made me feel like we were a team—he was looking after me, and I wanted to look after him. This was what it should be about, shouldn't it?

"It's Jake. Do you mind if I answer it?" I asked.

"Of course not. Shall I leave you to it?" He went to stand, but I pulled him back. His question was a reminder that we were still feeling out the edges of what our relationship looked like. Did I like privacy when I spoke to my brother? Did he like to shower in the mornings?

"Don't go."

He smiled and leaned back again.

"Hey," I answered my phone.

"How did it go? I've checked YouTube, but I couldn't find a clip," Jake said.

"It was good. I can send you the digital file. They said they'll send it through. Are you at work?"

"Yeah, are you back at the hotel?"

"Um, no. I'm staying with Dylan tonight." I stroked my hand over his thigh. I'd mentioned to Jake that I was seeing someone just before I'd left for Chicago.

"You are? If it's serious, I'm going to need to meet this guy. I hope he's looking after you."

I looked up at Dylan. "Yeah, it is for me, at least. He just brought me lemonade and cake."

Dylan slid his hand under mine and wound our fingers together. There was heat between us, as always, but this felt . . . more.

"Sounds like he knows how to get on your good side. Look, I'll leave you to it, but I'm serious. I want to meet him."

I laughed. "We'll see. You need to trust me. It's different now. I make better life choices."

"I know. I just worry." Jake had earned his right to worry about me. And Dylan had said that he wanted to meet him.

"Don't. I'm good. Send my love to everyone."

I ended the call and slung my phone on the table.

"He's worried about you?" Dylan asked.

"Always. I think there's lots of change in my life at the moment, and that makes me vulnerable."

He smoothed his hands up my arms. "Is it too much between us?"

I turned and traced his stubbly jaw with my fingers. "No. Is it for you? Are we going too fast?"

"Maybe on paper."

My stomach churned at his admission. I hadn't wanted that to be his answer.

"But it feels right," he continued. "In my heart, even in my head, it all makes sense. But I can understand why your brother might be concerned. What did he say?"

"He said that you clearly knew how to get on my good side." Should I tell him that Jake wanted to meet him? I didn't want unnecessary pressure on either of us.

"And?"

"And, you know, all the normal stuff?"

"No, I don't know. My brother's in the Navy. He has been married since he was twenty-two. I don't have sisters. So I don't know what brothers with sisters are like."

"Shit, your brother's in the Navy?"

He chuckled. "Are you wondering if you got the wrong James?"

I tutted. "Of course not. It's just that when you say stuff like that, I realize how much I need to know about you. I can hardly introduce you to my brother when I don't even know that your brother is in the Navy."

"I'm meeting your brother?"

I covered my face with my hands. "No. I didn't mean—"

"In your phone call, he said he wanted to meet me?"

I stayed silent, hoping I might disappear if I didn't respond.

"Beth, you know I can see you even if you're covering your face so you can't see me, right?"

I burst out laughing and dropped my hands into my lap. "Okay, you win. Yes, he said he wanted to meet you."

"Okay, good. I'll come over when we take ownership of Redux in two weeks. We can do it then."

"Just like that? You don't think it's too much too soon? I don't want us to burn out."

"Yeah, I said I wanted to. Why is it such a big deal? I'm not telling him you're knocked up."

I stretched to kiss his jaw. "Okay then."

How had Dylan gone from incredible sex and a tight ass to the guy who was flying to London to meet my family?

My stomach fluttered. Everything was just too perfect.

chapter THIRTEEN

Dylan

I'd told Beth that she didn't need to meet me at the airport, but now that I'd landed, I was delighted she'd told me that she was ignoring me and would be waiting for me.

As soon as I passed customs, I craned my neck to try to spot her in the crowd. Her beautiful smile and her plump red lips came into view first. Her grin was wide and she held her hands up high, as if she were a ring girl at a boxing match, except her sign read "Mr. 8A."

She was on the other side of a waist-high metal barrier, but that didn't stop me from leaning across and pressing my lips to hers. Her hands slipped around my neck and I let go of my suitcase so I could run my hands across her back. She smelled like lemons. I'd missed her. It had been sixteen days since I'd last seen her.

I rounded my hands around her ass and pulled her over the barrier. She clamped her legs around my waist. I wanted to be in private, to slide my tongue over her soft, pliable skin.

I dipped my lips over hers and she moaned. There was going to be a lot more of that very soon.

Blindly, I reached for my case and began to walk us forward. She pulled back from our kiss. "Hey. It's good to see you."

I chuckled. "The feeling is mutual."

She squeezed her arms and legs tighter. "Shall I get down?" I didn't want her to, but I knew we'd get to our destination quicker if she did. "Stop a minute, Dylan."

I let her down to the floor, bending to kiss the beauty spot on her cheekbone.

"I have a confession," she announced. "I'm not sure you're going to like it—I don't like it."

My gut twisted. Had she hooked up with someone? I tried not to give away my concern. Instead, I took her hand in mine and brought her knuckles to my lips. "Tell me." She was a beautiful girl; no doubt she was being hit on all the time.

"Sunday night dinner has kind of moved to Saturday night dinner, which means we have to go straight to my brother's from here." She screwed up her face as if she was waiting for me to lose it.

"Okay," I replied, relieved it wasn't something more serious, thankful there had been no one else. It was as if I was waiting for something to go wrong because everything was so right.

"Okay? That's okay with you?" She raised her eyebrows. "Because it's not with me. I want to get naked, like now."

I chuckled. "Yeah, me too. But look at it this way, unless

your brother kills me, we can stay in bed for the whole day tomorrow."

"Who's going to get me off, if you've been murdered? This is why we needed to get naked *before* you meet Jake."

I glanced at her. "You think you're cute, don't you?"

She cocked her shoulder. "Yes. And you agree with me."

I put my arm around her neck, pulling her toward me and kissing the top of her head as we headed toward the car.

"How come you organized a car?" she asked as we approached a man with my name on a sign. "I was going to take you on the train."

"The train?"

"Yes. Are you so spoiled that you can't take the Heathrow express?"

"Spoiled? Maybe I just wanted you to myself."

"I think you need to see how the rest of London travels. Come on." She grabbed my hand and started pulling me away from the car.

"I'm sorry," I said to the driver. "I'm not going to need you, just charge my account all the same." Beth pulled me toward a sign that said Trains. There weren't many women who could persuade me onto public transport.

As we stood on the edge of the platform, Beth's hand in mine, I wanted to ask her a thousand questions about her brother. I knew she was close to him, so it was important that I made a good impression. "Are you nervous about me meeting your brother?"

She glanced at me and moved closer so her body was pressed up against mine. "A little."

"Because you don't trust your judgment yet?"

I could almost see the filter in her brain start to organize her words. She didn't want to hurt me. She knew she was one of the only women who ever could.

"You can be honest, Beth."

She smiled and the train interrupted us. We climbed on board, stowing my luggage and finding a pair of seats. As we sat, she flung both her legs over my knee and brought my hand to her lap. I stroked her stocking-covered legs, wishing we were going to be alone soon.

"I didn't realize that that's what I was nervous about, but I think you're right. It's just that Jake has been part of my world, part of my sobriety, for so long that sometimes I forget that I'm separate from him. I've depended on him for so much. It's like the baking. That's something for me, and if it's a success then that's all on me. It's good, but scary. With you, you're my choice, too. I'm not used to making so many choices that don't involve my brother. So I guess I just want him to think I've done well. Especially because I'm invested."

I lifted her hand and kissed her knuckles, but didn't say anything. I wanted her to tell me how she was feeling.

She leaned back onto the window and stared at her lap. "I didn't expect it to be like this between us. It feels so good between us, as if it's . . ." *It. Forever.* I wanted her to finish the sentence. I wanted her to feel the same way I did.

She shrugged. "I don't know. I just want him to like you. It's important." She smiled at me. "But no pressure."

There was a lot of pressure. Because I'd not spent time with Jake and Beth together, I wasn't quite sure of the hold he had over her. If he didn't like me, what would this mean for us? She said she was invested, but I wasn't convinced that we'd survive if Jake and I didn't hit it off.

Sweat beaded at my brow. Fuck, I could have done with a night alone with Beth before this introduction. She calmed me, made me realize what was important. I needed that. Work was increasingly stressful. The Redux deal was a huge challenge, particularly as Raf and I were so far away. Almost all the projects we'd been involved with were domestic. Managing a company in another country was proving to be a challenge. On top of everything, I didn't want to fuck things up with Beth. Businesses could be rebuilt, but time and experience had told me women like Beth came along once in a lifetime. I didn't want what was happening at work to impact my introduction to Jake.

"So tell me about him. Does he like sports?" Would I have anything in common with this guy?

My phone rang. Damn, I should have turned it to silent when I switched it back on. I reached into my pocket for my cell and cancelled the call.

Alicia had been calling on and off since the gala. I'd not answered any of her calls. I kept meaning to work out how to block her, but hadn't quite managed it. I didn't want to keep anything from Beth, now just wasn't the right moment.

"You can take it."

"It wasn't anything important." My stomach churned. I should probably tell her that it had been Alicia. But I didn't want to spoil our moment together or have another discussion about my ex just as we were arriving to meet her family. If the situation upset Beth, I didn't want those feelings written all over her face when I met Jake for the first time.

There was a loud crash from behind the door as soon as Beth pressed the doorbell to her brother's house.

"They've probably just dropped the baby on her head. No biggie."

I chuckled.

A beautiful blonde woman answered the door wearing a fantastically wide grin. She glanced at me, pulled Beth into her arms, and squealed. "So glad you're here. Jake's just dropped a bottle of wine."

"Dylan, this is Haven."

"You're just as hot as Beth described," Haven replied and pulled me into a hug. I didn't quite know how to respond, so just hugged her back.

"Get your hands off him." Beth pushed us apart.

"Nice to meet you, Haven," I said.

"And you, Dylan. Come inside. Don't be put off by the stocks and rack we have set up back here. It won't hurt as much as you think it will."

I glanced at Beth but she was laughing nearly as hard as Haven. So this *was* going to be an interrogation. Something a good night's sleep and some naked time with Beth would have made more bearable.

We turned left into a huge open-plan living space running the length of the house. It would have been nice if it hadn't looked like they'd been robbed. Jesus, there was baby stuff everywhere.

Two guys stood in the kitchen. I recognized Jake from the airport but if I'd not seen him before, I would have known he was Beth's brother because of his reaction.

He strode toward me and held out his hand. "Dylan. Thanks for coming."

As we shook it felt as if we were locking horns. He made it clear that I needed to prove I was good enough.

I nodded. "Thanks for inviting me." We looked each other in the eye in a way that was almost primal. He was sizing me up, trying to get the measure of me. But his expression was as blank as I knew mine was. Business had made me the ultimate poker player, and I knew better than to let my nerves show.

"I'm not sure you're going to be saying that in a couple of hours." A process of elimination told me it was Ash who provided the warning and welcome interruption. She walked over, a baby on her hip, and kissed me on both cheeks. "Ignore Jake, his bark is worse than his bite. This is Maggie." She lifted up the baby's hand and made her wave.

I chuckled, the muscles in my neck loosening after my introduction to Jake. She was a cute kid. "Hi, Maggie. Nice to meet you, and you, Ash."

"Beer?" Luke asked, lifting Maggie from Ash. He offered me his hand. "I'm Luke."

"Good to meet you."

I would have been less nervous if we were all out at a late supper, in public, where at least I knew what to expect from my surroundings. I didn't see my brother often, and we were totally different kinds of people. We saw each other when we collided at our parents' house, not because we wanted to spend time together, but these guys seemed to genuinely like each other.

"Did you want that beer?" Luke asked again.

I glanced at Beth. Did they drink around her? She wasn't looking at me so I turned back to Luke. "No, thanks. Can I get some water?"

Beth snaked her arm around my waist, instantly calming me. "You don't want a beer?"

I couldn't remember the last time I'd had a drink. I was pretty sure that I'd not had one since I'd met Beth. "No. I have to concentrate later."

Even though we hadn't been together long, when we were in each other's company, I felt as if I knew every part of her. She was so unguarded; she shared everything so freely with me. Being here with her and her family reminded me how much I still needed to know.

She smiled at me, her hand rounding my ass, bringing me back to why I was there. Why it was worth being with her. I couldn't think of anything I wouldn't do for her. I was going to nail this thing with her brother. By the end of the evening, he'd know I was as invested in our relationship as Beth. I'd make sure of it.

Beth

It was great seeing Dylan amongst my family, but my palms were still a little sweaty. My gaze kept flitting between Jake and Dylan. As much as I wanted Jake to like Dylan, to support my decision to be with him, I also wanted Dylan to like Jake. If the two of them got along, then our group of five could expand rather than fracture.

The testosterone was clearly flowing, but Haven and Ash helped lighten the mood and Luke made a real effort to make Dylan comfortable.

I'd never hidden anything from Dylan, but introducing him to my family made me feel closer to him, as if he was seeing the whole of me, right from the beginning. And that's what I wanted. I wanted to be as close to him as possible.

"Why don't you boys go play pool?" Haven suggested, pulling me toward the sofa under the window at the front of the house.

"Does that mean you want to talk about penises?" Luke asked. He didn't stop for an answer, just grabbed his beer and headed out.

Dylan looked at me. Was he worried about what we were going to say? He bent toward me and kissed me briefly on the lips. I wanted to grab him by the collar and mount him. It had been too long since I'd run my hands across his hard body and felt him between my thighs. He frowned and pulled away, following Jake and Luke.

I turned toward my friends. Ash's hand was covering her throat and Haven was grinning.

"He's so hot," Haven said, collapsing back onto the sofa.

She was right about that, I thought as I sat down next to her.

"And so into you," Ash added, sitting on the floor in front of us, holding baby Maggie out in front of her.

"You look so good together. He's *so* hot." Haven pulled me into a hug.

"It's so good to see him." I hadn't realized how much I'd missed him until I saw him at the airport.

"It's like the air buzzes around the two of you. You can *see* the chemistry." Ash grinned at me.

I laughed. "That's just because I haven't been laid in two weeks."

"It's more than that," Ash said.

It felt like more than that. Physical attraction was where it had started, and I couldn't imagine ever getting to a place I wasn't floored by his handsome face every time I looked at him, but it was his sweetness, his honesty, and his kindness that made me miss him. "I think so."

"Are you in love with him?" Haven asked.

A small voice inside my head had been telling me I was in love with Dylan for a while now, but I'd been ignoring it. It felt stupid to admit it. Scary. He was the first guy who I'd even *kissed* sober. It was almost as if I was declaring my love for my high school boyfriend. I didn't want people to think I was being naïve, and I didn't want to have gotten it wrong. Did I know him well enough to love him? Had I seen the real him or just what I wanted to see?

"We'll take that silence as a yes," Ash said.

"I think I am," I replied.

"Think?" Haven raised her eyebrows at me.

"It feels soon, and maybe I'm wrong. Maybe I'm just grateful that he's nice to me and has a great ass. I don't have an awful lot to compare him to."

We all laughed, which made Maggie laugh and so we all laughed again.

Ash grabbed my hand. "I don't think it's that. You are the best judge of character I know."

"You think I'm a good judge of character?" I asked. "What about Louis?"

"Everyone has bad ex-boyfriends. You lost your mother and were dealing with your alcoholism. You're not that same person. I've always known you as thoughtful and wise; you really see through any bullshit that people throw at you." Haven grabbed my hand and squeezed.

I was still getting used to the Beth that Haven knew. And I still had all the same memories of the old Beth, which kept holding me back.

Looking at the baby, I made my confession. "I've never felt this way about anyone. I think that it's the first time I've ever really been in love."

"I think that's just fantastic," Ash said.

Haven released my hand. "You deserve to be in love, and have someone love you back."

"Don't be ridiculous." I laughed. "He doesn't love me back. From his side, we're having some great sex and that's okay."

"Just because you're having great sex doesn't mean he can't love you." Haven prodded me in the thigh. "There's no way a guy meets a girl's family if he's not serious."

I bit back a grin. Dylan had shown no reticence about meeting Jake. Things weren't just sex between us, but I wasn't sure *what* it was as far as he was concerned.

"I swear to God, sex is going to be this little girl's first word," Ash said, grinning at Maggie.

"Should I ask where my niece is?"

Haven shrugged. "She's somewhere around here." The look of horror must have shown on my face because she said, "I'm kidding. She's napping."

"Back to the sex," Ash said. "He has the look in his eye I saw Jake wear the first time I met him."

Haven frowned. "You were drunk the first time you met Jake, and besides, he was with another woman."

"Okay, that's true. The second time I met him, then. It's the same look. That's all I'm saying."

My heart clenched. The thought that Dylan might love me was overwhelming. I needed to go find him. I wanted him to tell me if it was true or not. I should confess to him how I was feeling, how happy he made me, how I was, even now, dreading him going back to Chicago. Within weeks he'd become a huge part of my life.

"I need to take it slow," I said, mostly to myself, in an effort to try to calm the jittery vibrations skirting across my skin.

"Not like Ash's version of slow," Haven said.

Ash slapped her on the knee. "Hey, it worked out with me and your brother. It just took a little time." She turned to me. "I think you should go with what you feel, Beth. If it feels good to go fast, go fast. As long as you're sober and having fun. Isn't that the most important thing?"

"I'm not really used to having to remind myself to put my sobriety first. Do you know what I mean?"

The girls shook their heads.

"It's just, when I'm with Dylan, it's easy to forget I'm an alcoholic." I paused, trying to think how best to say it. "I'm not saying I've had the urge to drink, just that *not* drinking isn't my focus when I'm around him."

Haven nodded. "Well, that sounds like he's a man who might just deserve you."

"You think that's a good thing?" I asked. I was pretty sure that the way he shifted my focus had been one of the reasons I'd been ignoring that I was in love with Dylan. If he made me forget I was an alcoholic, would that mean I was more likely to drink?

"It's a great thing. You keep telling me that you want sobriety to be at the center of your life and not alcoholism."

I nodded. That was true. Being with Dylan didn't make me want to drink. It made me forget to think about drinking in the first place.

Ash tilted her head and smiled. "I told you you were next."

Perhaps Ash had been right. Maybe it was my time to find my Prince Charming.

A piercing screech of a smoke alarm bled through our conversation and Haven leapt to her feet. "Shit. So much for Sophia's nap." She grabbed a broom and poked at the alarm.

The door started to open. "Okay, stop talking penises, we're coming in," Luke shouted just as the alarm stopped.

The boys filed in, laughing and chatting as if they'd all been friends for years. Dylan's gaze immediately found me. It was so good to have him here. I just hoped he felt the same.

About everything.

We finally took our seats around the table, everyone making room to ensure that Dylan and I sat next to each other. Dinner was Jake's responsibility, which normally meant we got some kind of stew, but today we had lamb tagine.

"So you all have dinner together every week?" Dylan asked as he passed his plate to Jake, who was dishing up food.

"Most weeks. We live just around the corner, and Beth's not far away," Ash said.

"And you three have known each other since—"

"Forever," Luke interrupted.

Dylan kissed me on the temple. I was surprised at how demonstrative he was. I reached across his lap and he grabbed my hand, clasping his fingers through mine.

As I looked back at the table, I locked eyes with Haven.

"When you boys were off playing pool, we told Beth how together you two look," Haven said to Dylan.

He nodded. "I guess that's how it feels, for me at least."

I squeezed his hand and smiled up at him.

"So, you're serious about her?" Jake asked.

"Jake. No," I said.

Dylan kissed my head again. "It's okay, Beth." He looked toward Jake. "Yes, I'm serious about your sister. It didn't start out that way. To be honest, it's taken me a little by surprise, but in my experience, sometimes the best things in life are the ones you least expect."

My stomach flipped and tumbled, but Dylan wasn't done.

"I think you're very special." He brushed his thumb across

my cheekbone. I knew how special I was to him. But did that mean he loved me?

Being with Dylan made me realize what I should have waited for. I wished I'd just been patient in the knowledge that he'd come to me rather than waste time on people who didn't deserve my love.

"I think you're special, too." My voice was small and my words few. I worried if I said more I'd lose it and ask him if he loved me.

His smile reached his indigo eyes and I craned my neck to receive a kiss from him. As much as I wished we were alone, it was nice to share this moment with my family. Hopefully Jake would lay off a little now.

I took a breath; Dylan's kiss affected me like a muscle relaxant. "But just because I'm special doesn't mean the hot sex has to mellow, right?"

He chuckled. "Give me a break, darlin', I'm meeting your family for the first time. You can't be saying shit like that."

"Yeah, for Christ's sake, Beth. I don't want to hear it," Jake said, scowling at me.

I shrugged as Haven and Ash laughed. The hot sex was an important thing to get clear. For now, I had to focus on how he treated me and how he made me feel rather than the words he was using.

Dylan

I put my suitcase in the cab while Beth gave the driver her address. Dinner with her family had been interesting. Good.

I'd said that I was serious about her, and I was. I wanted

them to know my feelings for Beth were more than I'd ever thought they could be. Beth had said a similar thing on the way back from the airport. I could tell how serious I was, not just from how I felt about Beth, but because of what I did for her. That I was here in London, meeting her family, spoke volumes. I wanted to see her all the time and know every part of her, inside and out. I wanted her to know how I felt.

Beth's family clearly loved her, which suited me. Although I was pleased to have met her family, I was overdue alone time with her. I wasn't sure she was going to survive the cab journey fully clothed. The admissions we'd made to each other, although skirting around the heart of the truth, were enough to make me feel more drawn to her than usual.

I stood to the side to allow her to step into the cab and found myself transfixed by her creamy white legs inviting me to slide my hands higher and higher. The only thing stopping me was the audience at the door. I turned to wave, and they responded with a chorus of goodbyes. As soon as we pulled out, I grabbed her and slid her across my lap so she was straddling me.

That was better.

"Hello," she said, cupping my face with her hands and placing a small kiss on my forehead. I didn't know which part of her to touch first.

"Tell me it's just you and me now for a few days." I stroked my fingers into her cleavage, relishing her warmth and softness.

"It's just you and me. I have food; I've baked. We don't need to do anything but—"

"Fuck."

She pressed her hands to my chest and swiveled her hips in that wicked way she had. She dipped her lips to my ear. "All night and all day."

I knew it still wouldn't be enough. "How long to your apartment?"

"Not long." She grazed her teeth up my jaw, sending spasms of pleasure right to my rock-hard cock. To my surprise and disappointment, she climbed off and sat next to me, clasping my hand in hers.

"We'd better wait until we're in private," she said, staring at my crotch. The outline of my erection in my pants was hard to miss.

"I thought you liked an audience?" I raised my eyebrows. I wasn't too keen on getting my dick out in front of the driver, but I wasn't sure I'd fight her off if she insisted.

She laughed. "It's different. I don't want to see my audience." She nudged me in the ribs. "So my brother liked you. And the others—well they were always an easier sell."

"Good." I grimaced, leaning my head back onto the seat, trying to focus on something other than the throbbing of my cock.

"Thank you for agreeing to meet him."

"You don't need to thank me. I wanted to. I want to know all the people who are important to you."

She sighed. "It's stuff like that."

"What is?" She wasn't making sense. I turned my head toward her.

"When you say stuff like that"—she shrugged—"it sounds like you mean it."

I smiled and pulled her to my side. "Of course I mean it. I told you, I don't lie." I bent, dropping the softest of kisses on her lips. "I meant it when I said I'm serious. And I think you are, too." We were on the edge of saying more, close to taking a final step onto more solid ground. The cab came to a halt and Beth glanced around. "We're here." She scrambled to open the door and climbed out.

We fought over who was going to pay the driver, which I loved. I won, of course, and I handed the driver some money and pulled out my suitcase. I wasn't sure what I was expecting when it came to Beth's place. It seemed odd that we were so far along in our relationship in so many ways but I'd never seen where she lived. What would I discover? That she was into taxidermy and her walls were littered with pictures of old boyfriends?

We walked up a small ramp to some glass doors that slid open as we approached them. The lobby, all granite, glass and low lighting. The entire wall to our left had water trickling down it, lighting up the bumps and spikes of the granite.

"Hey, Barney," Beth greeted the security guard behind the desk. "This is Dylan James. He'll be staying with me, so he'll be coming and going."

I nodded at Barney.

"No problem, Beth. Have you kissed Sophia for me?" Barney said.

"My niece has a way of making everyone fall in love with

her the instant they meet her," Beth said to me before turning back to Barney. "I just saw her. She's missing you no doubt."

We made our way to the elevators and as the doors shut, I turned to her. "Does Barney go to dinner with you?"

"No, silly. Jake and Haven have a place here. The penthouse, of course. For years Jake and I lived together in his old student place, then we each bought an apartment in this building."

That made a little more sense. "And they still use this place?"

"Less and less. It's big, but not very child friendly. My place is teeny in comparison. It's only got one bedroom."

One was all we needed.

The doors opened and I followed Beth out. "Here we are." She opened her door and kicked her shoes off as soon as she was inside. Goosebumps prickled my skin. Being here was the next step in our relationship. I liked her so much, loved her so much, that I didn't want anything I found out to disappoint me, to make me like her less.

The floors were dark, almost black, and everything was sleek and modern.

Beth glanced behind her at me. "Is it what you expected? It came furnished."

I nodded. I'd thought there was a bit of a disconnect; it didn't feel like her. I'd expected more vibrancy and plenty of color. "It's nice. Beautiful views." It was nice, and it did have a beautiful view, but something was missing. I left my suitcase and headed over to the floor-to-ceiling windows overlooking west and south London.

"Do you know, I really love it? I didn't expect to; I thought it would be more of a struggle to live alone than it has been."

My gut twisted. I didn't like the thought of her enjoying time away from me. Did she see us living together? And if so, where? Chicago? London?

"Can I get you a drink?" She walked over, her head tilted to the side in question.

"All I need is you."

She grinned and I could almost feel the atmosphere thicken. "Well, Mr. 8A, you have me. So what are you going to do with me?"

I growled and pulled her into my arms, bending to taste her neck. "Show me your bedroom."

She pulled at my shirt, freeing it from my pants, and slid her hands over my back. Her fingers were hot and eager. "I thought you'd never ask." She led me by my shirttail back down the corridor and into her bedroom.

There was more color, pinks and reds, in her bedroom. It felt more like the Beth I knew. "More windows," I said, lifting my chin in the direction of windows on one whole side of the bedroom.

"Wanna close the blinds?"

I pulled at her top, lifting it over her head. "No, I don't think I do." I dragged my thumbnails over the lace of her bra, relishing the feeling as her nipples hardened. How had I been with her all these hours without touching her like this?

I walked forward until she was trapped between me and the bed. She grinned as she undid the buttons of my shirt, then sat so she was perfectly positioned to take my dick in her mouth.

I was rock hard instantly. Just having that beautiful pout so close to my cock was too much. I shrugged off my open shirt and growled as she undid my pants.

She took my dick in both hands, twisting in opposite directions as she watched my reaction. Did she see my desperation for her?

"You seem pleased to see me, baby." She swirled her tongue over my crown and slid her lips until the tip of my cock was in her mouth. Her hands fisted around my cock with the perfect pressure.

"You're going to make me come," I said.

She took me deeper, as if she was daring me. She grabbed my ass, urging me closer and deeper. Was she trying to please me or herself? I wasn't sure it mattered.

I couldn't hold back as I stabbed forward, hating myself for losing control. For the first time in my life, I didn't want this to be about me getting off. Before Beth, getting a woman off was ultimately self-gratification. It turned me on to know the effect I could have on a woman. With Beth, I wanted her to climax because I wanted her happy; I needed to give her what she wanted. That desire went beyond sex and seeped into everything I did for her.

"I'm sorry, my sweet, you just look so perfect wrapped around my cock like that."

She released my dick. "Never apologize for wanting to go deeper. It's what I dream about."

As if to demonstrate she took me to the back of her throat as she glanced up at me, her eyes full of lust.

"Jesus, are you trying to kill me?" I cupped her face in my hands and wiped my thumbs across her cheekbones and that precious beauty spot. "That image right there is something I'm taking back to Chicago with me."

I pulled away, kicked off my boxers and pants, grabbed a condom out of my wallet and leaned over her, pushing her gently back on the bed.

"Hey, I thought I was in charge."

I balanced over her, between her legs. "I don't remember making you any such promise." I was always in charge in the bedroom, as I was in all aspects of my life.

"Can I try something?" She traced her index finger over my chest.

How could I resist that beautifully swollen mouth? "Anything."

She pressed her palms against my shoulders and I let her push me off her. What did she have planned?

I collapsed on my back, shoving my hands behind my head, not taking my eyes off her for a second.

Tentatively she climbed over me so she could straddle me. "Is this okay?"

I'd never let a woman ride me, not even Alicia. I liked to be in control, but I wouldn't deny Beth anything. I wanted whatever she did. I grinned. "Sure, knock yourself out."

She raised her eyebrows at me, reaching between us for my dick.

I held out the condom for her, and she pursed her lips. "Maybe you should do that bit."

She shifted back as I tore open the condom. I watched her, mesmerized by her hands on my dick. "It's all yours."

"I like that," she replied, her voice breathy.

"I like that you like my dick."

She rose to her knees and rested my dick right at her entrance. She threw her head back as she sank down. "I like that it's all mine. No one else's." Her voice was strained, as if my dick had pushed all the oxygen from her lungs.

She was so tight and warm and fucking perfect.

"That's right. All yours. And ready to fuck you all night."

Her eyes found mine as she gathered her breasts, teasing me as she pushed them up and together, grinding her hips in small circles above me.

It might just have been the best view I'd ever seen. I reached for her, smoothing my hands up her thighs and around her ass, encouraging her thrusts.

"It feels so good." Her words sounded like a prayer.

"It's always so good."

She screwed her eyes shut. "Always." Her movements became bigger, less controlled.

My racing heart took my breath away, and my skin thrummed everywhere it touched her.

"I love fucking you," she choked out.

That wasn't what we were doing. "I love making love with you," I replied.

I fucked *other* women; I made love with Beth. I felt her seep through my skin and become part of me from the moment

I touched her. And I knew that no other man had heard the sounds that passed from her lips when I made her come. During our first encounter I'd marveled at how responsive she'd been, but I'd come to realize it was *me* who did that to her, and in turn she opened me up and I allowed myself to feel more than I ever had.

She opened her eyes and gasped. She tightened and pulsed. I wasn't going to last long. "Dylan."

I couldn't hold back any longer. I needed her to know how I felt. "I love you, Beth."

I watched, fascinated and full of love as her orgasm exploded over her body. Her limbs shook and she collapsed on top of me. I rounded my hands over her ass and thrust up, desperate for my own release after witnessing hers.

"I love you, too," she whispered into my ear. "I love you. I love you. I love you."

There was nothing I wanted to hear more. A guttural noise exploded in my throat and my orgasm shot up my spine as I spilled into her, wrapping my arms around her, wanting her as close as possible.

I panted into her hair, breathing in the scent of almonds.

I needed to hold on tight. Beth was the only woman I'd ever need.

I could never lose her.

chapter
FOURTEEN

Beth

Don stood behind me with my case as I unlocked Dylan's door. It felt odd to let myself into someone else's house.

After Dylan's trip to London, it'd seemed ridiculous to insist on staying in a hotel. When he asked me to stay with him again, I said yes. If I'd known he'd smile as though I'd given him the whole world, I wouldn't have been able to resist in the first place. We loved each other; there was no need to pretend we didn't want to be with each other every second.

I stepped inside and grinned at the thought of being so close to Dylan. His scent surrounded me instantly; I could almost feel him. He'd stayed with me in London, and now here I was in his. We were beginning to share each other's lives, become more entwined, more together. And it felt easy, as if my anxieties got farther and farther away, my trust in myself and Dylan growing every time I heard his voice. There might be an ocean between us, but I'd never felt closer to any man.

"Would you mind running me into town if I just use the bathroom quickly?" I asked Don. I had a few hours before Dylan got home and wanted to pick up some ingredients at a specialty kitchen equipment store I'd found online. I also wanted to find a frilly apron so I could greet him as he'd requested.

Although I was meeting with the TV studio on Monday about a possible extension of my slot, and maybe a few stand-alone episodes, I wanted to make the weekend about us—I was hoping we'd spend most of our days together, indoors and preferably in bed.

I was uncomfortable with the attention I was getting from the breakfast show. I'd baked to distract myself from my drinking, not for attention, so it was as if I was in some way being misconstrued—a fraud almost. I was a home baker, not a TV personality.

When I'd set up the YouTube channel, and even when I signed up for *A Chicago Saturday*, I'd never really thought about the impact it would have on me beyond giving the last four years some meaning outside of keeping me sober. I liked the idea of sharing my love for baking with as many people as possible, and I hadn't really thought through the implications. That the interaction between viewer and presenter wasn't one way. I had to hear their opinions of my desserts, which could be kinda tough. Since the shows had aired, Amber kept asking me about interviews and photo shoots. She'd also suggested I get an agent and a publicist. I really wasn't sure encouraging attention was something I wanted.

I wanted to share without being shared.

Three of my six slots had already aired, the fourth was due to air tomorrow.

Apparently I was a hit.

It had all happened so fast.

"I could take the day off," Dylan said.

I hadn't even made it out of bed, yet I felt as if I'd been up for hours. I guess we had, trying to squeeze in every last drop of time together. Since I'd arrived in Chicago at the beginning of the weekend, we'd slept little, talked more and made love even more than that.

It was as if confessing we loved each other had stripped us bare. There was nothing between us anymore, no barriers, no walls. We were a unit. It was safe and intimate and I didn't want to let the world into it. I wanted to freeze time and just revel in this time together. My life had taught me that the bad times didn't last, but neither did the good. And although I knew I'd love Dylan for the rest of my life, I also understood that these moments together were special and needed to be savored.

"I just realized my flight's tonight, and we don't have any plans to see each other again." There was a tightness in my brow where I was scowling.

Dylan propped himself up on his elbow. "What do you mean?"

"I don't have any trips planned, and neither do you." I wasn't concerned. I just thought we should decide when we would next come together and come together.

He leaned over me, hovering above my mouth. "I'm flying over on Thursday," he said, then pressed his lips against mine.

I clasped his shoulders. What? "You're coming to London?"

"I am. But you know, we have to have a conversation about where we're going to live at some point."

I grinned. "We do?"

"Sure we do. I can't have my wife and kids living on a different continent, can I?"

"You're ridiculous." I laughed, throwing off the sheet and climbing out of bed.

"I'm not proposing." He followed me into the bathroom.

"Good. Because we've known each other five minutes."

I stared at him in the mirror and he shrugged. "I know. But I also know that I've never felt like this about anyone."

My stomach tugged and flipped. I loved hearing how he loved me because I loved him right back, just as hard. It was just so nice to hear him say it. It felt like we were . . . even. I'd never had that before. I'd always felt like I was two steps ahead of the guys I dated before Dylan.

"I'm not saying we have to have the conversation now, although that works for me. I'm just saying, at some point we need to discuss where we're going to live our lives."

He was right, but I didn't want to leave London and I couldn't see him moving continents when his business was here. Whenever I thought about it, I didn't see a solution, so I tried *not* to think about it. "Okay."

"Okay?"

I nodded. "I agree. At some point we'll need to talk about it, but right at this moment I need to get in the shower." If we came to an impasse, what did that mean? Would we be over if there wasn't a solution?

Dylan's phone buzzed from the bedroom and he forgot about following me in to the shower. Although I'd never say no to him, we both needed to get up and face the day. Sex was a great distraction, but real life intruded every now and then.

Dylan

"Stop calling me." I hung up before Alicia could respond, threw my phone on my desk and looked out at the city. Her calls were getting more frequent. Why was she so determined to contact me now?

If I hadn't met Beth, I might have been tempted to hear her out. I supposed there was a part of me that didn't want to have been wrong about her, that there'd been some huge misunderstanding between us that led to her leaving. If she turned out to be a hard-faced bitch, it meant I hadn't seen it. That I had a blind spot that left me out of control, someone who might be taken advantage of again, which wasn't something I liked.

Being with Beth had shifted things for me, shown me that what Alicia and I'd had was thin and flimsy. I'd never felt for Alicia what Beth evoked in me. I wanted to care for and protect Beth. With Alicia I'd felt obligated to provide for her, because that's what a man did, but it hadn't been about making her safe and happy, which is what I wanted for Beth. My sense of protectiveness over Beth was part of the reason that her leaving to go back to London today stung so bad. We'd had a perfect weekend and I wasn't ready to let her go.

Beth was thoughtful and kind—not just to me, but to all the people in her life. I grinned. Of course, she had the most incredible body. My phone vibrated on my desk; I turned my chair back around to see Alicia's name flashing. Again. This was seriously starting to get irritating.

"Fucking witch," I mumbled just as Raf walked in.

"What did you say?"

"I said 'fucking witch.'" I silenced my phone as Raf collapsed in one of the chairs in front of my desk. "This walnut desk is expensive; if it's going to get banged up I don't want it to be because Alicia was burning up my phone."

"Alicia?"

"Yeah. She keeps calling. Hey, do you know how to block a number?"

"Sure." Raf held out his hand and I tossed him my phone. "I didn't realize you two were in touch. I thought you hadn't seen her since—"

"We're not in touch. She started calling a couple of weeks back."

"You haven't answered her calls?"

I sighed and pinched the bridge of my nose. "I spoke to her briefly. I didn't know it was her; she's changed her number. She said she has a business proposition for me. I hung up."

"A business proposition?" Raf asked, fiddling with my phone.

Talking to Raf brought back some painful memories. The business that Alicia had convinced us to invest in, which went badly wrong, had rocked things between Raf and me and it had taken a long time to get our friendship back on track.

"Well, I hope you know better than to take her up on her offer." Raf and I had come to blows about the deal with Alicia—literally and figuratively. We'd agreed that we'd never let our personal lives get mixed up in business. "But, aren't you the least bit curious to hear her out? Isn't that what they call closure?"

"She dumped me for a richer guy. I think I got all the closure I need." It happened and I'd moved the fuck on.

"And you've not had a relationship since. It's like she chopped off your dick as well as your pride." Raf looked up and grinned at me.

"My dick is just fine. There have been plenty of women and now there's Beth."

"Beth is the first one who's had a name."

I shrugged. He wasn't completely accurate but he was pretty close. "I just wasn't about to make the same mistake twice. Sometimes you have to be patient to find what you're looking for."

"And Beth? She's the one you've been looking for?"

I nodded, though I hadn't been looking. Not even close. Beth had thrown me for a loop. She'd been entirely unexpected. But she was the best person I knew and the only woman I'd really truly loved.

"I need to tell you something about her."

Raf's eyes widened. "Does she have three boobs? Because I might have to arm wrestle you for her if she does."

"You're a sick fuck."

He stroked his jaw. "Hey, no kids and no animals, but anything other than that I'm willing to try once."

I shook my head and took a deep breath. "I don't want you to go off the deep end, but Beth is Beth Harrison, as in *Bake with Beth* on *A Chicago Saturday*."

Raf didn't say anything, he just stared out of the window.

"I should have mentioned it before now. They were in touch with her long before I met her and I've had nothing to do with her deal." Raf sighed. "Beth doesn't even know we own the company. I want to tell her but I wanted to tell you first."

"Is she the reason we didn't sell Raine Media?"

It was a fair question. "No. Well, maybe."

"Jesus." Raf stood abruptly and shoved his chair back. "We agreed not to ever let personal lives interfere with business."

"Look, I wouldn't have properly looked at the numbers if she'd not been there. I would have just gone along with whatever you wanted. But I swear, if I hadn't seen potential, Beth's presence would not have swayed me."

Raf's mouth was set in a thin, straight line. "This business partnership works because we don't lie and we keep our word to each other."

My gut twisted. I should have told Raf, but I also should have told Beth. I'd been trying to simplify things, but instead I'd made them much worse, made things a bigger deal than they had to be. When I got to London, it would be the first thing I did. Well, maybe not the first thing.

"You're right, I'm sorry." Raf had deserved to know the truth, and I should have told him before now. "It won't happen again."

"You're a dick."

"I'll let you have that one."

Marie raised her voice outside my door, something I'd never heard before. "He's in a meeting," she said, blocking the door to my office.

"He could never resist me in red." Alicia's southern twang pierced my ears.

Raf shot me a look and we both flew to Marie's aid.

Alicia grinned at me as if we'd just seen each other yesterday. "Dylan, darling, you're looking very handsome."

"What are you doing here, Alicia?" I barked as I steadied Marie.

"I'm here for you to take me to lunch, of course." She gently touched my arm, a small gesture that felt so alien. Beth was the girl who got to touch me.

"You need to leave, Alicia." We were causing quite the scene and the office gossips would be all over our little drama in a heartbeat.

She grinned, but shook her head. "I'm not going anywhere without you." She slumped down on the sofa. I was never getting her out of here.

I walked straight past her toward the elevators. If I had to leave my building to eject her, then that's what I'd do.

Within seconds, the smell of her heavy perfume caught up with me. "I've booked Giovanni's. This is going to be so fun, just like old times."

"I didn't say I'd have lunch with you."

"But you're going to. You forget, I know you, Dylan. You never could resist me."

"You're so wrong, Alicia. I just want you out of my building. Out of my life. If I agree to have lunch with you, will you stop this crazy stalker-ish behavior?"

"Absolutely." The southern accent had gone; it always did when she was being sincere.

"If you call me again after today, I'm taking a restraining order out on you."

"You have my word."

"Like I did when you said you'd marry me?" I shouldn't have said it. It made me sound like I was still bitter and I wasn't. I thought she was a bitch, and I was grateful I hadn't wasted more time on her than I already had, but I wasn't bitter. Until today I'd thought I hated her, but seeing her desperate, her tired tricks looked just that—tired. I didn't hate her. I felt nothing. It had just taken her showing up uninvited at my office for me to finally understand that.

"Marie, I'll be at Giovanni's, but I won't be longer than forty-five minutes."

Since our breakup there'd been a number of times Alicia and her husband had been scheduled to attend the same event as me—charity galas, business functions, that sort of thing. I'd always kept track of who was invited, and if I found Alicia's name on the list, I'd always pull out. Now I wondered why. I should have been fucking delighted she'd married some other sucker and left me to find Beth.

"See? I knew I could make you smile." Alicia grabbed my arm as we strode out of the elevator. I didn't make any pretense of trying to slow down for her. I needed this over with so I could get on with my life with Beth. I was pretty sure she'd be out of her meeting with WCIL anytime now and I wanted to know if she'd have more reason to be in Chicago from now on.

I checked my pocket for my phone to see if she'd messaged me and realized I'd left it on my desk. "This better be quick, Alicia. I have a busy afternoon."

"Come on, we'll have fun. We always had fun, Dylan, didn't we?"

"The gate to memory lane is closed and locked. I'm not interested in rehashing the good times."

"At least you admit they *were* good times."

I didn't respond. There was no need. She could live with her bad choices. I didn't need to tell her she was a bitch. She wasn't my problem, or my responsibility, anymore. I just didn't care.

"Here we are," she said breezily as we arrived at the entrance to the restaurant just a block from my office. They served quickly here, which was just as well.

"Mr. James, how nice to see you. Apologies, I don't seem to have a reservation for you, but I'll find you a table." I nodded at the host.

Alicia's practiced façade cracked. "I guess we'll get a nicer table if they know you," she said, her eyes flickering with irritation.

We were seated quickly and Alicia insisted on ordering a bottle of wine. I wasn't going to touch a drop of it, despite what she thought.

"So," she said dramatically as the waiter left. "I just want to set my cards out on the table so you know exactly why I'm here. I picked the wrong guy. I'm sorry. I should never have called off the wedding."

I chuckled. She'd picked the wrong guy because I turned out to be richer than her husband. Not because she loved me, not because she was dying without me, but because she thought she'd missed out.

"I think you made a fine choice. Bob's a decent man by all accounts."

She ignored my comment about her husband and continued, "You've done very well for yourself."

"So what you mean is you backed the wrong horse."

She shrugged. "I do miss you, Dylan. I know that no man will love me the way you did."

If I didn't know her, I might have fallen for her charm.

"And I miss our friendship and how wise you were. How you always took me seriously when I had an observation about business. Bob just laughs when I try to talk to him about work. And because you're such a good person and an amazing businessman, I thought that there was no one in the world I'd want to go into partnership with other than you."

She seriously thought I would go into business with her? She rummaged in her bag and pulled out a memory stick. "I know you'll love this, Dylan. And you'll love the projected revenues even more." Her eyes lit up. She really thought I might say yes.

She had to be shitting me.

Beth

As I climbed into the back of the cab on the way to the TV station, my phone buzzed in my pocket. I'd packed all my bags in case I didn't have enough time after the meeting. A car was due to pick me up to go to the airport at six, but I was pretty sure the station was going to want me to sign something before I left. And I still wasn't sure I was ready to commit to it.

The weekend with Dylan had been wonderful, easy and perfect. I didn't need an excuse to come to Chicago, but Dylan meant I was going to be here more and more so I might as well have something to keep me busy while I was here and *A Chicago Saturday* might be a good option.

I told the cab driver where to go and checked my messages.

Amber: Don't listen to it. It's all bullshit. Bryan found you on YouTube, you know that. Can't wait to see you at 11.

I read it twice and couldn't make any more sense of it the second time. I would've assumed she'd meant to send it to someone else if she hadn't mentioned seeing me at eleven. What was it that I shouldn't be listening to? Perhaps she'd gotten me mixed up with someone else?

It was a short drive to the television studio and Amber was waiting outside as the cab pulled up, her near-constant smile gone, her eyes downcast and her lips pursed. My stomach churned as I paid the driver and opened the taxi door. Maybe they'd changed their minds about offering me an extended run on the show. I took a deep breath. It didn't matter. It didn't affect my relationship with Dylan, and it didn't mean I couldn't spend as much time in Chicago as I wanted. This was no big deal. I hadn't enjoyed the publicity side of things anyway. Maybe it was a blessing in disguise.

"How are you holding up?" Amber pulled me into a hug. "I thought we'd go around the side entrance where there are fewer people. Not that anyone is taking any notice. I just thought you might prefer it." We walked around the side of the building.

It was nice of her to be concerned, but I didn't really understand why we were going ahead with the meeting if they were just going to say they didn't want to work with me any longer. They could have just called me.

"I had no idea you were even dating him," Amber said, and suddenly the world started to tilt. I stopped so I didn't fall over.

"Dating who? What's going on, Amber?"

"Dylan James. He's super-hot, so I'm not surprised. You make a great couple, though that has nothing to do with why we offered you the job."

"How do you know who I'm dating?" I asked, scanning my brain for answers. It must have been the benefit. There'd been press there and Dylan was a well-known public figure.

"You know, from the internet."

Amber used her pass to unlock the door and we stepped inside. Amber rushed us into a conference room where Bryan was waiting for us.

He cocked his head to the side and said, "How are you holding up? Don't let these bloodsuckers get you down. We know the truth. I fucking found you on YouTube." Amber had said something similar. I didn't understand it. "It had nothing to do with who you're dating. The press are just looking for bodies to pick over them. You're going to be the next Martha Stewart, so consider this your coming-out party. You just need to stay strong."

"Hang on." I put my hands up. "We need to back up here. What are you talking about? Why are you both mentioning Dylan and the press?" My gaze flicked between them. "Have they discovered we're dating? Why are they so interested?"

Amber and Bryan glanced sideways at each other. "Have you not seen the story?" Amber asked in a small voice.

I heard the rumble of a tidal wave in the distance, a warning that things were about to get serious. "What story?" I asked, and I took a seat. "You guys are really starting to freak me out."

Bryan took a deep breath and shook his head as he took a chair opposite me.

Amber sat next to me and said, "Have you not seen it? There's an article in the *Sun-Times* about women sleeping their way to the top—they mention you in there."

Sleeping my way to the top? My stomach churned. Baking was something I'd done on my own. I hadn't had any help from Jake, and I hadn't met Dylan until recently, and anyway how would he help? This was why I wasn't convinced about extending my time on *A Chicago Saturday*. "But you asked me to meet with you before I even met Dylan."

"Exactly," Bryan said.

"We know," Amber said, trying to reassure me. "It will blow over. And it's just small town gossip. Ignore it."

"I don't understand how dating Dylan matters. I mean, I know he's rich and well-known, but he can't get me my own show. Can he?"

"And that's what I told the press when they called. I told them Dylan has no creative control over *A Chicago Saturday* or WCIL. He just doesn't get involved with daily operations."

"Wait, what? What do you mean 'doesn't get involved'?"

Amber shrugged as she fiddled with her phone. "I'll show you what they wrote. Be strong. I think they're just trying to start trouble, or they're naïve about how much the moneymen get to control creative content. Really, who knows?"

Moneymen? Why would Dylan have creative control over *A Chicago Saturday*? Investors?

"But while we're getting our cards out on the table, it would have been good to have a heads-up. We could have had a PR plan, just in case something like this caught fire," Bryan said.

Amber offered me her phone. "It Still Pays to Sleep with the Boss." What the fuck? I began reading the article.

New baking sensation A Chicago Saturday's Beth the Baker just happens to be sleeping with the owner of WCIL and Raine Media . . .

I couldn't read any more. Dylan owned WCIL? That couldn't be true. I dropped the phone on the desk. He would have told me. He assured me he'd never lie. I stood up, aware that Amber and Bryan were speaking but I couldn't make out the words. I turned to the door. "I have to leave."

Had I been unknowingly sleeping with my boss? There must have been some kind of mistake. They must have this all wrong. I spluttered out some excuse to leave. I fumbled in my bag, pulled out my phone and pressed call as I hit the sunlight.

I spotted a cab where I'd been dropped off, and I headed toward it. Dylan would explain. He'd be able to make sense of it. He'd tell me that he *used* to own Raine Media. His phone rang and rang. I climbed into the back of the cab, mumbling Dylan's office address at the driver.

The phone went to voice mail. I couldn't remember that ever happening before. He always picked up. The rumble of the tidal wave grew nearer. It was as if I'd woken in an alternative universe where nothing was as it should be.

We pulled up outside his office; for a fleeting moment I thought that maybe he didn't actually work here—there was a possibility that everything I thought we'd had was a gigantic lie. I tried to shake off that feeling. I imagined Dylan grinning at me as I surprised him in his office and he pulled me into his arms, telling me that the *Sun-Times* had mixed him up with someone else, or had thought he owned Raine Media when in fact he owned a different media company. Yes, that's what would happen.

I headed inside. "Beth Harrison for Dylan James," I said to the security guard at the front desk. "If you could just call up for him—"

He handed me a security pass. "Take lift five to floor sixty-two. His assistant will meet you there."

Everything felt unfamiliar as I made my way to the lift. I wanted Dylan to make me feel better, to make me feel good in the way no one else could. Perhaps I'd become more dependent on him than I had realized. How could I have gotten myself in so deep, so quickly? I didn't really know anything about him. I hadn't been to his office before, and I'd only met his business partner at the gala. I'd never met his parents and other than the fact that he was in the Navy, I knew nothing about Dylan's brother. How could he be bringing up where we lived our lives when we knew so little about each other?

I stepped out of the elevator and a slim, gray-haired woman smiled warmly at me. "Beth? It's so good to finally meet you. Dylan's spoken of you often. He always gets me to clear his diary when you're in town."

I smiled, soothed by her words. "Can I see him? I need to speak to him urgently."

Her brow furrowed. "I'm afraid he's just stepped out for a lunch appointment. But he said he'd be quick if you want to wait."

I checked my phone, willing it to flash with Dylan's name. "Actually, it's really important. Can I ask what restaurant he went to?" I pushed the elevator button to go back down to street level. "I just need to give him a quick message before I leave for the airport, and I'm afraid I can't wait." It was a lie and it almost stuck in my throat as I said it, but at that moment, my need to see Dylan, to see that everything was fine, overwhelmed my need to be honest.

Marie was uncomfortable with my request but my face must have convinced her of my need to see him. "He's at Giovanni's just on the corner of this block. Turn left when you get out of the building and it's on the right."

I smiled at Marie as I stepped into the elevator car. "Thank you so much."

I hardly noticed the wind as I charged up the street and into the restaurant.

I scanned the diners, trying to find him.

"Hello, miss. Can I help you?"

I continued to search the faces of the patrons as I replied, "I'm looking for Mr. Dylan James." I spotted his profile. He was taking a sip from his water; his strong hands looked like they could crush his glass if he held it just a fraction too tightly. I exhaled, feeling like finally I was where I should be. His face broke into a grin, but it wasn't directed at me. He was looking at the person opposite him. I followed his line of vision . . . I stepped closer. Her red hair was unmistakable.

He was having lunch with Alicia.

The color and the noise of the restaurant all seemed to blend together in a huge complicated web and I spun, desperate to get out.

Nothing was what I thought it was.

As I tried to leave, something hit my leg and the sound of broken glass echoed in my head. "Sorry," I whispered.

I felt people looking at me and ran toward the door and out into the sunlight. I needed to escape.

I tripped out onto the sidewalk just as a cab was dropping someone off. I clambered into the back before the driver even switched on his light.

In the distance, I heard my name being called as I closed the door. "Please, can we get out of here?"

The driver pulled out. "Where to, miss?"

I took a deep breath. I wanted to be at home. "Chicago O'Hare, please."

chapter
FIFTEEN

Dylan

I wasn't enjoying Alicia's company, but she wasn't irritating me either. It was an hour of my life that I was never going to get back, but I wasn't emotional. There was no feeling for her left in me, and I felt celebratory at the realization. I was desperate to get back and call Beth. Perhaps I could convince her to change her flight, stay the night. I had so much to tell her.

The sound of smashing glass caught my attention, and I looked up and saw her as she turned and headed toward the door. What was she doing here?

I stood and headed after her. If she'd seen me, and I was pretty sure she had, why hadn't she come over? Shit, she'd seen me lunching with Alicia and had probably assumed the worst.

I headed outside and looked left and right, trying to see where she'd gone. I reached into my pockets for my phone. Damn, I'd left it in my office.

Where had she disappeared to? I stepped back into the restaurant. "That woman who was here a minute ago—"

"Yes, she came in looking for you, but seemed to change her mind when she saw you. I hope everything . . ."

I didn't stay to hear the rest, and instead I ran back to the office.

Where had she gone? It must have been a shock to see me with Alicia, but it wasn't as if she'd found us naked together. Beth knew how I felt about her and that Alicia wasn't a threat, didn't she?

As I stormed through the glass doors on the 62nd floor, Marie greeted me. "Beth was just here. Did she catch up with you?"

I stopped before I reached my office. "She was here?"

"Yes, desperate to give you a message. I hope you don't mind, I told her where you were having lunch. I'm sorry you missed each other. Should I get her on the line?"

"No, that's fine." I grabbed my phone from my desk. I had two missed calls from Beth, both from the time before she walked into the restaurant.

Fuck.

I called, heading out of my office toward the elevators.

Her phone just went to voice mail. I hung up and travelled down to meet my driver. She was probably headed to my place. If nothing else, she needed her luggage. It would be fine. I just needed to see her and explain.

"Can we go back to the brownstone, please?" I asked Don as I slid into the backseat. "As quick as you can."

I opened the door before the car came to a complete stop, then took the stairs to my front door two at a time and let myself inside.

"Beth?" I called and listened for her response, any kind of sign she was here. Nothing. Perhaps she was on her way?

Her luggage was still by the door, so I dialed her number, again.

Voice mail. Again.

I needed her to pick up, to stick around and let me explain I'd gone to lunch with Alicia to get rid of her. Fuck, I should have had security throw Alicia out. Why had I indulged her?

I wanted Beth, but where was she? My heart was thumping through my chest and my skin itched. I shrugged off my suit jacket, throwing it on the couch.

I typed out a message.

Dylan: Can you pick up? Alicia came by the office and made a scene and refused to leave unless I had lunch with her. She's a maniac. Please call me. I love you.

I stared at my phone, willing her to call me.

Impatient, I called her.

Voice mail. Again.

Fuck. Would she have gone to her father's? I was ashamed to say I had no idea where he lived. She didn't mention him often. To Beth, her family seemed to be all about the people she surrounded herself with in London.

She'd have to come back to collect her luggage before leaving for the airport. I'd just sit and wait, try not to overreact—and keep calling until she either turned up or answered.

Dylan: Where are you? I love you. Pick up.

Maybe she had gone to a meeting—or a bar. My gut twisted at the thought of being the one who had caused her pain. All I wanted to do was make her happy. Why had I been such an idiot?

I'd been avoiding the most obvious phone call I should make. I had to call her brother. This wasn't just a lover's tiff. Beth could derail her recovery, and I had to do everything I could to ensure that didn't happen.

I dialed Marie and got her to call me back with Jake Harrison's number. It didn't take her long to find it. It was late in London, but I was pretty sure that Jake wouldn't mind me calling. He'd kick my ass, but he'd want to know about Beth.

I punched his number into my phone.

"Hello?" Jake answered. "Beth?"

My stomach twisted and I took a deep breath.

"Jake, it's Dylan James. I'm calling about Beth."

"I warned you about hurting her."

"I know and I'm sorry, but it isn't what she thinks."

"Don't call me again, and leave her alone. She deserves better—"

He sounded like he'd punch me if I were in hitting distance. At that moment, I'd be happy to let him. It might help me focus on something other than the pain of not having Beth right beside me. "Can I just explain? It wasn't what she thought it was—"

"Unless you can tell me that you don't own Raine Media and didn't neglect to tell my sister that she was working for you, and that you didn't have a cozy lunch date with your ex-fiancée, there's nothing I want to hear from you. Leave my sister alone, you piece of shit asshole."

Jake ended the call. I tossed the phone on the stairs next to me and thrust my hands into my hair, waiting for the blood pounding in my ears to lessen.

She'd found out I owned Raine Media.

Why on earth hadn't I just told her and Raf? Why hadn't I just let Raf sell the fucking thing? Then I wouldn't be in this mess. I had nothing to hide. It was no big deal. Things were just so great between us, and I didn't want anything to spoil that. I wanted her to know, but there hadn't been the right time to tell her.

It wasn't as if I had any influence over the hiring process. They'd contacted her before we met. It shouldn't be a big deal.

I wondered how she'd found out, and how long she'd known. Had Jake run a background check on me or something?

I jumped when my phone rang. My heart sank when I realized that it was just Marie.

"I'm trying to keep this line free, Marie. Is this urgent?"

"I just think you should take a look at the *Sun-Times*. There's an article there about Beth that I can't imagine she'd be too happy about."

Jesus, was there a full moon? This day was just getting worse. I grabbed my tablet from the kitchen and brought it back to the stairs. I wanted to be waiting when Beth came back.

I searched the *Sun-Times* website.

Fuck.

Fuck.

Fuck.

Well at least I knew how she'd found out about my owning Raine Media.

But I should have told her. I'd been an idiot.

I dialed her number again.

Voice mail. Again.

I tapped out a message.

Dylan: I just saw the *Sun-Times* article. I should have told you. Please come home so I can explain, there's history to this. I had nothing to do with you getting this job. I love you. I'm sorry.

There was nothing to do but wait.

I loosened my tie as a sense of dread passed over me. I checked the time. It was almost six. She had to be here soon. It had been hours.

My doorbell almost induced a heart attack. I jumped to my feet. Finally, she was here, though I hated she wasn't using her key.

I threw the door open, but found a man in a chauffeur's uniform instead of Beth.

"Airport ride for Ms. Harrison." Shit, it was the car I'd asked Marie to arrange this morning.

I closed my eyes. Was she running late or was she drunk in some bar because I'd been a dick?

Neither option sat well with me.

"Ms. Harrison is running a little late. May I ask you to wait?" If Beth did come back, I wanted her to have a way to get to the airport.

The driver shrugged. "I get paid whatever I do."

I was pretty sure Beth would want to be back in London as soon as possible. I just couldn't imagine her missing her flight. I closed the door and went back to my tablet, checking the departure board at O'Hare.

The flight to London was on time and there hadn't been a plane that she could have made if she'd tried to fly earlier. If she wasn't planning to pick up her luggage, perhaps I could find her at the airport and explain.

I raced upstairs, grabbed my passport and burst out of the door. "Don," I called as I flew down the stoop. "Airport. As quick as you can." He had the engine started before I grabbed the door handle.

If she wouldn't come to me, I knew her favorite table in the first class lounge. She had to be there.

Less than thirty minutes later, I stood at the ticket desk, repeating myself. "I *need* to be on the nine-ten flight to London Heathrow."

"I understand that, sir, but unfortunately that flight is fully booked."

"I'll pay whatever it takes. Please just let me on that flight."

"I'm afraid it's not a question of money. We just don't have any seats left. Not even in economy."

I wasn't ready to give up. "Can you just tell me if Beth Harrison checked in?"

The check-in woman scowled at me. "You know I can't tell you that, sir."

I did, but I was used to being an exception. I grinned at her. "Are you sure?"

"I'm sure," she replied, unmoved by my pathetic attempt at flirting.

"Okay, then I need a seat on your next plane to London." Hopefully I wouldn't need to use it. I could find Beth on the other side of security and explain, convince her to stay.

"You're in luck," the check-in woman said. "I have five seats left in economy on the nine-fifty flight."

I really hoped I wouldn't need that ticket. It had been some time since I'd flown economy. At least I'd get through security with a boarding pass. I rummaged in my wallet and pulled out my gold traveler's card. "I presume I can get into the lounge with this?"

"Of course, sir. I'll get you an invitation."

My feet wouldn't stay still. I prided myself on my ability to keep my composure at all times, but it wasn't working for me today.

The check-in woman pretended she didn't notice my fingers tapping against the desk. "How many bags are you checking in today?"

"None."

"Carry-ons?"

"I don't have any," I replied. Perhaps I should have brought Beth's luggage with me. No, I wanted her to come home with me. I didn't want her getting on that plane.

Finally, the clerk handed me my boarding pass and invitation to the lounge, and I streaked off through security, clinging to the hope that when I saw Beth she'd understand.

I needed things between us to be back where they had been.

In a short space of time she'd become my whole world. Her openness and vulnerability had drawn me to her—my heart ached that I'd abused that and not been as forthcoming with my own emotions.

I didn't bother checking the faces in the lounge. I knew where she'd be hiding. I rounded the corner to find three empty tables.

Shit.

I was certain I'd find her there.

How had I been so wrong? Perhaps she wasn't planning on making her flight. Nausea floated in my stomach. I shook my head. I couldn't think like that. Not yet.

I spun around and headed out of the lounge and toward her gate. The flight wouldn't be boarding yet, but if she was going to fly she'd have to come to the gate at some point. I'd wait until the last passenger boarded, at least that way I'd be sure that she was okay.

I dialed her number again.

Voice mail.

I shoved my phone back in my pocket, trying to find the correct gate.

There were three people seated nearby the desk. None of them were Beth. I sat in the seat nearest the door to the gangway, determined not to miss her, and waited.

People filled up the seats around me. Not one of them was Beth. Eventually they started to call people to the aircraft. First class was up first. No Beth. Then business class and then economy. Still no Beth. I checked my watch. Twenty minutes until they were due to take off and the queue had disappeared completely.

The thought of never seeing her again crawled up my throat and made me choke. I couldn't lose her. It just wasn't possible. She'd changed me forever and I knew that my love for her would last the rest of my life, whether we were together or apart.

Fuck. She wasn't flying.

I felt her before I saw her. My heart surged in my chest, and I stood as her beautiful red pout came toward me.

"Beth," I said, a mixture of relief, love and sadness in my tone. She looked so broken. She glanced at me and then looked away as she handed her boarding pass to the flight attendant.

I couldn't have lost her, could I?

I just had to explain, make her see, remind her how much I loved her.

Beth

I half expected him to show up at the airport, but I'd thought I was safe when I got through security. Of course he had managed to get through somehow. He probably owned the airport as well. No doubt he'd heard about the *Sun-Times* article and had some spurious excuse about how come I'd been the last to know he owned the company I'd been working for.

I didn't understand why he hadn't told me, but I wasn't about to ask him for an explanation. I needed space. He was so seductive, and I wanted not to be feeling like this so badly, that I didn't trust myself to stop and hear an explanation.

There was no point; whatever my heart might want, my logical brain couldn't be convinced. I'd caught him in several lies, and after I'd told him how important honesty was to me. My heart twisted—walking away would be the hardest thing I'd ever done, but was exactly what I had to do.

I couldn't be the woman I was with Louis, grasping for explanations, holding on to the impossible because I had to hold on to him at any cost. I would never be like that with a man again. I'd never be such a fool.

"Beth, please just wait a second," he said as I handed my boarding pass and passport to the flight attendant. "Alicia came to the office and refused to leave unless I went to lunch with her. It was entirely unexpected, and I would have told you as soon as I saw you. I wasn't hiding anything."

Unable to digest what he was saying, I glanced up at him. I shouldn't have. I could drown in those indigo eyes. They were misleadingly kind. I looked away, desperate to have some distance so I could keep my clear head. I needed to be in London. I'd debated going to a meeting before I left Chicago, but called my sponsor instead and cried for thirty minutes solid before I could explain to her what had happened. It'd felt surprisingly good to tell someone about it. How betrayed I felt. How much I loved him. How stupid I felt. How much I wanted it to have never happened. I didn't say any of that when I'd called Jake after to tell him I was okay and on my way home.

I *was* going to be okay. I wasn't going to drink, and I didn't want him to worry if Dylan did something stupid and called him before I did.

My first instinct wasn't to bury my feelings with alcohol, which was both shocking and comforting. What I wanted was to run home, not to get shitfaced. I guess that was what people called progress. I clung to that feeling as Dylan kept talking.

"Beth, please look at me. I need you to understand how sorry I am. I can explain it all. Can you just stay?"

I wanted to sink against his hard body and feel his arms smooth over my back, but I knew I couldn't think about that, not now.

The flight attendant handed me my boarding pass and passport. I smiled and turned to Dylan.

"I believe you're sorry that you got caught. At least I found out who you were before I got in too deep." I walked away. It had been my turn to lie. It hadn't happened before I got in too deep. I was way out of my depth and drowning.

Dylan shouted after me, "Beth, don't say that. Don't pretend you're not in this as deep as I am. Please don't leave."

When I knew I was out of sight, I stopped. I couldn't take another step. Crashing sideways into the wall, I slid to the floor, sobs shaking my body.

I cried because I felt foolish and I was embarrassed for having been so easily taken in. But most of all I cried because I'd never see him again.

I loved him. And I knew I'd love him for the rest of my life.

How long would it take for that to pass? I'd never fallen for anyone like I'd fallen for Dylan. He'd made all my previous encounters feel so meaningless. If only he could have been the man I thought he was.

When I heard footsteps behind me, I pulled myself up.

Just a few more steps and I'd be on my way home and able to start rebuilding myself once more.

***

"I just got through security, and I can't face public transport. I look like I've been crying for nine hours straight." I wore my sunglasses despite the fact that it was the middle of a gray winter's day.

"I could have come to get you. I'm sorry, I didn't think," Jake said.

I headed toward the taxi line. "Don't be. I'm not in the mood for company. I just want to go home, shower and go to bed."

"And you'll come over for dinner tonight? You know if you don't Haven will just come to you. If you come here at least you can leave when you want to."

It was the last thing I wanted to do, but Jake was right; Haven would insist on coming over and I knew my brother would only worry if I stayed home and felt sorry for myself. "Okay. I'll come to yours, but I'm not bringing anything. There's no way I'm baking."

"No, that's fine."

"Can you make sure you have cake? And ice cream?"

"You've met my carboholic wife. We have both at all times. We just never tell you about the store-bought cake in the fridge."

I managed to smile slightly. "Okay, I'll see you later."

The journey to my flat passed in a nanosecond. Whether it was warp speed or sleep, I wasn't questioning it. I just needed a shower and my duvet.

As I opened my purse Dylan's scent hit me. The woodsy, masculine smell that his skin had, which was always so comforting. I couldn't stop the tears as they rolled down my cheeks.

I stripped off what I was wearing and set the wash to hot, naked as the day I was born. I loved how comfortable Dylan was naked and how his attitude encouraged me to be more accepting of myself.

I needed a shower so I scooted into the bathroom, covering my chest with my crossed arms just as Dylan hated me to do. A good shower could cure almost anything.

I let water cascade over me, taking with it my tears. God, I'd not expected to come home like this. I'd let myself imagine that Dylan and I might have something special, something long term. How could I have been so wrong?

I turned off the faucet and wrapped myself in a towel. Someone was banging on my door. Haven?

I opened the door and stood, open-mouthed, as I came face-to-face with Dylan.

"What are you doing here?" I asked. I was pretty sure he hadn't been on my flight.

"I need to talk to you. To explain." His jaw was clenched and he looked tired.

I just wanted him to hold me and tell me it had all been a horrible dream or something. I wanted to rewind and pick up in the moment just before I left his brownstone, when my heart only ached at the thought I wouldn't see him for three days. I didn't want to be here, standing here in front of him, my heart in pieces.

I shook my head. "There's nothing to say. You need to go." I started to close the door but he put his hand out, stopping me. "Really? You're going to force yourself into my apartment?"

He let go instantly and I shut the door, resting my forehead on the wood as I turned the lock.

"Beth, please. I'm so sorry. You have to believe me. I've seen Alicia twice since she called off the wedding. The first time was with you, then when she turned up to my office about thirty minutes before you came to the restaurant. I'm not making this up."

I started to cry again. I so wanted to believe him. "What about Raine Media, Dylan? Why didn't you tell me you owned it?"

I heard him sigh. "I don't have an answer for you. Not a good one, anyway. Raf and I have some history with business and my exes, and I hadn't told him you were involved in WCIL. It didn't seem important, at first because we weren't that serious, and then I never found the right words. Things were so perfect; I didn't want to ruin it. I should have said something, but we were thinking about selling and I just didn't want to complicate things, with him, with you. In the end I've just made things so much worse."

He sounded sincere and I so desperately wanted to believe him. I wanted to hear about the business issues with his ex. Did he mean Alicia? But I didn't want to give in to him. I didn't want to be the weak woman I'd been with Louis. The woman who believed every lie because I didn't trust myself. "Dylan, I can't . . . I don't know . . . You should go."

"I love you, Beth."

My heart urged me to tell him that I loved him, too, but my head wouldn't allow it.

"I don't think so. I need the people in my life to be completely honest with me. To be gentle with me. To act like they love me, not just use the words." My heart felt like someone was ripping it into shreds. I'd finally opened up to someone and it was as if history was repeating itself.

"I know. I fucked up. I'm not good at this, but it's new. And you don't tell me everything, either. Can you tell me you've shared everything about your ex?"

He was right. I'd never mentioned my pregnancy and the way Louis had told me to get rid of it.

"You don't talk to me about your meetings or your sobriety."

I couldn't argue with him. Jake was the only one that really knew the ins and outs of my struggle to stay sober. Partly because it wasn't much of a struggle anymore, but also because he'd seen me at my worst and loved me anyway. I knew he wouldn't judge, or reject me. But was that comparable with what Dylan had kept from me? My head spun. I wanted him to be right, for us to be able to work through this, but I didn't want to be made a fool of.

"We don't know everything about each other. Not yet, Beth. But I want to hear all your stuff and I want to tell you all mine. I want all of you, and I want you to have all of me."

"Please, Dylan, I can't. You need to go. I need time." I didn't want him to go. I wanted to stay close until the pain passed.

"Can we talk tomorrow?" His voice was small and sad. Despite how I felt, I hated that.

"I don't think so. I need some space. Some time to heal." I wasn't thinking rationally. It would be so easy to open the door and for him to say all the right things, but if I did that, we would never be the same—the trust had gone. A part of what we'd had was destroyed forever.

"Then let me help you, be there with you. Please, Beth, I can't lose you."

"You should have thought of that before you lied or hid what you knew would be important to me."

"I'm not leaving London before I've made this right." He sounded so certain that it was something he could do. But I wasn't a business deal to be negotiated. Unless he could turn back time, I wasn't sure how things could ever be right.

My stomach churned. Part of me desperately wanted to open the door and be pulled into his arms. My head was telling me to walk away. "I need you to leave. I'm going to get dressed." I headed down the corridor, ignoring him as he called my name. I collapsed on my bed, my wet hair soaking the pillow, and began to sob.

chapter SIXTEEN

Dylan

While Marie's line rang, I stared out of the window onto the Georgian and Edwardian buildings of Portland Place. The views of the Georgian terraces from the Langham in London were very different from the views of the river from Beth's hotel room in Chicago. But I knew Beth didn't stay there for the view. It was all about the cakes and desserts. Even though I was in London, staying at the Langham brought me closer to her somehow.

"Marie, can you arrange to have my laptop couriered to me? And can you speak to Dawn and ask her to pack my things for a two-week trip? Also, send the luggage already in my hallway as well." Dawn was my housekeeper who came in three times a week.

"You're going to be in London two weeks?" Marie asked.

"I don't know." I'd stay for as long as it took. "But it will be as if I'm there. No need to cancel anything. I'll do everything on video or phone. Can you put me through to Raf?"

"No problem."

"Dylan, what's going on?" Raf asked when he came on the line.

"I'm in London—"

"What the fuck? We've got that tech start-up coming in in an hour."

"I know. I'll dial in. Look, I think I'm going to be here a while, I just . . . I'll handle everything from here. Marie is couriering my laptop and stuff to me. I can work remotely. You won't notice I'm gone."

"Of course I'm going to notice you're gone. We have a mountain of work here, all these strategic plans to review. You never take vacations, so why the sudden trip? Are you trying to screw with me?" Raf and I rarely argued and the last thing I wanted was to fuck things up with him as well.

I took a deep breath. "I fucked things up with Beth and I need to set things straight." Somewhere along the way, Raf and I had stopped talking about personal shit. He teased me about being celibate from time to time, and I made sure I told him he was a man-whore on a regular basis, but other than that, everything had been about business between us for a long time.

But now I needed a friend. "I don't know what to do. I'm afraid I've lost her."

Raf sighed. "What did you do?"

"What didn't I do? She caught me having lunch with Alicia yesterday."

"What do you mean *caught* you? I was there; Alicia forced you into having lunch with her. That wasn't your fault."

That wasn't entirely true. "Yeah but I should have told Beth before I went. In fact, I just shouldn't have gone."

"You really like her, don't you?"

"I love her, man."

"Wow. Well, good for you. So lunch with an ex isn't a great idea, but it's not a capital offense as far as I can see. Can't you just explain it to her?" Raf was very black and white. It was part of the reason his relationships never lasted. If only life were that simple.

"And then there's Raine Media. I never got around to telling her we owned it."

"You fucktard." Raf had a knack of getting right to the heart of the problem. He hadn't lost his touch. I was a fucktard.

The corners of my mouth twitched as if remembering how to smile.

"So when you told her, she went postal?"

I shrugged off my jacket. "If only. The *Sun-Times* ran an article about how she was sleeping with her boss."

"Jesus, man, that's how she found out?"

I nodded even though he couldn't see me. "That's how she found out. She wants nothing to do with me and it's killing me. I can't leave London until I sort this shit out. I need you to cut me some slack. I'll be able to get through loads of stuff in the mornings here while you're still sleeping. I'm not going to leave you to hold the fort—I'm not that stupid."

"I know it sounds weird, but I'm fucking ecstatic. I mean not that Beth wants nothing to do with you. That part blows. But the fact you care enough about someone to go after them?

I wasn't sure it would happen, and as much is it stings now, I'm pleased for you."

Raf might be an asshole when it came to women, but he was a good friend. I'd missed this side of him. "She isn't just someone, and I'm not just finally getting back on the horse. Whatever Alicia and I had doesn't come close to what I feel for Beth." I sat on the bed. "I feel like a fucking douche for hating Alicia for so long. She set me free. I couldn't be more grateful, but if I don't make it right with Beth, this is the woman I'll never recover from." Telling Raf was like going to confession; it felt good to explain the gravity of the situation.

"Then you gotta do what you gotta do. You've got plenty of weapons in your arsenal. She won't be able to resist you for long."

"I don't know about that. Honesty is the most important thing for her, and I've just trampled on that. I don't know if I can ever get her back." A darkness tugged at my chest. Losing Beth forever was too painful to think about. She'd brought me to life, and I didn't want to go back to an existence without her.

"Look, we've built our considerable fortunes on turning the shitty situations companies find themselves in into million-dollar opportunities. You've just got to apply the same planning and precision to your personal life. I know you can turn this around."

Perhaps he was right. My instinct was just to camp on her doorstep and beg her forgiveness constantly. But maybe I needed to be slightly more strategic, a little more patient. Perhaps I needed to give her the time she'd asked for.

"Thanks, man. I appreciate it."

"Anytime you need me to call you a fucktard, you know I'm here. Now fuck off, I've got a meeting to prepare for."

I managed a half-chuckle. "I'll call to you in the meeting."

I hung up, and went straight to the phone on the low table by the sofa and dialed room service. Perhaps eating a lot of sugar would assist me in coming up with a plan to win around Beth, and get my life back.

I'd been in London a little over two weeks, and I had something of a routine now. I got up and went for a run. On my way back through the hotel, I'd place an order for four cakes and desserts to go. Then I'd shower, grab my laptop and head down to collect the patisserie box. This morning, like the last fifteen before them, the doorman flagged me a cab.

A few minutes later, he'd drop me at the café across the street from Beth's building, where I came every day. I'd not spoken to Beth; I was trying to be patient, but I was having a hard time of it. I missed her. I wanted some kind of reassurance that she'd forgive me, someday.

"An Americano with a chocolate biscotti?" the waitress asked.

"Yes, please."

Beth left her building around ten every day. The first couple of times I'd seen her from my seat in the café, my heart had pinched as I took in her sad eyes and turned-down mouth. I'd taken joy from her and couldn't have felt worse about it.

When I was sure she wasn't coming back, I paid for my coffee and biscotti, then slipped inside her building to deliver my gift. The security guard had taken pity on me, and as long as I made my entrance when no one was looking, he was happy to let me in. I made my way up to her floor, taking in a deep breath in the hope of catching the scent of her hair.

The doors pinged open and I headed left toward her apartment. I set the box down on her welcome mat. The print of a giant pink cupcake on the mat always made me smile. I'd started to wonder if I should be leaving her a note along with the cakes. I didn't want to push her, but I wanted her to know I was here.

I turned back to the elevator and pressed the down button. Sometimes I went back to the café, but lingering felt increasingly like I was stalking Beth. Today I'd just go back to the hotel. I'd set up a virtual office there, and I had a day of calls that would take me late into the London night.

As the doors to the elevator opened, I came face-to-face with Beth.

She took my breath away. Her smooth, pale skin with the flash of red lipstick contrasted so perfectly with her almost black hair. But there was an unfamiliarity in her eyes that was like a knife to my chest.

We both froze, not knowing what to say or how to react.

"I was just leaving," I said as the doors started to close. I moved to one side and held them open so she could get off.

She stepped out of the elevator, her eyes firmly on the ground. "I didn't realize you came each day."

"You didn't think the cakes were from me?"

"I thought you'd be in Chicago. I assumed you had them delivered." Her voice was small as she continued to stare at the ground, but I couldn't take my eyes off her. I drank her in, desperate at having spent the last two weeks without her.

"I told you that I wasn't going until we had a chance to talk. I can't give up. You mean too much. You've become the reason I get up in the mornings." I took a breath. How could I convince her to give us a second chance? "Tell me it's not too late. Tell me you can imagine not being together, because when I shut my eyes, all I see in my future is you."

She didn't say anything, but she didn't leave either. I wanted to reach out to touch her; I wanted so desperately to feel her skin against mine.

"It's hard, Dylan. I need to keep my heart safe. I can't go back to how I was—weak and vulnerable. You know that."

She didn't feel her heart was safe with me? I cringed. "I'm so sorry, my sweet. Tell me what to do."

She lifted her eyes slightly, but she still didn't look at me. "I don't have an answer for you. You should be in Chicago. Raf and—"

"I need to be wherever you are." I reached for her, but she shrank away and turned. "Try to imagine your life when we're not together. If you can do that, then tell me and I'll walk away, broken, but I'll be out of your life forever."

"Don't, Dylan. I can't. Not yet."

Nausea seeped into every part of my body as she went out of sight. I stumbled into the elevator. I needed to be able to breathe, needed fresh air. What got to me the most was that Beth didn't sound angry. Her voice was full of sadness. Anger I could have coped with, but that look of disappointment on her face killed me over and over again.

Walking back to the hotel, replaying our encounter in my head, I cringed. What were her words? *Don't, Dylan. I can't.* But there'd been something after that. *Not yet.* My heart pounded as rain dampened my hair. *Not yet* implied that there was a future. But for what?

To speak?

To touch?

Jesus, waiting without any promise of resolution was killing me. I was so used to getting what I wanted, when I wanted it. Beth had turned everything on its head for me in every way.

Beth

I looked down at my doorstep to the now-familiar pink-striped patisserie box from the Langham. It had been a little over a week since I'd run into Dylan. How long would the daily deliveries continue? Right or wrong, I enjoyed receiving them. It took the edge off my sadness that he seemed so genuinely sorry.

"What's that?" Haven asked.

"Cake."

"Is that a regular delivery?"

"I guess you could say so." I stooped to collect the box. "It's from Dylan."

"Really? How do you know? Do you get them a lot?"

"Every day." I put my key in the lock.

"He has them sent every day? Seriously? That's so sweet."

"Hey, you're supposed to be on my side. And he doesn't send them, he delivers them." I opened the door and put the box on the console table while I took off my coat. Haven was unusually quiet. She'd come over because she wanted a hand making a birthday cake for Jake. I got the impression it was just an excuse; she wasn't much of a baker.

Haven dumped the shopping bags she'd been carrying on the counter and started to unpack. "Shall I put these in the fridge?" She held up two blocks of butter.

"No. First rule of baking is that everything has to be at room temperature when you start."

I set Dylan's delivery next to the shopping and opened the box. I swear he must be making special requests. There was no way the Langham had such variety.

"Whatcha got?" Haven peered over my shoulder. "Wow, they look good. Does he pick them out himself?"

I shrugged. The Bakewell tart looked delicious. There were a couple of things I didn't recognize. I resisted the temptation to dig in, closed the lid and put them in the refrigerator.

"So, he's in London?" Haven asked. "I mean, if he's delivering you cake every day . . ."

I thought it was a little odd Haven hadn't focused on that fact. "Yeah, I think so."

"For how long?"

"I don't know. He said . . ." He'd said he'd wait for as long as it took, but he'd have to go back to Chicago soon, wouldn't he? I should be pleased, but as much as I couldn't bring myself to have a conversation with him, I was glad he was close. "He said he'd be around a while. I don't know when he'll go back."

"He's here on business?"

I was pretty sure he hadn't abandoned his company, but I was equally sure he would be most effective in Chicago. It must be inconvenient being in London. Perhaps I didn't want to have the final conversation because ultimately I didn't want him to leave. And I wasn't sure I was ready to give him up just yet. "I guess."

"I thought you hadn't talked since you left Chicago?"

"Grab a wooden spoon," I said, handing Haven some caster sugar and a mixing bowl. "I ran into him a week or so ago when he was leaving the desserts. That's how I know he's delivering them." I pulled out some scales from the cupboard and set them on the counter.

"Did you talk?"

"When I saw him?" Haven nodded. "Not really. I'm just so scared of ending up someone's fool again. I feel trapped, like I can't go back to him because it will mean going back to the old Beth who glossed over so many signs with Louis. But I can't move forward either, because the thought of Dylan not being in my life is just too painful to contemplate."

"But Dylan and Louis aren't the same person. I've met Louis. You're right, he might as well have 'asshole' tattooed on his forehead, but you were young and vulnerable and your mother had just died. You saw what you needed to see."

Was Haven right? Would Louis have had the same effect on me if I hadn't been grieving?

I pointed at the sugar and Haven opened it. "You're one of the wisest people I know, but even you don't get it right all the time. Are you sure Dylan's not just human rather than an asshole?"

I took the bag of sugar from Haven and poured out two hundred and twenty five grams, thinking about what she'd said. Was I making Dylan pay for my previous bad judgment? "I'm not saying I'm perfect. Far from it. I'm saying the opposite."

"I know. But I wonder if Dylan had been perfect up until then for you. He'd gotten everything right, but that was never going to last. He's bound to fuck up, and so are you. That's just life. You can't expect him to be perfect any more than you can expect perfection in yourself."

Did I want to erase the possibility of any fuck ups in my life, to try to make everything perfect?

I turned on the oven then rounded the counter and took a seat on a stool opposite Haven. "Now add two hundred and twenty five grams of the butter." I rested my chin on my hand. Since I got sober, I'd existed in a bubble that kept me safe and happy and only allowed people I knew I could count on in. Jake was my constant. He pissed me off at times, but I never doubted his honor or his desire to see me happy. I'd immediately liked Haven, but I didn't open up to her often. I didn't want to put myself out there to be judged or rejected. Feelings like that didn't belong in my bubble. In my world, I was safe and sober and happy. Steady.

As close to perfect as I could get.

"You think I'm trying to make everything too—?"

"It's like how the pastry on an apple pie is supposed to be flaky, golden and crisp to be good. But sometimes it doesn't come out that way. But you know what? It's still delicious."

"But Louis' problem wasn't soggy pastry."

"No, his apples were rotten. That's the point. Dylan's not rotten, he's just not perfect. Edible if you like." Haven grinned at me and raised her eyebrows.

Dylan had been my first attempt at seeing what life was like beyond my safe haven. I'd thought he'd be a good time, a bit of fun. I hadn't expected to fall in love with him.

Haven tipped the bowl toward me. I nodded. "Yup. Now you add the flour. The same amount as the sugar and butter."

"Don't you have a mixer for this shit?"

"Not for beginners. You need to feel the texture of things when you stir so you know it's right."

"You're a hard-ass."

I shrugged. "You think I've been too hard on Dylan?"

"It doesn't matter what I think. All I'm saying is that people fuck up, but it doesn't mean you have to cut them out of your life. Thank God your brother is so forgiving. I can be a maniac at times."

I grinned. I saw Haven and Jake do things they shouldn't all the time, but they seemed to forgive each other and love each other anyway. Was that how it was supposed to be? "So you think that because of Louis, I've overcorrected with Dylan?"

Haven smiled. "I don't know. Did you?"

Maybe. I'd wanted him to fit into my perfect bubble. Perhaps I should hear him out, see if there was a way through this for us. The thought was terrifying because it meant turning my world upside down and reinventing the rules I'd created for myself. But he'd been right—picturing a future without him was impossible.

"But how do I know? How do I separate asshole from human?"

Haven grinned at me. "You know as much as I do. You're always going to get assholes. You can't protect yourself from that. I just think that you need to dust yourself off. You're strong; you can handle whatever life throws your way. You've proven that. If you hear Dylan out and feel in your heart that he's playing a game, then toss him aside. But I don't think he would be in London, delivering cake to your doorstep every day, if he was an asshole. The guy is lava-hot. There's going to be no lack of women wanting to take your place. He doesn't need to chase one halfway across the world."

My stomach churned at the thought of Dylan with someone else. Or with Alicia. She was an idiot for the way she'd treated him. As much as I didn't want to repeat my mistakes, I didn't want to repeat hers, either.

"Remember," Haven continued, "when you were accepting all the bullshit from Louis, your judgment was affected. Your true feelings were covered by the booze."

I let Haven's words sink in. Perhaps sobriety meant I could trust my heart. I reached for my phone. Should I message him? Reach out and see how my heart felt with him?

"The answer's yes, you should text him," Haven said.

"You a mind reader now?"

"Don't overthink it. A message isn't going to make or break you."

She smiled as I hesitantly typed out a message.

Beth: Thank you for the cakes. I love Bakewell tart.

I hadn't put my phone down before it buzzed in reply.

Dylan: I want to give you everything you've ever wanted. I want to be the man you deserve.

My heart squeezed and my stomach flip-flopped. There was no question that he still had a hold over my body, heart and soul.

"I'm guessing that wasn't the reply of an asshole," Haven said with a smile.

I shrugged. Maybe not.

chapter
SEVENTEEN

Beth

I'd been to a meeting every day since I'd returned from Chicago. Recovery gave me a single focus and a pass to put everything else aside and just concentrate on my sobriety. But it was as if the meeting today had been designed for me. If I didn't know better, I would have thought Haven had put together the agenda. The last words of the speaker rang in my ears as I put up my umbrella and started the short walk back to my apartment. "Remember, AA is meant to provide you with a bridge to normal living. It's not here to cocoon you from all the difficulties that life will throw at you, but instead to help you navigate them without alcohol."

Talking things through with Haven had helped me see that I was expecting Dylan to be perfect. He'd kept things from me, but I hadn't even let him explain himself. I owed him that. I owed me that. I couldn't turn away the man I was in love with so easily. I couldn't walk away from the only man I'd ever really loved because I was scared. Haven was right; I needed to hear him out, then see what my heart told me.

I didn't regret texting him.

I hadn't responded to his reply. I didn't quite know what my next move was. The following day I'd received two patisserie boxes. One with four cakes, each a different variety. The other held four Bakewell tarts. I was beginning to worry Dylan may be a feeder.

My heart skipped as I pulled the door to my building open. What would I find today? Maybe I'd run into Dylan again. I checked the time on my phone. He was probably long gone.

My heart beat faster as I got to my floor at the thought of Dylan in my building. I turned toward my apartment as I stepped off the lift, but didn't see the usual pink-striped box on my doorstep.

Normally Dylan would have been and gone by now. My heart went from skipping to thudding. Why no delivery, and today of all days? Had he finally gotten sick of waiting around for me? My forehead became tight and I took a deep breath, trying to neutralize the prickling of my skin.

I pulled out my keys but couldn't bring myself to unlock the door. Had he flown back to Chicago without telling me?

I rested my forehead on my front door as I tensed, releasing my grip around my phone. I couldn't exactly message him asking where my cake was. That seemed a little . . . selfish.

My stomach churned. I was at a crossroads, and whichever path I chose from here would be a one-way street. I could pretend I didn't notice the lack of delivery and let Dylan slip away, or I could take action and have a conversation that was long overdue.

I headed back down to the lobby to speak with the doorman. Barney must have been letting Dylan in.

"Hey, have you seen Dylan today?" I asked, trying to sound nonchalant. I was sure I was failing miserably.

Barney looked a little guilty. Given we never came or left together, it was probably clear that he knew that Dylan and I weren't on the best of terms. "Not today. Should I not let him in? I can say no next time he tries."

I smiled. "No, that's fine. I just wondered how he always knows to come when I'm out. Do you know?"

Barney glanced at his feet. "He usually waits at the café across the street until you've left. He told me he had some making up to do, and I know that feeling. I figured you would have told me if you didn't like getting the gifts he brings."

I nodded. "Yeah, I would have. It's not a problem. He didn't mention if he would be coming today, or if he was going back to Chicago?" I was grilling my doorman for information. How had it come to this?

"Afraid not. Shall I tell him you were asking if he shows up?"

I had a feeling he wasn't going to be back. That maybe he'd finally given up.

I couldn't blame him.

I headed out of the building and grabbed my phone. Perhaps I could catch him before he left for the airport. My chest squeezed at the thought of not having him close to me anymore. How could I expect him to hang out in London indefinitely until I grew some balls and decided to have a conversation with him? What had I been thinking?

I headed across the street to the café. I burst through the door, and heads snapped in my direction. I didn't care how much attention I was attracting. There were less than a dozen tables and only two that had people at them. Dylan wasn't one of them.

I stepped back out into the street, looked left and right for a cab with its light on.

It wasn't a long journey to the Langham, but it felt as if it took as long as a flight to Chicago. He'd never said that that was where he was staying but it was the only place that made sense.

I scanned the heads of the people in the lobby as I made my way to the reception desk. "Can you tell me which room Dylan James is in, please?"

The blonde woman smiled at me. "I'm sorry; we can't give out the room numbers of our guests."

Shit, I should have thought of that. "Right." I pulled out my phone and called Dylan. I just needed to know he hadn't left.

No answer.

I turned back to the receptionist. "Could you put me through to his room?"

"Please hang on." She tapped away at her computer and scowled. "I'm afraid Mr. James has checked out."

My stomach sank. I knew it. I'd been an idiot not to agree to a simple conversation with him. No wonder he'd lost patience. "Did he check out today, or yesterday?"

The receptionist winced. "I really shouldn't say, but if it's any help, I did see him this morning."

"Thanks so much." I didn't quite know where to go. His phone had rung before going to voice mail, so he couldn't be in the air yet. Should I head to the airport to try to catch him before he boarded? The flights to Chicago generally stopped for the day after lunch, so I'd have to hurry.

I spun and charged toward the door.

"Beth?" Dylan's silky voice washed over me and my knees nearly gave way with relief. I turned and had to hold myself back from flinging my arms around him. His brow was furrowed. "Are you okay?" he asked as he held his hand out, then stopped himself and pulled back.

I stepped toward him. What was I going to say? How was I going to explain what I was doing here?

He raised an eyebrow at me. "You here for a refill? I'm sorry; I haven't gotten to your delivery today. I had some stuff to take care of."

"I'm not here for cake." I should have planned it better; I should have thought about what I was going to say. I'd been so concerned about finding him that I hadn't thought beyond that. "I wondered if . . ." I took a deep breath. "I thought maybe you left, and we never got a chance to talk."

"My sweet, I told you I wasn't leaving until I'd made things right. I've let you down about a lot, but I wasn't going to go back on that promise."

"But you checked out and . . ." I looked down at the carry-on he always travelled with.

"Marie found me an apartment just around the block. I wasn't going far."

He was so close. I couldn't bear that he wasn't touching me, so I reached for him. "I think maybe it's time for that talk. I mean, if you want to. And we don't have to do it now. I'm sure you're busy and you've got things you need to be doing. Just whenever—"

"I have nothing that would ever stop me talking with you."

Dylan

The reality of being apart from Beth for all these weeks had left me starving for her. Not being able to hear her voice, stroke her skin, breathe in the remnants of her baking that permeated her hair was torture. I knew with more certainty each and every day that I was prepared to do whatever I had to in order to win her back. And now here she was, taking the first step toward me. What we had felt so fragile, I didn't want to push and scare her off, but all I wanted to do was pull her against me so I could feel her heartbeat next to mine.

I resisted. "Let me get rid of my carry-on." I turned and quickly left my suitcase with the concierge before returning to Beth.

I glanced around the lobby. "Should we go and have some cake? Or we could go for a walk. It's cold, but sunny."

"A walk sounds good."

I smiled, wanting to see in her eyes what she was thinking. Had she come to me knowing how this would play out? Was she going to try to send me home? I had to suppress my impatience, and stop myself from asking her to skip to the heart of the matter. Instead, I gestured to the hotel exit. "Shall we?"

She nodded and stuffed her hands in her pockets. We descended the small stoop, then headed north up Portland Place. We walked slowly in silence, our eyes firmly on the path in front of us. I so desperately wanted to touch her. I'd been hoping for this opportunity for so long and now that it was here, I didn't want to fuck it up. I took a deep breath. "I—do you want me to . . . Can I explain?"

"You don't need to. I've heard what you've said, and I've thought about nothing else—"

Had I lost her?

"Can I ask you a question?" she asked. Her hair fell over her face. I longed to see her eyes, and perhaps forgiveness in them.

"You can ask me anything," I replied.

"What was lunch like?"

"With Alicia? Honestly?"

She turned to me, her eyebrow raised.

"Sorry, of course. It was okay. Good, even."

Beth stopped in her tracks and covered her face. I tried to pull her hands away. "Good because I realized how I'd been angry at her for all these years for no reason. I don't care enough to hate her anymore." My fingers finally persuaded her hands from her face, revealing glassy eyes. I stroked my thumbs over her cheekbones, brushing my favorite part of her, the beauty spot on her left cheekbone. "And in a way I was even grateful because if Alicia and I had gone through with the wedding, I wouldn't have met you."

She tilted her head and closed her eyes, yielding to my

touch. My body filled with relief. I allowed myself to hope she believed me.

She sighed and moved away from me, restarting our walk.

I did everything I could to resist pushing her, asking if she forgave me.

"And Raine Media? Did you have anything to do with my contract, or their second offer?"

I pushed my hands through my hair. "No, I really didn't. I don't have time to get involved with that kind of detail. And anyway, I've seen your videos and tasted your baking. You don't need my help."

Beth tucked her hair around her ears as we continued to walk forward in silence.

"I'm learning how to do this, the relationship thing. Alicia and I were kids when we started dating. You know there's been no one serious for me since then—except you. I'm really sorry, Beth. Please don't give up on us."

She stopped again just as a woman walking her Highland Terrier came from the opposite direction. I moved to the side to let the woman pass. I could feel Beth's stare as I nodded and something stopped me from looking back at her. I was worried about what I might find. I couldn't bear to see that hurt look in her eyes I'd spotted back in the restaurant when she'd seen me with Alicia. I couldn't handle it if I saw coldness. So much of her beauty came from her warmth. I didn't want to be the guy who changed that. "You can't know how sorry I am," I said, focusing beyond her shoulder.

She tugged at my lapel and I could resist her no longer.

"I'm sorry, too," she whispered as she gazed up at me, her eyes sad but still warm.

I shook my head. "No, you have nothing—"

She placed her index finger over my lips to stop me. "You've made your apology. Now let me make mine."

She'd done nothing wrong, what did she have to apologize for? My gut clenched. I hoped she wasn't about to tell me there was someone else.

"I'm sorry. I shouldn't have just run away. I should have stayed so we could talk. But more than that, I'm sorry for being so hard on you. You've borne the brunt of a hell of a lot of baggage." She tugged on both lapels of my coat. "Haven pointed out that I was overcorrecting, and she was right. I was so concerned that what happened with Louis didn't happen again, so determined not to go back to the weak Beth I'd been before, that as soon as things were anything less than perfect, I threw in the towel." She slid her hands over my shoulders. Even through my coat, my skin lit up from her touch. I was mesmerized by her beautiful red pout and the way her lips pushed together and out with each word. "The way you've treated me . . . you deserved a fair hearing, and I didn't give you that. I didn't trust my judgment; I'm sorry for that. I knew you better than I let myself believe."

"I'll never not forgive you anything," I replied. "But you don't need to apologize for holding me to a higher standard. I want to meet it and exceed it. I want to be the man who deserves you. I mean that."

She smiled her huge smile at me and it warmed me.

It gave me hope.

"I'll do whatever you need me to."

"I forgave you before you explained." She slid her finger across my lips. "I just need you to do one thing."

My heart exploded with her words. I wanted to hold her close, eliminate the gap between us. "Name it." I expected her to ask me to move to London, sell Raine Media, or refuse to see Alicia ever again. I'd do any and all of it.

"Kiss me," she said.

My breath caught in my throat. That was it? My heart squeezed in my chest and I took a deep breath. "I think I can do that." I snaked my arms around her waist as she brushed her fingers over my jaw. I'd not touched her in so long; I wanted to get this right. As she parted her lips, my nerves dissolved and desire passed over me like a cloud. My eyes flickered from her eyes to her lips and back again.

I bent down and took her bottom lip between my teeth, and groaned. It had been too long since I last tasted her. I wanted to tease her, make her desperate, but I couldn't hold back. I cupped the back of her head, holding her close as I slipped my tongue into her hot mouth.

It could have been minutes or hours later when Beth pushed against my chest. Only then was I aware of the catcalls and shouting of some kids coming down the path.

"I think we're putting on quite the show," Beth said.

I couldn't tear my eyes away from her red, swollen mouth. My dick throbbed uncomfortably in my trousers.

"Want to show me your new apartment?" she asked, trying to hide her face from the teenagers who were laughing as if they'd caught us naked.

I guess we couldn't hide what we had.

"I really do."

I grabbed her hand and pulled her down the street. Perhaps a cab would be better, quicker. I glanced around as I continued to stride down the sidewalk. I looked down at Beth who was doing a half run, half walk beside me. "In a hurry?" she asked with a laugh.

"I really am. I've waited so long to have you in my arms; I don't want to waste a second of our time together. Am I walking too fast?"

She grinned and stuck out her hand. "Only for a girl in heels." A taxi coming toward us pulled up to the curb.

Beth

Dylan hadn't let go of me for a second since he'd kissed me. And what a kiss. My head was still dizzy from the warmth of his lips. I'd almost let myself forget how he felt against me— so hard and hot and determined. No wonder I'd fallen so fast for him.

We climbed out of the cab precisely four minutes after we got in, and Dylan's fingers were closed around mine every second.

The cab drove away, and Dylan pulled me against his chest. "It feels so good to have you back." He grabbed my shoulders and held me away from him as he searched my eyes for something. "I have you back, right?"

I smiled. "Yeah, you have me back. I don't think you ever lost me really."

He led me up the stoop to an old oak door. "It didn't feel that way. I hated being apart from you."

I squeezed his hand. I'd hated being apart from him, too. I shouldn't have left it so long. But I couldn't have regrets. I had to believe that whichever path brought us here was the right one; we were stronger now. The time apart had been a transition from a fragile relationship built on sex to something we knew could weather a storm. That couldn't be a bad thing.

"Maybe I should have kept the room at the hotel. I could have ordered cake."

"I don't need cake."

"Isn't that blasphemy for you?"

I laughed. "I think it's okay as long as I'm giving it up in favor of an orgasm."

"My sweet, I promise you that."

We turned left out of the elevator and down a dark hallway. "I think it's this one."

"It better be this one. I'm getting impatient."

He shot me a lascivious look and raised an eyebrow. I tilted my head toward the door as if to say *Get on with it*, and he dipped his head and ran his tongue across the seam of my lips. It was a prelude to sex in a way our kiss on the street hadn't been. That had been about a need to be close, reunited. This kiss was all about wanting each other naked.

He smiled and turned his attention back to the lock as I started to undo the buttons on my coat. My skin burned where I needed him to touch me.

He held the door open and I stepped inside, shrugging my coat off as I walked. The hallway was long and dark. The door slammed behind us and the room went black as the corridor light cut off. The atmosphere shifted and I could almost taste the lust flickering between us. I turned and felt the heat rolling off Dylan's body. I pushed my hands up under his coat and suit jacket, slipping them over his shoulders. He shrugged them off as I trailed my palms back down over the contours of his chest. He hissed as I went lower, finding him hard and wanting.

"I've missed this," I whispered.

He pushed his palms against my breasts. "I've missed these."

I laughed. "I've been keeping them safe for you."

My giggle was curtailed as he pulled open my blouse, scattering buttons across the floor. Pushing my breasts up and together, he bent and took a lace-covered nipple in his mouth, scraping his teeth across the puckered flesh, then sucking and soothing them against his tongue. I moaned. "You feel so good."

My fingers fumbled over the button at the back of my skirt. I released it and the skirt slid down my legs. Dylan's hand found my sex instantly, grinding his palm against my clit.

I pulled at his shirt. I needed us naked already. We were a flurry of hands and mouths and fingers and tongues, pulling and grabbing, sucking and biting.

When we were both naked apart from my panties, Dylan reached around my ass and lifted me up, his hard cock rubbing against my clit as I wrapped my legs around him. "Come on.

I need to see you to believe you're real." He pushed open the door to our right. "Shit. Bathroom."

I laughed as he tried the next one. "Fuck." A closet. I circled my hips, desperate to pull him into me. "Where's the fucking bedroom?"

Inside the next room was what we were looking for. "Thank fuck for that." He leaned forward, releasing me onto the bed, grabbing my ankles, and pulling me to the edge of the mattress. He pulled at my panties. "I need to be inside you; are you ready? Please be ready."

I pressed my hand to his, palm against palm, and pulled him over me. "I'm ready. So ready."

"Fuck, condom," he spat as he moved away from me but I wouldn't let go of his hands.

"Do we need one?" I asked. Was he tested regularly? I was on the pill.

His eyes widened, looking right at me. "I was tested a month or so ago. Are you—"

"I want to feel you with nothing between us," I said. He didn't need to be convinced.

I moaned as he pushed me up the mattress with his first thrust. I'd forgotten how big he was, and how needy his fucking was, as if he couldn't get enough. He stilled deep inside me, panting against my neck. "Did I hurt you?"

"I'm so wet for you, I can take it."

He groaned and dragged himself out of me. I felt the loss of him as he retreated. I clasped his ass, trying to pull him back. I needed him to fill me, wanted him as close as possible. He looked at me and slowly pushed back inside, more controlled this time. The concentration strained across his face. I smoothed his scrunched brows with my fingertips. "You feel so good."

I squeezed my muscles around him.

"If you do that I'm gonna come in a nanosecond. I want this to be good for you," he said.

"You're always good for me," I whispered.

He closed his eyes sleepily as if I'd just given him the best gift in the world.

I pulled him on top of me, then pushed him to his back while he was still inside me.

I circled my hips and he lay back, his arms reaching for my breasts. He pinched both nipples between his thumb and forefinger and spikes of pleasure ran up my spine. I threw my head back and gasped.

"You are so beautiful."

"Are you talking to my boobs?" I grinned as I slid my hips up to meet his, resting my hands on his chest.

"Jesus, that's deep." His hands slipped to my waist, his thumbs circling my hipbones.

"I feel it, baby." I rocked back and forward. I loved the way that he didn't seem to know where to look. His eyes roamed my body as if he were trying to pick his favorite part.

"So fucking beautiful. I don't ever want to be without you again."

His words woke my orgasm, fizzing around my edges. "I know. I need more."

His fingers pressed deeper into my skin, pulling me closer,

deeper and faster. My limbs weakened with desire. And of course he knew. He understood my body better than anyone.

He flipped me over onto my back and took over. "Like this, my sweet?" I arched, bringing us closer. The shift in angle made us both gasp.

"Beth, I'm so close."

I could only look at him in response as my climax pushed through every part of me.

"Oh God," he called out as he watched me shiver and shake beneath him as he emptied himself into me.

His arms collapsed, and he fell, leaning all his weight on me. I was pinned and loved it. I smoothed my hands over his back and breathed in the musky smell that was unmistakably him.

"I love you," he mumbled into my neck.

"I know," I replied, tightening my legs around him.

He shifted to his side, pulling me with him, staying inside me. "I'm never leaving." He hitched my leg up over his waist and his hips rocked soothingly backward and forward. I reached between us for my still-throbbing clit.

"Hey, I've warned you about that." He batted my hand away and took over, circling a single finger around the nub of nerves. "Such a greedy girl," he whispered. "But I want to give you everything."

Within seconds, the urge to climax was on me again. His fingers on my clit were too much, and as he thickened within me, my skin tightened and my breathing hitched. His movements were still small and intense as he watched me, but it was as if every possible feeling was concentrated and more profound.

I trailed my fingers down his chest, enjoying the heat transferring between us. I wanted to share everything I could with him. I squeezed him and he groaned. "You're so perfect."

"Dylan." I wasn't perfect and I didn't like that that was how he saw me. I could only let him down. "You know that's not true."

He continued to rock in and out of me. "What I know is that you're perfect for me."

The beginning of my orgasm rumbled at the base of my spine. I got it now. Perfect for each other didn't mean getting everything right, it just meant not giving up, trusting each other and being in it forever.

Dylan's fingers changed direction and I squirmed against his touch, wanting to hold off my orgasm, wanting to stay like this for a while.

"You don't need to save them," he said, reading my thoughts. "Our future is just going to get better and better in every way." He sped up his hip movements and bent toward me, licking a hot, damp line across my collarbone as I threaded my hands through his hair. "I'm going to spend the rest of our lives making you feel like this."

I believed him. He loved me. I just had to let him, feel worthy and love him right back.

I molded into him and let my climax overtake me, flowing from my skin and across his as he jerked inside me, calling my name over and over.

He felt like mine.

He felt like forever.

epilogue

Beth

"It makes more sense for you to be in Chicago," I said as Dylan handed me the strawberries. We were having *another* conversation about where we were going to live.

I poured the cream into my mixer and started the machine. I was making strawberry and white chocolate hearts *mille-feuille*. Puff pastry was a killer, but the first batch I'd made this morning was the best I'd ever done. I was trying out recipes for a new cable cooking show launching in the UK in four months that had given me a dozen fifteen minute slots. Baking was no longer about my past. It was all about my future. Our future.

Dylan grabbed a strawberry from the bowl beside me. "You have this new show, so it makes more sense for me to be where you are." In the weeks since we'd been back together, Dylan hadn't been back to Chicago and I hadn't questioned it, wanting everything to stay as it had been. Dylan had barely been back to his apartment. He certainly hadn't slept there. We'd spent every night together, and I couldn't imagine anything else. If that meant I had to move to Chicago, then so be it.

"But be practical, that's where your business is."

"But you're here. You're happy here and that's what's *most* important to me. And now that the Redux deal has gone through, Raf and I need to be on top of things. I can make London work." He checked his messages, dropping the discussion as if it were a done deal.

"Well, maybe for six months or something." I stopped the mixer and waited for Dylan to respond.

He looked up at me. "We're not living in the fifties. I can do what I need to by video conference. People are used to it now. It's not such a big deal. I want you to be happy, and I can always fly back when I need to. Raf's cool about it."

"You've spoken to him?"

He shrugged. "Of course."

"Before you spoke to me?"

"Beth, I've seen you with your family. It's important to you to be here with them. As much as I love Chicago, it's just a city to me. This is your home. Anyway, I like the thought of our kids having British accents." He pulled me to his chest. "Have I told you how much I like you in this apron?"

I ignored his perverted apron obsession. "Kids?"

"Yeah, I was thinking five or six, but maybe six is too many."

"Oh yeah, but five is perfectly fine? You don't have to push them out of your vagina."

"We can start with one and see how we go." Dylan

threaded his fingers through mine and traced his thumb across my wrist.

"Okay then." I rested against his chest. "But not yet. I'm young and . . ." I'd thought about having kids in the abstract. Spending time with Sophia and Maggie convinced me I wanted children but it wasn't something that I saw happening to me in the near future. Life fundamentally changed when kids came along. Dylan and I would be together forever, but I just wasn't ready to share him yet.

"I'd like a few years just you and me, if I'm honest," Dylan said, echoing my own thoughts. "We can borrow Maggie or Sophia if we want to practice. But let's spend a few years married on our own. I've not tasted everything you can bake yet."

I laughed. "Did you just propose?"

Dylan shook his head. "Nope. You'll know when I do. I haven't bought a ring yet."

"Okay then." I frowned. "What if I want to propose to you?"

"Well, I guess we'll see who gets there first." He kissed me on the forehead.

"Okay then." I looked up at him and stroked his jaw. "Dylan?"

"Yes, my sweet?" He dropped a small kiss on my lips.

"Will you marry me?"

He smiled and shook his head. "You a little impatient?"

I turned in his arms. "Always."

"Me too, baby, me too. But I'm not answering that question, so you're just going to have to wait until I have a ring. Anyway, though I hate to interrupt this moment, I smell something burning."

"Shit." I pulled out of his arms and raced to the oven. "Holy crap. I knew it was a fluke. I'm hopeless at pastry."

Dylan slid one arm around my waist and turned off the oven with the other. I looked up into his indigo eyes.

"You're perfect, for me," he said, kissing my neck. "You don't need to get everything right the first time. We learn more from our mistakes than we do our victories."

I smiled, grateful I had Dylan to remind me not to be too hard on myself, or him, whenever I forgot. Neither of us was perfect but we were perfect for each other.

If you enjoyed Indigo Nights, please leave a review. Good reviews really help indie authors!

For Jake and Haven's story, read What the Lightning Sees

For Luke and Ash's story, read The Calling Me Series

Other Louise Bay Books

Faithful

Hopeful

The Empire State Series

acknowledgments

I can't believe I just typed 2016 into the copyright page. I've been publishing for less than two years and it feels like I should have been doing it all my life. I love creating characters that you like to read. I hope I continue to do that during 2016 and beyond.

Thank you for reading Beth and Dylan's story. It was a difficult one in many ways. I've known a number of alcoholics and I understand that recovery isn't as easy as Beth makes it look. I understand the pain that addicts and friends and family of addicts endure as a result of addiction. Luckily for me I get to write things the way I want to write them. I know that Beth and her family struggled with her addiction more than we ever saw in this book or in What the Lightning Sees. But some of you may know that I like to write love stories and that's what I wanted for Beth-I wanted her next chapter to be about love not about addiction. I hope that makes sense to you.

To all my champions and cheerleaders-thank you. I hope I can pay it forward.

Elizabeth-so often, in the space of ten minutes I go from wanting to punch you in the face to wanting to kiss you on the mouth. It's a good job we live thousands of miles from each other! Thank you, thank you, thank you.

Karen Booth-thank you for being there. 2016 is going to be your year my lovely.

Jessica Hawkins, thank you for your support and help. I can't wait to read what you have for us next.

Jules Rapley Collins-I'm sorry for all the hot sex in this book #sorrynotsorry. Megan Fields I believe you will find your own Dylan James. Thank you both for all your support.

Thanks to Jacquie Jax Denison, Lucy May, Lauren Hutton, Kingston Westmoreland, Lauren Luman, Mimi Perez Sanchez, Ashton Williams Shone, Tina Haynes Marshall, Susan Ann Whitaker, Vicky Marsh, Sally Ann Cole, Elaine Hudson York, Karen Isopi, Athena Grayson and Colleen Flynn Vermilye. You girls rock!

Twirly, ahem, I've not heard from you ALL DAY. Where are you?

other books by
LOUISE BAY

THE NIGHTS SERIES

(each book is stand alone, focusing on a different couple)

Parisian Nights

Promised Nights

Indigo Nights

OTHER BOOKS

The Empire State Series

Hopeful

Faithful

the nights
SERIES

Parisian
NIGHTS

The moment I laid eyes on the new photographer at work, I had his number. Cocky, arrogant and super wealthy-women were eating out of his hand as soon as his tight ass crossed the threshold of our office.

When we were forced to go to Paris together for an assignment, I wasn't interested in his seductive smile, his sexy accent or his dirty laugh. I wasn't falling for his charms.

Until I did.

Until Paris.

Until he was kissing me and I was wondering how it happened. Until he was dragging his lips across my skin and I was hoping for more. Paris does funny things to a girl and he might have gotten me naked.

But Paris couldn't last forever.

promised NIGHTS

I've been in love with Luke Daniels since, well, forever. As his sister's best friend, I've spent over a decade living in the friend zone, watching from the sidelines hoping he would notice me, pick me, love me.

I want the fairy tale and Luke is my Prince Charming. He's tall, with shoulders so broad he blocks out the sun. He's kind with a smile so dazzling he makes me forget everything that's wrong in the world. And he's only man that can make me laugh until my cheeks hurt and my stomach cramps.

But he'll never be mine.

So I've decided to get on with my life and find the next best thing.

Until a Wonder Woman costume, a bottle of tequila and a game of truth or dare happened.

Then Luke's licking salt from my wrist and telling me I'm beautiful.

Then he's peeling off my clothes and pressing his lips against mine.

Then what? Is this the start of my happily ever after or the beginning of a tragedy?

The Empire State Series

Anna Kirby is sick of dating. She's tired of heartbreak. Despite being smart, sexy, and funny, she's a magnet for men who don't deserve her.

A week's vacation in New York is the ultimate distraction from her most recent break-up, as well as a great place to meet a stranger and have some summer fun. But to protect her still-bruised heart, fun comes with rules. There will be no sharing stories, no swapping numbers, and no real names. Just one night of uncomplicated fun.

Super-successful serial seducer Ethan Scott has some rules of his own. He doesn't date, he doesn't stay the night, and he doesn't make any promises.

It should be a match made in heaven. But rules are made to be broken.

OPEFUL

Guys like Joel Wentworth weren›t supposed to fall in love with girls like me. He could have had his pick of the girls on campus, but somehow the laws of nature were defied and we fell crazy in love.

After graduation, Joel left for New York. And, despite him wanting me to go with him, I'd refused, unwilling to disappoint my parents and risk the judgment of my friends. I hadn't seen him again. Never even spoke to him.

I've spent the last eight years working hard to put my career front and center in my life, dodging any personal complications. I have a strict no-dating policy. I've managed to piece together a reality that works for me.

Until now.

Now, Joel's coming back to London.

And I need to get over him before he gets over here.

Hopeful is a stand-alone novel.

FAITHFUL

Leah Thompson's life in London is everything she's supposed to want: a successful career, the best girlfriends a bottle of sauvignon blanc can buy, and a wealthy boyfriend who has just proposed. But something doesn't feel right. Is it simply a case of 'be careful what you wish for'?

Uncertain about her future, Leah looks to her past, where she finds her high school crush, Daniel Armitage, online. Daniel is one of London's most eligible bachelors. He knows what and who he wants, and he wants Leah. Leah resists Daniel's advances as she concentrates on being the perfect fiancé.

She soon finds that she should have trusted her instincts when she realises she's been betrayed by the men and women in her life.

Leah's heart has been crushed. Will ever be able to trust again? And will Daniel be there when she is?

Faithful is a stand-alone novel.

let's CONNECT

If you enjoyed Parisian Nights, please leave a review. Good reviews really help indie authors!

I love hearing from readers – get in touch!

Instagram me

@louiseSbay

Tweet me

twitter.com/louisesbay (@louisesbay)

Friend me

www.facebook.com/louisesbay

Like me

www.facebook.com/authorlouisebay

Pin me

www.pinterest.com/LouiseBay

Friend me

www.goodreads.com/author/show/8056592.Louise_Bay

Circle me

https://plus.google.com/u/0/+LouiseBayauthor

Find me at home

www.louisebay.com

30593438R00195

Made in the USA
San Bernardino, CA
27 March 2019